The Moon
IN
Her Eyes

Book Two

A Witch's Tale

Nikki Broadwell

Airmid Publishing
Tucson, Arizona

The Moon in Her Eyes

This is a work of fiction. All names, characters, events, places and ideas presented here are a product of the author's imagination.

Cover by Perry Elizabeth Design
Formatting by Polgarus Studio

ISBN-13: 978-0-9979941-7-9
ISBN-10: 0-9979941-7-7

Airmid Publishing

Disclaimer

This story is meant for entertainment purposes only.
I invoke artistic license for my rendition of events
either past, present or future.

Imagination is the only weapon in the war against reality.
~Cheshire Cat~

Chapter One

Shapes coalesced out of the darkness. I was suddenly afraid. Grandma had assured me that I was a member of this ancient order of witches that went back a thousand years. But I wasn't convinced as I watched the inky blackness from my place by the fountain, terrified of what was to come. I had recently turned eighteen, the age in which I was supposed to take my place within their ranks. Who was I to join this sacred group? And yet here I stood in front of the fountain, in a European city I'd never heard of before tonight. Aside from the shadows I could see nothing beyond the fountain, no city lights, no streets, no buildings, a dense blackness filling in the space beyond, as though this fountain and these trees were an island unto themselves.

A larger than life stone statue rose from the fountain's center, water cascading from the open mouths of serpents entwined around the legs of Luna, the Roman goddess of the moon. Her naked body was voluptuous and sensual, stylized curls coiling down her back, her form twisted at the waist as though she had just this moment turned to watch the moon rise. And rise it did, full and enormous above the tree line to the east. Pale light found me, linking me with the goddess, both of us pulsing and radiating as the orb lifted into the dark sky. A shiver went through my body as I realized the enormity of this moment. Because now I could see the many faces, all of them focused on me—both female and male, their clothing archaic and dark.

All the bizarre circumstances of the past month drifted through my mind as the witches took shape, landing one by one on the ground in front of me. Now I knew I'd followed the obscure instructions in *Witches of the World*, properly. Thirteenth page, thirteenth line down, Grandma had told me…the words written there disappearing a moment after I read them. I hadn't needed anything beyond those words to find my way here, only asking to be shown.

It all began around a month ago on the day my sister Jean arrived in 1694 Salem where I'd been living with the Wampanoag tribe. From that point on my life no longer seemed my own as I followed a twisting trail that brought me to this turning point in my life.

Chapter Two
1694

K *ehtannit is with us,* the natives chanted in Algonquin,
dancing in a circle. It was the night of the full moon,
its bright face a promise in the dark sky. Legs lifting, faces
turned upward the tribe moved as one, the murmur of
female and male voices blending together like a prayer. *Our
hunt will bring meat to last through winter. Nikommo keep us safe—
Great Spirit, Kehtannit, is with us.*

Since I was white, and not really a member of the tribe,
I sat alone by the fire. I pulled the deerskin cape around my
shoulders against the chilly air. Fall was upon us and the
tribe would need good hunting to provide food to last
through the cold winter to come. Samoset danced with
them, his long hair loose and shining in the moonlight. He
was painted tonight, a black mask across his eyes, red
streaks on his cheeks. His chest was bare, and he wore his
decorated breechcloth, formal leggings beneath. Beaded
armbands on his upper arms caught the light as he turned.

He looked formidable and strong, separate from me and not of this world. I glanced down at the tattoos he'd painstakingly worked into the skin of my upper arms before our marriage vows. His arms held the same dots representing the yearly thirteen moons and the swirling lines that signified the path through them.

Tonight was a *Nikommo* night, the name of one of many spirits who watched over us. Seldom seen, this spirit lived in the fir trees and brought success to the hunting and fishing done at this time of year. I had yet to see this creature, but Samoset had told me many stories in our one year together. He described him as elf-like sometimes, in animal form others. *Nikommo's* antithesis, *Hobomock*, was the *manito*, or spirit, feared most by the Wampanoag people. Also known as *Chepi*, the word for ghost, this evil creature could appear as deceased loved ones, tricking tribe members into following him. Medicine men and self-styled witches were particularly susceptible to his trickery, I'd heard, their gifts leaving them more vulnerable to abuse from the dark spirits.

Coming from the future and having read the myths surrounding tribal life, I hadn't taken any of this very seriously. But the more I lived with the Wampanoag the more I realized that being a witch made me susceptible to such a creature. According to tribal lore the *Hobomock* preyed on those who were able to locate water and game and who knew when danger was coming. My ability to travel through time could be mined by evil if I wasn't careful.

The medicine man, Joseph, and a very old woman, who called herself Appause, after the moon, were the wise ones the Wampanoag consulted in times of need. It was only

Samoset who made use of my talents and who trusted me for who I was. By all accounts I was an outsider married to their sachem, Samoset, but not entirely trusted. I let out a heavy sigh, wishing I was one of them, but until Samoset and I had a child I had a feeling my status would remain as it was—a white woman who traveled with them.

"Em?" I came out of my meanderings, realizing that the dancing and drumming had come to an end. Samoset stood next to me, his masked eyes scaring me for a moment. He had the look of a spirit himself, his eyes pools of darkness.

I smiled up at him. "Are you ready for bed?"

He shook his head, gesturing to the forest. "Need time. You sleep."

It was deep in the night when Samoset joined me in the *wetu*. His hair was damp from swimming, his skin cool where it touched mine.

"Where have you been? I was worried."

"I go to ocean. Sit. Swim. Think."

"What were you thinking about?"

Instead of answering his mouth sought mine, the length of him pressing against me. He tugged at my loose nightdress, pulling it over my head before removing the loincloth that still lay between us. I let out a gasp as he entered me, surprised by his urgency. But a moment later I was lost as always, caught up in the magical world we created together. We soared into the treetops and even further into the stars, our moans and cries joining the creatures of the night. We clung together as darkness turned into dawn. And then we slept.

It was a week after *Nikommo* night and most of the men had taken off into the forest to search for game. Samoset had been one of them, his hair braided, the beautiful carved bow he'd inherited from this father across his wide shoulders. After he left I shirked my sewing duties with the other native women to wander off into the forest alone. Something pulled at me and I needed to be in nature for it to show itself. "Is it Samoset?" I asked. Since *Nikommo* night I hadn't seen much of him. I wondered again about his behavior that night, as though he couldn't get enough of me. Samoset was disappointed that I didn't yet carry a child. Maybe that was the reason for his intensity. It was the right time for me, something I'd explained a few days earlier. But we'd tried before, our timing impeccable, and no baby had come of it. I was sixteen when we first met, a virgin, but with Samoset's patient instruction I had learned what it meant to lie with a man, to be part of his life and he part of mine. I loved him and I did want a child—didn't I?

My gaze went to the lengthening shadows that signified the coming season and what this would mean for us. Soon we would move to our winter home where we would sleep with the rest of the tribe in the *nush wetu*, the permanent longhouses built inland closer to the mountains. We would not have the privacy we had in our summer *wetu*, something we would both miss.

My mind wandered into the past to my previous life in the town of Danvers, Connecticut. My family was still there, but since living with the tribe I hadn't visited. I loved them and missed them all, but Samoset did not want me to leave. He worried that something would happen to prevent me from returning. Thinking back to several time-traveling anomalies I understood his concerns.

My life here was good. I was with the man I loved and I felt connected to the forest and all the creatures that made it their home. I knew where and when to search for mushrooms, nuts and greens. I respected all life, including the ants that collected on our ground-up nuts, to the bees that pollinated the flowers on the blackberry bushes.

But I did have a concern. Could it be the timeline difference that prevented me from conceiving? If I couldn't get pregnant Samoset would surely turn away from me, wife or not. As Sachem he was expected to bring a child into the world; according to the tribe a baby was long overdue.

Since *Nikommo* night several tribe members had begun to watch me, their furtive glances worried and somewhat fearful. I saw them talking with Samoset, pointing out the beautiful Indian women who would be happy to share his bed and his life. He hadn't spoken to me of this, but I saw it and I knew. Should I tell him of my fear or keep it to myself? If I told him it might hasten his defection.

I heard the screech of an owl, a dark portent according to the tribal elders. Shivering, I watched it fly soundlessly through the trees, disappearing into the shadows. Owls could signify death, but I knew better than to take this literally. Death could mean rebirth—something new beginning. Maybe this time my womb held the seed of new life.

I was still contemplating meanings when my younger sister abruptly appeared out of the ether. I let out a gasp and stepped back, stumbling and nearly falling in my surprise. It had been over a year since I'd last seen Jean, my thoughts brought sharply back to 2016.

"What—no hug?" My sister glared at me out of narrowed blue eyes, freckles standing out in the cool shadows of the conifer forest.

I laughed uneasily and moved forward, feeling the tension in her shoulders as my arms went around her. Jean had never believed me when I told her I'd been traveling back and forth to 1692, my tales of saving nine people from being hung as witches making her laugh out loud. And now she was here? "So I guess you believe me now?"

Jean stared at me. "What are you talking about?"

I looked her over, noticing how her body had filled out, baby fat gone from her cheeks. She was taller than I was. But with my height topping out at five foot two that wasn't saying much. "Don't you remember how you questioned my ability to time travel?"

She scoffed. "Not really. Maybe I didn't like you disappearing all the time and leaving me to deal with Mom and Dad. They were always so…"

"So controlling?"

She scoffed. "I guess that's one way of putting it."

"Why are you here and how did you find me?"

"Easy enough, Emmy. Your psyche has always been an open book to me."

It was? I frowned, trying to place this person in my memory. "You're saying that you followed my energy signature?"

"I thought of you, pictured you in my mind, and whoosh—here I am."

I thought of my portal, the two oak trees that I had to pass between to get from future to past and back again. It had taken months before I realized I no longer needed them. Apparently Jean was more accomplished at traveling through time than I was. "Since when have you been able to do this?"

Jean scrunched her pale eyebrows and stared at me. "What is *with* you? Where's the village, anyway?" she asked, looking around.

"Come on," I said, leading the way through the forest. "It's close to the ocean."

Her nose wrinkled. "I thought I smelled salt air."

Jean's gaze roamed across the small summer *wetus*, her mouth opening when she noticed the tribe members going about their daily business. It was summer and in this culture clothing was optional.

I followed her gaze to my friend Numee, attempting to see things as Jean did. The young Indian woman was naked to the waist, long hair covering her upper body as she worked with a tool to tan deer hides.

Jean was now scanning the dome-shaped houses formed from cedar saplings and covered with loosely woven reeds to let the breezes blow through. Beyond the dwellings a circle of smooth river stones lined the community fire where we gathered for meetings and celebrations. And behind the fire pit stood the long woven racks where deerskins were stretched to dry. Chickens pecked in the dirt due to my prowess as a thief, the chicks taken before we left Salem for the deeper wilderness. Aunum, the mastiff who had adopted me, arrived next to my left leg, his wary amber eyes on my sister. "It's okay," I said soothingly, placing a hand on his wide head.

Jean seemed at a loss for words, her gaze coming back to me. "This is…so rustic!"

"Yes, well it is the sixteen hundreds, you know. What did you expect?"

She shrugged. "I don't know. Pictures I've seen make it look well, you know…different."

I turned to watch Samoset's mother walk by, Weetamoo's calm gaze going to my sister who was dressed in skin-tight low cut jeans and a T-shirt that exposed her midriff. The older woman disappeared into a dwelling.

I noticed the piercing in her belly button. "Mom let you do that?" I asked, pointing at the gold ring.

"Mom doesn't care."

Mom had always been a stickler about ear piercing and dying our hair—she didn't believe it was proper. And here was my sister with blue streaks in her blond curls, a belly button ring and several piercings in each ear. On her feet she wore impossibly high black boots.

Hair dye was nothing new to the Wampanoag, many of who had red streaks in their long black hair. Black tattoos were etched into the skin of their forearms, streaks of color on their cheeks and foreheads; they didn't seem at all surprised by my sister's attire.

My jeans had been discarded long ago, and now I wore a dress I'd fashioned from a pilgrim cotton dress Samoset had given me shortly after we met. I'd shortened the hem to knee length and cut both sleeves off at the shoulders—alterations to accommodate the warm weather. Faded from many washings, it was my signature summer outfit. In the winter I put it away and dressed like the Wampanoag women in the warmer deerskin skirts and tunics.

"Nice dress," Jean said sarcastically, looking me over. "Do you ever bother to bathe?"

I was suddenly aware of the dirt under my fingernails, my hair thick and oily where it hung down my back. My dress was ripped in several places, the brown of mud permanently stained into the fabric. "Why are you here, Jean?"

Jean straightened and sniffed, pushing a few wayward strands of glossy hair behind her ears. "Grandma sent me. Mom and Dad split up. The government's gone crazy and the new president is like some Nazi general or something. He's doing stuff that's unconstitutional and getting away with it because he has both houses of congress behind him."

My sister had never paid any attention to politics, and last I'd known, Grandma was living in 2011 with one of the men we'd saved from being hung as a witch. Sam and Grandma had moved in together and seemed very contented with their life. "Why is Grandma there?"

Jean stared at me defiantly. "I don't know. She just arrived one morning and stayed."

That explanation made no sense. My grandmother was devoted to Sam. She wouldn't just leave him for no reason. "And this Grandma told you to come find me?"

"What do you mean 'this Grandma'? What other Grandma do we have?"

"She has a life in 2011, right?"

Jean shrugged and frowned. "What do I care? All I know is she's been living with us for a while and trying to help. Mom has seriously gone off the deep end. If you weren't so selfish you would have known this."

I held up my hand. "Stop right there. I came to 1692 to keep those demented idiots in Salem from burning witches. I would hardly call that a selfish act. Now tell me again why my little sister, who used to complain about everything I did, is here to ask for my help?"

Her lips compressed. "It's your country too, Emily. A lot of schools have closed due to lack of funding. Money is being funneled into the military and the uber wealthy. I thought you might give a care, but I guess I was wrong."

I thought of my devoted parents. In the world I knew they couldn't have split up.

"Mom's going crazy and Dad just sits at his new apartment pretending nothing's…" her voice drifted away when Samoset approached, a bow slung over his shoulder.

Through her eyes I saw him anew—copper skin, glossy blue-black hair filled with bits of leaf and twigs, and eyes the color of onyx. His cheekbones looked chiseled, remnants of red paint still on his face. He had just arrived from the hunt, blood speckling his hands and forearms. He looked untamed.

He frowned, staring at me. "Em?"

I came out of my examination and took his hand. "Samoset—meet my sister, Jean."

Jean stared at him, her mouth falling open. Her face turned beet red. "I…hello…" she finally managed.

"Hello," Samoset said, breaking into a wide smile. "I have heard of you many times." He turned to me again. "We need fresh water source. Can you…?"

I laughed. "Can I use my witch intuition to find a new

one? I thought we were leaving soon."

"We go but need water before move. Stream dry up."
He pointed to the clear blue sky. "Dry time. Need rain."

"Let me finish talking with my sister. She came a long
way to find me."

"From future?" he asked, watching her curiously.

"Yes, I came from the future," she answered, "which is
seriously fucked up right now."

"Jean! Language!"

"Are you kidding me? You're worried about me using
the F word? Give me a break."

I let out a snort. "I guess I'm taking on the mom role."

"Yeah, whatever. If you need to search for water I can
come along."

I stared at her fancy boots. "We'll be climbing through
brush. I'll lend you a pair of moccasins."

When Samoset wandered off Jean followed me into our
dwelling. "Wow, this isn't what I expected," she said,
looking around. "This is kind of cool."

I followed her gaze to the woven mats on the floor, to
our cozy place at the back where we slept. It smelled of
rushes and sweet grass. I climbed into Samoset's and my
sleeping space and fetched the moccasins from where I'd
stashed them. When I turned she was right behind me, her
interested gaze going to our bed and the small bits of
feathers, stones and shells that sat in niches I'd fashioned
to hold them.

"You and Samoset—wow."

"What do you mean?"

"He's a hunk and a half, Emmy. Do you have sex with
him?"

"What do you think—does sex still repel you?"

She scoffed. "No. Brian and I, we…he kissed me and felt me up, and I have to say I liked it. We haven't done it yet, but…"

"Make sure you use birth control."

Her gaze met mine. "Planned Parenthood is gone. I have no way to get birth control now."

"Because of the new president?"

"Yup. He's taken away women's rights—no more abortion, not even to save the mother's life—free health clinics are gone. The religious right has taken over. I don't have the money to go anywhere else. And I can't ask Mom."

I could hardly believe what she was telling me. "Why does Grandma think I can help?"

"Maybe she hopes you can deal with Mom, who has basically gone into some kind of death spiral."

Samoset was standing outside the doorway when we left the *wetu*. "You go now?"

"Yes, Samoset. I'll find water. You should come along and bathe. Your hands…"

He looked down. "Deer blood."

"I know what it is, I just think you should wash it off."

He shook his head. "More to come."

"Yuck!" Jean said, staring at him. "Do you butcher the deer?"

"Butcher?" He looked at me.

"Yes, Jean. They kill the deer and thank it for giving its life to feed us. They skin it right there and drain the blood before carrying the carcass back to camp. We cook the brains and then use them to tan the hides—we rub them into the hides to soften them. Every part of each animal is eaten and used to make pouches and clothing. For instance…" I glanced at Jean who had turned pale. "You eat meat, right? This is way more humane than how they kill cattle."

"I know—it's just…"

"At first Em feel like you," Samoset said. "Now understand ways."

I grabbed my sister's hand, dragging her away from where she stood rooted, gaping at Samoset. "As soon as I find water you're taking a bath," I called to him over my shoulder.

I followed the path into the woods, my mind calling out to the water spirits. We were in a drought and I would have to search far and wide to find another spring to use until we left for our winter home. As we walked Jean carried on a non-stop monologue, taking me back to the future where the memory of the screech of traffic, the heavy bass of radios, and the shrill sound of police sirens, reminded me of why I was here. Just hearing her fast-paced chatter had replaced my normal calm with the familiar urgency from the twenty-first century.

I climbed through brush, holding up branches for Jean. Samoset assigning me this 'job' was a joke. Every native here had a sixth sense from living in harmony with the earth. He did it to make me feel a part of things and so I could get into the tribe's good graces. Lately I'd been blamed for lack of water, lack of food, sickness, and the various raids that came about because of the encroaching white man. It had been my idea to move the tribe far from Salem to an area I knew from history would remain safe for the foreseeable future. But my time traveling seemed to have altered the past and we'd already encountered many settlers who coveted the land for farming. In Wampanoag eyes my arrival from another time, another place, made me a *Hobomock*, or *chepi*.

Jean crashed through the brush, her loud voice startling birds and a small herd of deer that jumped out of our way and leapt into the shadows. "Try to be more quiet," I whispered, watching a fawn hurry after its mother.

"You're going too fast," she whined. "I didn't sign up to take a hike in the woods."

"You said you'd come with me—now quit whining and let your senses take over. You're a witch same as me, and maybe with the two of us we can find water sooner rather than later." I heard her frustrated sigh, but after that her footfalls weren't quite as loud and she stopped talking for a while.

It must have been close to an hour before I felt the tingle I was waiting for. I stopped, putting up a hand when I noticed Jean about to say something. I turned in a circle allowing my senses to reach out. We were in a former boggy area that was mostly dry after the drought, but there was something...

I slowly walked on, stopping to scrabble in the dirt when some little voice ordered me to. When I looked up, Jean was nowhere around. "Jean?"

"I'm over here," I heard her call. "I found water."

I headed toward her voice, emerging out of the woods into a small clearing where I heard the unmistakable burble of a stream.

"It's here," she said from where she knelt in the soft dirt.

"Good for you!" I complimented, bending down to see how much water we were talking about.

"The spring's up there," she continued, pointing behind us to a rocky outcropping.

I followed her up the small hillside where a deep pool had collected within the hollowed out rock. Without thinking I stripped off my clothing and climbed in. Jean watched for a minute before she did the same, both of us sinking into the water with twin sighs of contentment. Jean gazed at me across the pool. "This is heaven."

I smiled and sank beneath the water to rinse my hair, running my fingers through to loosen the oil and dirt. I had no shampoo but the natural oils in my hair had kept it healthy and shiny. My mind went to my bathroom at home, the array of hair products, skin creams, make-up and deodorant that lined the shelves.

When I emerged from my bath my sister was sunning herself on a rock, her naked body glistening as her fingers combed through the short tangle of curls. Some of the color had come out, leaving behind a blue-blonde halo.

I climbed up beside her and took my waist long hair in my hands and squeezed out the excess water. "What a spot you found. Now tell me how you discovered the spring, Jean."

"I did what you told me to do—let my senses guide me. After that it was easy."

"Maybe your elemental is water," I said, watching her. I was surprised to see her so relaxed, and doubly surprised that this modern girl had managed to allow her senses to do anything. "I'm impressed. You should stay here. That way you don't have to worry about what's happening in the future."

She shook her head, her bright eyes turning dark. "They need me back there. Mom would freak out if she lost another daughter. You need to come home and help. Grandma said. And besides, I don't know anything about elementals."

"Grandma hasn't explained the elementals to you? That doesn't sound like her. And why she sent you to find me is kind of surprising."

"She said that unless you were pregnant I had to convince you to come back—at least for a while." She glanced at my body, which had filled out since my time with the Wampanoag. "*Are* you pregnant?"

I shook my head. "I may not be able to conceive because of the time difference."

Jean shuddered. "Ugh. A baby sounds terrible."

"I have to ask Samoset about going with you," I said, ignoring her. "He may not want me to."

Jean's eyes widened. "You'd let him decide? I thought you were so independent, such an emancipated woman. Remember that rally you led in high school to protest the computer shutdown?"

"What? I don't remember that."

"Oh come on, Emmy. You were the one who organized the entire thing. You had half the school carrying signs. Our computers were useless until they got the grid back up."

"Why did it get shut down?"

She frowned. "Are you for real? The government wanted to show us how much control they had over our lives. It's way worse now."

I racked my brain trying to remember the event. "I seriously have no memory of that at all. As to Samoset, we're a team, Jean. He doesn't control me. We love each other. I don't think he'll say no but I still have to talk it over with him."

"I never want to get married," my sister announced, pulling on the clothing she'd left discarded on the boulder. "We should get back. I need to go home." She stared at me pointedly.

I reluctantly dressed, pulling my damp hair into a loose braid before setting off. On the way I pointed out a cougar skulking through the brush around fifty yards from us, grabbing my sister before she let out a scream. "He's hunting one of the older deer. See the footprints there? One of the herd is lame. He'll kill it and eat it. It's the way of nature to cull out the infirm."

Jean moved closer. "How far is the village?"

Samoset frowned, his dark eyes meeting mine. "Is not good plan."

"Grandma is there."

"Grandmother has left Plymouth and Sam?"

"I guess so—seems odd, I agree."

"I need you here. We move camp. You will not find."

"Are you going to our winter camp? I know where it is. Besides, all I have to do is think of you and I'll find you. I've done it a million times."

"May make new village. Scouts say white man close."

"You're planning to build new longhouses? Where?"

"I do not know. Is why you need to stay."

"You're being silly, Samoset. I can always find you."

"Have had trouble in past, Em."

I touched his arm. "I think I have to go with her. I want to see Grandma, and the government is…" I shook my head. "I don't know what's going on, but according to Jean we have a president who is slightly crazy."

"Not slightly," I heard Jean call from where she eavesdropped.

"Bad sachem?"

"Yes. Very bad sachem."

"What can you do to stop? I have seen your future villages—too big."

"I don't know, but I do know I have to go."

He let out a long sigh and pulled me into his arms. "Not stay long, Em. I need you."

I laughed and pulled away. "You don't need me. You go off every day with the men and leave me at camp to cook and wash and sew and all the rest of it."

"You do not wish to hunt. But we go together to catch fish and mollusks."

What he said was true. He'd virtually begged me to go along on their hunting expeditions but I couldn't stand to see them kill the animals. Despite my bravado in telling Jean all about it, I was still squeamish about skinning and tanning the hides as well as turning the entrails into pouches and other useful items. My modern sensibilities would not be quelled. Fishing was fine, time spent in Samoset's canoe relaxing and enjoyable. And I could deal with trapping the rabbits and the partridges. It was the bigger game that got to me. But winter was coming and that meant turning meat into jerky and digging tubers where we'd planted them in the spring.

"I promise it won't be more than a few days." When I stood on tiptoe to kiss him he pressed his mouth to mine—but when his eyes flicked to Jean watching us he quickly pulled away.

"Come on," Jean said impatiently, tugging at me.

I gave Samoset one last lingering look before I took her arm, letting her lead us forward in time. No portal for her. It was straight into the ether without a moment's hesitation.

Chapter Three

I gazed up and down the street—our street, Randall Lane. The grass in yards was dried and brown, trash under bushes, plastic bags hanging from tree limbs. This was not a wealthy part of town but it had always been tidy, the residents watering and mowing and planting flowers in their front yards. Why hadn't anyone cleaned up? Our red brick ranch house with green shutters looked as it always had except for the boarded up windows. "What's with the windows?"

"The religious right doesn't like Mom. They call her a heathen. They threw rocks one night and another night they burned some kind of weird effigy in our front yard. Things are really bad."

As though to illustrate her point a car rolled down the road, a megaphone blaring. "Church is mandatory!" the male voice yelled. "If you don't attend there will be consequences."

"Church is mandatory?" I stared at my sister. "Since when?"

"Since these ideologues took over our government.

They refuse entry into the country to anyone who isn't Christian, and the ones who live here are required to go to church to prove they belong. The borders between Canada and Mexico are closed."

"What about other religions—Buddhism, Judaism, Muslim, Hindu and all the rest?"

"They've either converted or been arrested. There's a lot of secrecy—it's hard to get information now. Do you remember that weird news group that called themselves some name that had bright in it—the ultra right, or part of the alt-right or something? They've kind of taken over."

"White supremacists?"

Jean nodded, heading toward our house. Before we reached the door it flew open, revealing my grandmother. She pushed gray strands back from her face, her worried gaze turning into a smile when she saw me. "Emeline, my dear!" She pulled me into a hug.

"Grandma, why are you here?"

A puzzled expression appeared on her face. "I'm here because of your mother, of course. She needs my support."

I was about to ask about Sam when my mother appeared. "I thought I'd never see you again," she whispered huskily, pulling me into a hug.

I could feel every rib, her body stick thin.

"Your grandmother has been a godsend," she said once we pulled apart. "I had a nervous breakdown due to Henry's departure."

"Yeah, what's with Dad leaving? I can't believe he'd abandon you."

Mom's eyes filled. "He's always had that independent streak. You know the one."

No, I didn't know. My last impression of my father was of a man devoted to my mother and unable to do anything for himself.

"How is your Indian?" Grandma asked, her bright bird-like eyes moving across my body. "No baby yet?"

"Samoset is fine, and no baby. Not for lack of trying."

She let out a snort. "Not the worst of fates, I would imagine."

"Grandma!" Jean said, horrified.

"Have you seen the man, Jeanie?"

"Well, yes." Her gaze went to the floor as a blush moved up her neck, turning her cheeks pink.

I ignored the interchange, turning to my mother. "What's happened to you? You look like a scarecrow."

"Emeline, your mother doesn't need to hear that. She's doing the best she can."

Since when did Grandma stand up for her daughter? They'd barely been speaking the last time I'd been here.

Mom tried to smile. "It's hard without your father to support us, dear. And with the recent violence we may have to move."

"Move where? Because of money?"

Mom looked at Grandma, seemingly unable to go on.

"Henry is no longer paying the mortgage on the house. It may be foreclosed," Grandma supplied. "And this has become a target neighborhood for the religious right."

Grandma ushered us inside and closed the door, locking it carefully with several extra deadbolts. We all followed her into the kitchen where the smell of baking bread reached my nostrils. The familiar scents brought back memories of my childhood when life was carefree. Now a pall hung over us, despite the homey aroma and my grandmother's butter stained apron, which I'd never seen her wear. As far as I remembered she'd never baked in her life.

She removed two golden loaves from the oven. "Now, Theresa, I fixed you a good meal," she said, watching my mother. "And I expect you to at least attempt to eat it. I do not want to have to fetch the doctor again." She lifted what looked like a meatloaf out of the upper oven and left it cooling on a rack. "Sit everyone."

"How long have you been here?" I asked my grandmother as she dished out meatloaf and placed slices of warm bread on plates.

"Several weeks," she said vaguely, waving her free hand in the air. "I've been trying to get your mother out of this town but she refuses to budge."

I glanced at my mother who looked about to cry. "Is this violence all over the country or just here in Danvers?"

Grandma scoffed as she placed plates in front of each of us. "It's everywhere, dear, but there are places in the country where we could be safe. I agree about not abandoning the fight for Danvers, but if we stay much longer we could become victims."

"Henry won't leave and with things the way they are he can't cope on his own—you know that, Mother."

"He divorced you, Theresa. Why are you still making excuses for the man?" Grandma sighed. "If your house is foreclosed and the political situation
doesn't take a turn for the better, you'll have to do something, with or without Henry."

Mom let out a sigh. "Henry wants nothing to do with me."

"Theresa," my grandmother said sharply, "it is time for you to stand up for yourself. Henry was once a good man, but with his recent activities I would no longer place him in that category."

"What activities?" I asked just before stuffing a buttered piece of bread into my mouth.

"He's going along with everything that fool in the White House says," my mother explained. "He's turned into a yes man."

"That isn't fair!" Jean cried. "He only did what he did to keep his job."

"What did he do?"

My sister gazed at me. "He signed a waiver that took away his individual rights."

"Lots of people signed that waiver, Jean," my mother said. "It's why we're in this predicament."

"But that's the backbone of our constitution!" I shouted.

My mother shook her head, her eyes closing. "Not anymore."

Grandma rapped sharply on the table with the back of her fork. "Let's eat, shall we? All this talk is enough to make me lose my appetite."

I watched my mother take very small bites, finishing only a quarter of her food before putting her fork down. "Lovely dinner, Mother, but it is too much for me. Enjoying food seems wrong when so many people are suffering."

My grandmother glared at her. "If you don't eat you will have little energy to do anything about those suffering people, Theresa. You've let yourself sink into despair, and until you reclaim your strength you are useless to the cause."

The cause. I wondered exactly what that referred to. "Are we planning to march?"

Grandma stared at me. "I thought Jean explained everything we've been doing. Despite a recent decree that forbids it, people are taking to the streets."

"But you just said if we didn't leave…"

"We're doing it anyway," Jean said loudly, her fork clattering onto her plate. "If they want to throw me in jail, fine. I refuse to give up."

"Facism—is that what we have now? Or would you call it a dictatorship?"

My grandmother turned to face me, her blue eyes flashing. "The name for it doesn't matter. What matters is that we stop it before our country turns into a place we don't recognize."

"Sounds like it already has," I muttered, thinking about the car and the megaphone, the edicts to keep people from entering the country, my father signing away his rights as a citizen. "What's happening with the refugees from all the wars we've caused?"

"Stranded at the borders or sent back," my mother muttered, staring down at her plate. "Planes have been mostly grounded, normal folk unable to get from one place to another. But the wealthy continue on as though nothing has changed."

"How did it get this bad?"

"Slowly so that we didn't notice it happening until it was too late," Grandma answered. "First it was the illegal election of this man, done by gerrymandering and suppressing the vote. After that it was the ultra conservative congress and the president taking away our rights, one by one. People stood up, but the ones in charge chose to ignore us in favor of their cushy jobs. I honestly thought marching would help us, and I still do, but now the police have been given authority to jail people for saying an unkind word about what's happening. And that piece of paper we've been forced to sign is another nail in the coffin of democracy."

"But you didn't sign it, right?"

"Only because they haven't gotten around to us yet. In the end we will all sign it, Emeline."

"Your grandmother thinks we can march and have an influence, but I have my doubts," Mom said, shaking her head. "Your father has already succumbed. We're next."

"Do not say that, Theresa. There's still a chance if we can gather with others."

"And where do we find these others?" Jean asked. "When I venture out of the house, all I see on the streets are the police."

No one answered that question.

The rest of the meal was eaten in silence, and when we finished I got up and cleared the table. I washed the dishes and placed them in the dish rack, half-listening to the conversation going on between my grandmother and Jean. Outside the window the grass had turned brown, flowers un-watered and shriveled up. Trash sailed by on the wind. There was no sign of birds or the squirrels I remembered.

"The library is first on the agenda for tomorrow," Grandma said. "They cannot close it."

I turned. "They want to close the libraries?"

"Tax dollars are being allocated to border security and the many wars that are raging around the world."

"But we have Internet, right?"

"The Internet has been restricted to only news from inside the country—and most of what we hear is propaganda, geared to make us think everything is going well." She paused, her troubled gaze meeting mine. "I'm sorry to have to be the bearer of such bad news."

"And I thought I'd have a hard time living in the 1600's. I already miss my simple life with Samoset and the rest of the tribe." I frowned. "I can't waste time fighting for a cause we can't win."

My grandmother pursed her lips. "The price of freedom is eternal vigilance."

"Maybe so, but I don't want to end up in jail and unable to get home." I was about to ask about Sam when Grandma continued.

"I've always fought for what I believed in."

"What if this is a fight that can't be won?"

"Well then, all of us, including you and Samoset, can…"

I shook my head. "He's sachem now, Grandma. He's not going anywhere."

"Perhaps there's a place in the world where people have learned their lessons about war," she said dreamily, ignoring me.

"People will never learn," my mother intoned.

I was asleep in Jean's room when I heard someone pounding on the front door. I got out of bed and padded into the hallway. "Grandma? Mom? Should I answer the door?"

My mother appeared from her room, bleary-eyed. "It could be your father. I'll go."

I watched her stumble down the stairs, pulling her robe closed as she went. A minute later I heard raised voices and then my Mom shouting, "No! Absolutely not! Why should I?"

"You will comply, Mrs. Chase, or we will have to use force."

"Mom?" I hurried to the stairs, but by the time I got there two uniformed men were dragging her away. "Mom!" I ran down the stairs and out the open door just as they pushed her into the back seat of a black car and drove away. I ran after the car shouting, but it disappeared into the darkness, the taillights fading until I couldn't see them anymore.

"Emeline, what in the world?" I heard my grandmother call.

I ran back to the house, my bare feet barely registering the rough gravel as I hurtled through the door. "They took Mom!"

Grandma stared at me, her eyes widening. "I was afraid of this. Her name is on a list of those who refuse to attend church."

"What about you? You don't go, do you?"

"I'm not an official resident here." She slammed the door shut and locked it. "Henry needs to be notified, that is if he hasn't been arrested as well."

"Can you call him?"

"There are no more private cell phones, dear, at least not for the masses. First thing in the morning we will pay your father a visit."

I barely slept, my thoughts on my mother and what had happened. I had no idea where they'd taken her or anything else about what she might be going through. I was a newbie in this world of violence and repression.

It was five a.m. when I dressed and headed downstairs. Grandma was already in the kitchen, a cup of tea in her hands.

Without speaking she poured me a cup. We seated ourselves across from one another at the table.

"I am very worried about Theresa," she said. "She is not strong right now and if they harass her she will head into another tailspin. Your father may have some suggestion, but I think my only option is to pull in some debts."

"Debts? What are you talking about?"

"I used to have friends in high places in Danvers. If a certain person is still around he just might be able to help us."

I frowned. "When was this, Grandma? I thought you went into the past a long time ago."

A far away look appeared on her face as she continued. "I worked as a secretary for one of the most influential democratic senators for a while. He was very fond of me."

"Fond—do you mean you had an affair? How long ago was this?"

She smiled, staring into the distance. "He was married and a lot younger than I."

"When?" I asked again.

Her gaze met mine. "Why is that important?"

"I was just trying to establish a focal point. This doesn't match up with what I thought I knew about your life. Do you know if he's still in Congress?"

"I would imagine he is, unless they've booted him because of his liberal views."

"Maybe he changed his views in order to get along."

"Not Rory. He would never compromise his position." She gazed at me, her eyes bright. "The library has access to the Internet. I'll send him a quick e-mail."

"How will you get his response?"

"The library computer, dear. It's the only way. He represents Massachusetts."

"I don't understand. If he's still in Congress wouldn't he be fighting against the monster in charge?"

"The good ones fight but it gets them nowhere. He's a member of the minority party."

"At least we still have parties," I muttered.

"They would dearly love to have only the one party—I assume that's what all of this is about. But so far they haven't managed it."

"I can't believe this. I've only been gone a year."

Grandma stared at me with a puzzled expression. "One year? This has been going on for several years and has only come to a boil recently."

I was about to question that statement when Jean padded into the kitchen rubbing her eyes. "Why are you up so early? Where's Mom?"

I glanced at Grandma, waiting for her to answer. "Jean, come sit next to me," she said, patting the chair. "Have some tea."

Jean frowned and looked at me before sitting next to Grandma. "Emmy? What's going on?"

"Mom got arrested last night."

Jean's eyes widened, and then her face crumpled. "I

knew it! I saw it happen in a vision. Why didn't I tell her?"

I reached across the table and took her hand. "It wouldn't have changed anything."

Jean was crying now, her hands covering her face. The hollow sobs were disturbing, setting my teeth on edge. "Jean, Grandma has a plan."

Jean looked up and wiped her eyes on her sleeve, sniffing.

"As soon as you're dressed and we've all had a bite to eat we'll head to the library. From there I expect to speak to your father. Once he's on board I'll attempt to contact Rory McCord."

"Dad on board? I doubt it," my sister said, looking skeptical.

"Despite the divorce I know Henry loves your mother. And with the way he feels about you and Emeline, I'm sure he'll join us."

We dressed and ate a silent breakfast, my mind whirling in several different directions. It seemed impossible that things had deteriorated this much in the time I'd been gone. And I was about to find out just how bad things really were.

Chapter Four

The three of us trooped down the sidewalk single file, Grandma in the lead. There were ruts and broken pieces of concrete that prevented us from walking together, that and trash and broken glass that littered the roadway from one side to the other. I saw only two cars on the road, and they looked official. When we turned right toward the library we could hear voices raised in anger. Grandma stopped when a gunshot rang out.

"What in the world now," she muttered, squinting into the distance.

"It looks like the cops are arresting someone," Jean said, squinting at the clump of police.

Another shot echoed and this time a person fell. "The cops are shooting people!" I yelled, pulling Jean back. "We can't go out there!"

"We'd better see what's happening," Grandma said, walking forward toward the chaos.

I grabbed her arm. "Grandma, are you crazy? Do you want to be rounded up and shot too?"

"I will use Rory McCord as my 'get out of jail free' card," she assured me, heading toward the fracas that was becoming louder as each moment went by.

I ran to catch up, walking next to her. "If you get yourself shot I'll never forgive you," I muttered.

My grandmother laughed gaily as though she'd done this a thousand times. I stared at her for a moment, wondering about her sanity. This was not the sensible Grandma I knew.

Once we reached the crowd of people and cops we realized the true extent of the violence. Several bodies lay on the ground, blood pooling around them. The cops were wearing riot gear, the other civilians cowering and covering their tear-streaked faces.

"What is happening here?" my grandmother asked the nearest cop.

He turned toward her, his face obscured by the mask he wore. "The library has been closed for safety reasons. These people are breaking the law."

"Trying to get inside," my grandmother acknowledged, nodding sagely. "It is the only access to Internet, you know," she added, looking up at him.

"That's not my problem. Take it up with your representatives."

"You don't sound in favor," my grandmother said.

"I'm neutral, ma'am. I'm doing my job."

"I need to send an e-mail to Senator McCord. Where can I do this?"

The cop shrugged and turned away to deal with another hysterical person, his hand going to his gun. The action stopped the woman in her tracks, her eyes going wide when she saw it. "I must get in touch with my husband," she begged him. "Where can I go?"

He shook his head, holstering his gun. "I don't have that information. Now all of you need to disperse," he shouted loudly, "before anyone else gets hurt!"

Grandma grabbed my arm. "Come with me."

She dragged us away from the library and down the street to a recessed doorway. "Once they leave we'll break in."

I stared at her in disbelief. "Don't you think they'll guard the place?"

"No, I don't. Once the people leave they'll head off to do some other nasty piece of their job. Without access to the internet we are like rats in a cage."

"More like sheep, if you ask me."

"No, Emeline. Sheep put up with things—these people are attempting to fight back. But if things escalate any further they will give up."

I nodded, thinking of the three still forms on the ground. We waited for nearly an hour before the area outside the library cleared out. The bodies were placed on stretchers and moved into a van, the bloodstains left to show what happens when citizens disobey the law.

"Hurry," Grandma hissed, walking quickly toward the library. Jean and I followed her, both of us horrified by what she planned to do. If an alarm went off we could end up just as dead as the others.

"Grandma, no!" I hissed, watching her standing on tiptoe to reach a window. A moment later she had managed to pry it open using a broom left behind by some maintenance person.

"Give me a leg up," she ordered, staring at me out of over-bright eyes.

"Let me do it," I said, moving toward the window. My arms were strong from living with the tribe and I pulled myself up easily, pressing my body through the narrow opening. Once inside I dropped to the floor, taking a moment to let my eyes adjust to the darkness. No alarms yet. I moved to the front door and loosened the locks, swinging it open for my waiting sister and Grandmother. "Why isn't the alarm on?"

"I doubt they set alarms, Emeline. It is only lately that the library with its Internet has become susceptible to unlawful break-ins."

"Like us?" I let out a humorless laugh and closed the door behind them.

The bank of computers sat in a room behind the front desk. When I turned one on, the whirring sounded way too loud. I glanced around nervously.

Grandma shook her head. "The police are long gone. This is small potatoes compared to what they've been employed to do these days."

Before I could move the mouse Grandma had shoved me aside and was seated and searching. "Jean," she said without looking up, "give your father a call please. I think he still has his landline. Phone is on the front desk."

Jean nodded and headed off. A few seconds later I heard her voice echo out of the silence. "Dad? They arrested Mom."

I turned back to see Rory's name appear on the screen, my grandmother's fingers flying across the keys. She clicked send and sat back. "Now we wait."

It was a half hour before Grandma got her answer, a

short message that read: *For you I would risk everything. What do you need?*

"Wow, Grandma, I thought you said it wasn't a love affair."

She smirked. "Did I say that? We were very fond of one another." She typed in another message. *My daughter has been arrested. Can you help us get her out?*

I can certainly try, came the reply a moment later. *Luckily I happen to be in town this week. Meet me at the county courthouse on the corner of Main and Vine.*

Jean arrived, her cheeks wet with tears. "Dad says he can't do anything about Mom. He seems to think that if he comes out of his apartment he'll be thrown in jail too. But why would he? He's done everything they asked."

"Because he's a coward," Grandma whispered half to herself. She took hold of Jean's hand. "I heard back from Rory. He's promised to help. Now come along girls. We need to get downtown as soon as possible."

Chapter Five

Chaos was the only word to describe the Humvees driven by police in riot gear rolling up and down streets, the people running to get away from them, and the screaming and shooting in the distance. Most shops were closed up tight, paper cups, plastic bags and cardboard detritus collected against the doorways. Windows were either broken out or hung open, screens hanging by an edge. Curtains flapped in the breeze. It felt like some distant future I'd already visited and didn't want to be in again.

Grandma paid no attention, walking with head held high and back straight. Jean and I followed her like two nervous baby chicks. "It's all in the attitude," she whispered, glancing back at us. Grandma had always been sure of herself, but in these circumstances her behavior seemed foolhardy.

When we reached Main Street she turned right onto Vine, scanning for Rory. "He should be here by now," she muttered worriedly. The courthouse looked abandoned, no one sitting on the steps leading up to it, no one coming or going through the wide glass doors. A moment later a tall gray-haired man emerged from behind a pillar and walked quickly toward us. He pulled Grandma into his arms, closing his eyes as they embraced.

When he released her he had tears in his eyes. "I never thought I'd see you again, Rebecca. You look wonderful."

Grandma smiled up at him coquettishly, surprising me. It didn't seem the proper expression for a woman her age, especially when she was living with another man. I was beginning to think that her explanation about their relationship had left a few things out.

"I'm very glad to see you too, Rory." She glanced at us. "My granddaughters are concerned about their mother. Is anything being done about this thug in the white house?"

Rory glanced around furtively and took hold of my grandmother's arm. "Let's take this conversation somewhere more private." He led us down the steps and around the back of the building, stopping by a doorway that led into the basement of the courthouse. He opened it with a key and took us into a dark hallway, stopping there to talk. "I've been doing everything I can, but we are locked in the grips of the monster we created. If it hadn't been for the slow eroding of our constitution we wouldn't be in this predicament. The presidency holds too much power now, and the courts have been stacked. I'm only here because of my long standing connections, but if they get their way this country will have only one party."

He glanced up when the sound of shouting reached our ears. "This is martial law, put into place because of supposed terrorism. This is the week for town halls but they've all been cancelled due to the recent new rules. As far as your daughter, I have already called the jail and organized her release." He glanced at Jean and me before turning back to Grandma. "You must get away from here. If you stay and fight, you will be caught up in it and either killed or thrown in jail. I know you well, Rebecca, but this time you have to let it go. Please." He held on to her arms, staring into her eyes.

She shook her head. "How can I give up? Without people like me they get away with it, Rory. The citizens must organize in order to stop this."

Rory frowned. "They've already gotten away with it. You've seen what goes on. The police have been militarized and given the authority to shoot those who they deem a threat. News has been suppressed, reporters jailed for telling the truth—whistle-blowing is now a federal offense. It's too late for any of us. All we can do is hope that this tyrant is assassinated, which is a very real possibility. Unfortunately there are others of like mind to replace him; unlimited power and money are quite seductive. Maybe I should opt out and come with you."

Grandma smiled sadly. "I know you aren't serious. Perhaps when this is all over?"

I wanted to scream, 'what about Sam'?' but I kept my mouth shut.

Rory turned to me. "You have to convince her." When the sound of shots rang out he turned back to Grandma. "I have to get back. Go to the jail and ask for your daughter. She will be released into your care." He bent and kissed Grandma full on the mouth before holding the door open for us and locking it once we were out. He gave Grandma a sad smile before striding quickly toward the main street.

I stared at my grandmother who seemed stunned, her eyes filled with unshed tears. "Let's go," I said, tugging her arm.

She let me lead her in the other direction, where we skirted along the back of the courthouse and hurried toward the jail.

Mom looked haggard and exhausted, her eyes red-rimmed. Her robe had been replaced with an orange jumpsuit. "How did you get me out?"

"Rory," Grandma said simply.

"Senator McCord? I thought he was dead."

"Not dead yet."

"He really likes Grandma," Jean said. She'd been oddly silent and it was good to hear her voice.

Mom smiled. "Your grandmother has always been able to wrap men around her little finger. Wish I'd inherited the ability."

"It's just an attitude, Theresa. You have to cultivate it."

"Where's Henry?" Mom asked, looking around.

"He's decided to take the cowards way out," Grandma answered. "He's a lost cause."

Mom got a wild look in her eye. "I have to see him."

When she headed off alone Jean and I ran after her. "Mom, it's dangerous out here," Jean said, grabbing her arm.

She twisted free. "And where I've been isn't? Henry is all I have."

Jean stopped dead. "What about us?"

Mom turned, her expression softening. "I didn't mean

it like that, Jeanie. Your father is my man, my support. I love him and always will."

"Even though he's behaving like an imbecile?" Grandma asked, joining us.

"He's afraid. He's never been part of the world. He's an academic and spends most of his time in books."

"The absent-minded professor?" Grandma said sarcastically. "He's let you down one too many times, Theresa."

"I don't see it like that." Mom walked purposely away without glancing back.

I sighed, shrugging at Grandma before the three of us followed.

It was hard getting there, what with the commotion on a lot of streets and the megaphones blaring warnings. We skirted down side streets and along alleys, trying to avoid the worst of it. When we finally reached the apartment complex I got a bad feeling in the pit of my stomach. There were no Humvees here, nothing but silence and trash blowing everywhere. "Looks deserted." I glanced at Grandma.

"It is not deserted," Mom said, heading toward the entrance. A second later she disappeared inside.

Grandma let out a huff of annoyance. "Come along, girls. If your mother feels this is necessary then I suppose we must support her."

The inside of the building was dark, the sound of hollow footsteps reverberating as Mom ascended the metal stairs. The elevator was no longer in service, just like everything else in Danvers. Once my eyes adjusted I followed her, listening to my sister's heavy breathing and the gasps coming from my grandmother as they climbed after me.

"Henry? Open this door!" I heard Mom shout.

By the time we caught up to her the door was open, a haggard replica of my once robust father standing there. "Theresa, what in God's name are you doing here?" He glanced at the rest of us, his demeanor going from surprised to angry. "What is going on here?"

Mom ignored him, muscling her way by him into the apartment. Something must have happened in jail to make her so brave all of a sudden.

Dad was still standing there when Jean, Grandma and I walked past him. He reached for my arm. "Emily? When did you get back?"

"A couple of days ago. Jean came to the past to get me."

"Don't give me that time-traveling nonsense," he said, frowning. "You've been shacked up with some guy and ignoring your family."

I didn't answer his accusations, my gaze going around his darkened apartment made even darker by the pulled shades. It smelled musty and like stale food and dirty clothes. "When did you last eat?" I heard Mom ask, emerging from the kitchen.

Dad shrugged. "Don't rightly remember."

Mom grabbed his arm. "You don't look at all well, Henry. You need me to take care of you."

Dad seemed dazed, staring at her blankly. "Aren't we divorced?"

"Yes, we are, but that doesn't mean I don't still care for you." Mom bustled back into the kitchen and I heard her humming as she banged pots and opened and closed cabinets and the refrigerator.

I moved around the apartment, putting up shades and

gathering discarded clothing off chairs. "Where's your washing machine?"

Dad shook his head. "Not enough water to do a load. I've been re-wearing things."

"I can tell, "I answered, looking him over. His hair was over-long and dirty, his face unshaven. He'd aged a decade since I'd last seen him.

Grandma came up behind me, her hand on my shoulder. "We can't stay here," she whispered.

"Why not?"

"Because the police have cleared out this building. Your father is the only tenant left."

"How did you come to that conclusion?" Jean asked, joining us.

"I took a look around."

I looked at her. "By 'look around', you mean…"

"Didn't you notice my absence? I've been checking other apartments. The electricity is off and there is no one else here."

"Henry? None of your burners work." My mother stood in the doorway with hands on hips.

"Haven't worked in a while," Dad mumbled.

The squeal of sirens burst out, the sounds coming closer. "Oh my god," Jean muttered. "We have to get him out of here."

"Yes, we do," Grandma agreed.

Somehow we managed to get back to our house safely with Dad in tow. It seemed the chaos had been driven to the other end of town, the shouting and sirens fading as we hurried along deserted sidewalks toward our house on the edge of the city center. As far as Dad's apartment, I was sure he would have died there if we hadn't come when we did.

"We have to regroup," Grandma said as she heated water for tea. "I'm beginning to see what Rory was trying to tell me."

"You want to take everyone back to 2011?"

"2011? Why that particular time? If anyone can do such a thing it would have to be you or your sister, Jean. I'm thinking of the future when this maniac is no longer in office."

"But Grandma, you're a witch too."

"No, Emily, I am not a witch."

Not a witch? A shiver went down both my arms.

"I suggest the early part of the century," Mom interrupted. "That way we can enjoy the inventive and creative time period filled with bohemians."

"I think the future would be better, Theresa, when the human race has come to its senses.

"Or annihilated itself," I muttered under my breath, trying to take in Grandma's pronouncement. "And I'm not going anywhere without Samoset."

Grandma stared at me, her eyes narrowing. "Maybe you should just leave now, Emeline. Jean can take us where we need to go."

In the kitchen Mom was placing a plate of meatloaf and fresh bread in front of my father. I heard her laugh and his laugh in response. My sister was a witch and my grandmother wasn't a witch. Something was seriously off.

After dinner my father and mother left the kitchen and headed up the stairs to their bedroom. Somehow during the meal my mother had managed to bring him out of himself, his cheeks turning from pale to a healthy hue. His eyes had never strayed from her, getting brighter as the meal progressed.

"I wonder what went on during your mother's time in jail," Grandma mused, watching them. "She seems quite invigorated."

"Maybe some hard-ass ladies gave her a pep-talk," Jean said.

I laughed. "You did say your ability with men was an attitude, right Grandma?"

Grandma's cool gaze met mine. "Perhaps she listened for once. Now are you planning to help, or run back to your safe little life in the past?"

Chapter Six

When I came downstairs the following morning Mom and Dad were already sitting together at the kitchen table making goo-goo eyes at each other. I ignored them and poured coffee. I stood at the sink wondering if the sun had decided to go on permanent vacation. When Grandma arrived I heard a huff of annoyance come from her before she said, "You two need to snap out of it. We have a lot of work to do today."

I turned, watching the look of embarrassment that crossed my mother's face. "Really, Mother. Henry and I are only catching up."

"You're in a fantasy world, Theresa. The look in your eyes is exactly the same one I saw when you first met Henry. You have three grown children now—you and Henry are no longer lovebirds. And we simply don't have time for this sort of nonsense."

Three children? Dad didn't say a word as he rose from his chair and went to the coffee machine. He met my gaze and looked away.

"Aren't you being a little harsh?" I whispered when Grandma moved by me.

"We're in a situation here, Emeline. Your mother has a way of disappearing into her own little world, and it is neither the time or the place for it."

"I heard that, Mother," Mom said. "Now what's your plan?"

Grandma had a faraway look, her eyes unfocused. "It is still in process, but I've thought a lot about what we've seen and what Rory said—it may be too late for us to make any kind of impact here without being jailed or hurt. If Jean will take us, can we agree to go to the future?"

I thought of one of my time travel trips with Grandma. We'd accidentally traveled into a dangerous dystopian future. "Grandma, remember what happened last time."

She stared at me. "What are you talking about?"

"You and me. We went to some kind of horrible future together. Don't you remember?"

"No, I do not. You and I have never done any such thing together. Now are you on board or not?"

Dad's eyebrows shot up as he sat down next to Mom, a cup of coffee in his hands. "Please don't start this witch nonsense again, Rebecca. It isn't good for Theresa and it's why I couldn't stay."

Mom put her hand on his arm. "Now Henry. I've told you about our family," she said soothingly.

From the expression that appeared on Dad's face Mom had to be a witch—either that or my father had fallen completely under the spell of her feminine wiles. His eyes went suddenly soft, focused on her. He'd never been one to take control or force things his way, and since their divorce he seemed even more diminished. I chalked it up to near starvation, loneliness and fear. But there was something changed about him that I couldn't quite put my finger on.

"Whatever you think is best, Theresa," he said, placing his hand over hers.

"What about where you live, Grandma—nothing weird is going on in that timeline."

She shot me a look. "What are you on about, Emeline? I haven't settled anywhere for very long. I'm a gypsy at heart and I go where the wind blows me."

"But…what about 2011?"

"That again? Why would I wish to go to a time I already lived through?"

"Because of Sam?"

"Who is this Sam?"

A little warning voice in my head said, *this is definitely not your world.* I looked around at my family who all seemed almost normal. It *had* to be my world. Now that I'd spent time with them I *wanted* it to be my world. But if Grandma had never been with Sam…

"Emmy? What's wrong?" Jean asked.

I glanced at her and then addressed Mom. "Why did you let Jean dye her hair and pierce her belly button? And what about her clothes?" My *real* mother would never agree to Jean baring her midriff or wearing high-heeled boots, or to the thick mascara and lipstick Jean had applied.

"Emily, what has got into you? Your sister is in high school. How she comports herself is her business."

"No, it isn't!" I shouted. "You've always been strict

about this kind of stuff, Mom. You never even let me pierce my ears!"

Mom glanced at Dad, her expression bewildered.

"Emily, why are you attacking your mother? She's done the best she can under the circumstances. At least your sister isn't into heavy drugs. You were a horror back then. I certainly hope you've cleaned yourself up."

Heavy drugs? "Are you saying I was into drugs? I never touched the stuff! You were adamant about that when I lived here. Does Jean smoke weed? And how would you know? You haven't even been here."

"Stop it!" Jean shouted. "Why are you arguing about me as though I'm not even here? And if you must know I've been smoking for a year now. What of it? Mom smokes too."

My mouth fell open. When I glanced toward Mom she wouldn't meet my gaze. "Mom, is this true?"

Her eyes pleaded with me, her hands making odd movements like she was working her way through a set of mudras. "The cannabis eases things, Emily. Your brother Robert's disappearance, this political situation, and then Henry..."

"I don't have a brother," I began, backing warily toward the door. "And the Grandma I know is a witch," I continued, "a witch who helped me save Sam, the man she loves and now lives with." Before anyone could respond I turned and ran for the front door, struggling to loosen the bolts. By the time I had it open both Grandma and Mom were there. When Mom grabbed my arm I wrenched away and took off in the direction of my portal of oak trees without looking back. In my haste I'd forgotten completely that I didn't need them anymore.

Chapter Seven

"Emeline, for goodness sakes!"

I helped my grandmother stand, brushing off her long black skirt as I looked around the familiar seventeenth century house. When I heard Sam whistling in the backyard garden I threw myself into her arms, nearly knocking her over again. "I just came from a parallel reality, Grandma. I'm so glad to see you. That other Grandma wasn't even a witch!"

Grandma chuckled. "Me not a witch? That is a hoot. Whatever happened to take you away from Samoset? He's all right, isn't he?"

"Samoset is fine—at least he was when I left him. Jean came into the past to get me, said you sent her. The country had been taken over by some thug who proclaimed himself king or something. Danvers was basically under martial law. We were trying to stop it, but..."

"Come, sit and have a cup of tea, you're positively white."

I let her lead me to the little table against the wall where

I lowered into a ladder-back chair. "I'm so relieved to be here. But how could that Jean find me in my past? We live in parallel worlds."

Grandma put the kettle on the stove and busied herself with adding tealeaves to a brown crockery teapot. "Time anomalies are difficult to understand. I wouldn't have thought it possible for her to enter your world from another parallel reality, but it does happen occasionally. But why are you here, dear?"

"I guess I was thinking about you when I ran between the two trees."

"The two trees? You don't still use them, do you?"

"I forgot I didn't need them. I was kind of freaked out."

She poured boiling water into the pot and put on the lid, the aroma of Earl Grey wafting toward me. A moment later she was placing tea mugs and the pot on the table. "Cream?"

"No, thanks," I said, picking up the pot to pour.

She placed a hand on my arm. "Wait for it to steep for a few moments. I'll just call Sam and let him know you're here." I watched her head out the back door, heard the murmur of talking before Sam followed her back inside. Sam was a burly man, his skin ruddy from the sun. His smile warmed my frozen heart.

"Emeline! So very good to see you."

I stood to hug him, the smell of sweat and damp earth somehow comforting.

He sat and waited as Grandma found another mug and poured tea.

"Sam has turned our garden into quite the money-maker," Grandma said, sitting next to me. "He sells flowers and vegetables and berries at the local farmer's market nearly every week until the weather grows too cold. In the winter we have a greenhouse for tomatoes and the odd vegetable, but mostly we hole up in here by the fire." She smiled, placing a hand on his knee.

"And the others? Are they still happy at Plimoth Plantation?"

"Aye, they are," Sam answered, glancing at Grandma with a twinkle in his eye. "As are we."

"I can tell," I said, taking a sip of tea.

"I expected to see a baby by now," Grandma said, looking me over.

"The other Grandma basically said the same thing."

"She knew about Samoset?"

I nodded. "Everything was pretty much the same except her not being a witch. Jean is a witch in that timeline—not sure if she is in this one."

"She is but she doesn't accept it," Grandma answered.

"Still? I thought she'd grow into herself. When did you last see them?"

"Five months ago I went forward in time to visit. Danvers was just the same."

"Dad was with Mom?"

"Of course. He would never leave your mother."

"That's what should have clued me in," I muttered.

I stayed another hour and then said my goodbyes, anxious to be home with Samoset.

Before I left she smiled and pulled me close. "Now don't forget to keep in touch! When the baby comes I want to know about it."

I wanted to ask her about time travel affecting

conception but it was too late, Samoset's face in my mind pulling me into the ether. Grandma and Sam turned wispy and indistinct and then faded away as I was taken back to 1694.

I landed in an unfamiliar room within the longhouse, Samoset sitting bolt upright when he saw me. It was quite dark but I could still make out his smile as he reached to pull me into his arms. "Gone a long time—too long," he whispered, his lips on my neck.

I pulled back. "Less than a week, Samoset."

"A week." He counted it out on his fingers. "Longer," he insisted, continuing to count until it seemed he'd indicated a month. "One moon," he said, his hand going to the side of my face. "Enough time to build new longhouses." He stared into my eyes.

"An entire month?"

"I worry you not come back."

"I will always come back, that is unless something terrible happens."

When he kissed me I felt safe and loved and I had to admit, turned-on. He tugged at my T-shirt and pulled it over my head, his lips sliding down to my collarbones. I sighed, reveling in the warmth of him. I was very aware that other tribe members lay close by—just on the other side of the freshly woven mat hanging next to our sleeping pallet. I could hear their soft snores.

"Where are we?" I whispered, watching him kneel in front of me. I could barely make him out other than his outline and his earthy smell.

"Far from settlement, far from sea and river. Tribe worried after attack."

"What attack?"

"Talk tomorrow, Em. Make love now," he whispered. He pushed me gently backward and before I could ask another question he'd stripped me naked, the length of him pressing urgently against me. I held back the cry in my throat, muffling my face against his shoulder as our bodies joined and began the magic dance.

Chapter Eight

I woke to soft gray light sifting through the pole and bark walls. It was not yet dawn but Samoset was already up and sitting cross-legged, his eyes focused on my face. I stretched languidly and reached for him but he only stared at me solemnly. "Must talk before tribe wakes," he whispered, handing me my jeans and sweater. The air was cold and I quickly pulled them on before following him outside. He set out for the forest and I hurried to catch up, wondering what was so important to take us from our warm bed this early.

He stopped next to a group of boulders, climbing up before reaching for my hand. Once we were settled I waited, frightened by the serious expression on his face. He gazed into the distance seeming to need to collect his thoughts.

"Is this about the attack? Who attacked you?"

"White men, trappers come to old village. Friendly, eat food and laugh. But come back in night and take woman, steal food and hurt many."

"I'm so sorry, Samoset! Who did they take?"

"Numee."

Not Numee! She was my friend, the sweetest person I'd ever met. When I let out a sob Samoset smoothed my tangled hair back and kissed the spiral on my forehead, a tattoo I'd had done back in Danvers when I turned sixteen—the year I became a witch. The spiral was an ancient symbol representing eternity and growth, but right now it seemed tawdry and stupid in the face of what had happened in my absence. Why hadn't I known about this?

"Tribe say attack Em's fault. It was Em who picked site of village, Em who said we would be safe."

I tried to take in what he was saying. "The tribe blames me? What did you say?"

"I tell them no, cannot be. Em my wife."

"But how could it be my fault? I wasn't even here when it happened."

"I explain all that. They no listen, say *Hobomock* come through you."

I stared into his troubled eyes. "*Hobomock*—the evil spirit?" Tears welled and spilled over. The tribe hated me.

Samoset placed his hand on my shoulder. "We will hunt and find trappers and bring Numee home."

"Will you kill them?" I asked, wiping my face with my sleeve. Killing a white man would be bad for the Wampanoag and would get them into trouble with the colonists. It was best to let these situations die down in their own time. But Numee being gone was hard to bear. "Maybe you can get her away from them without resorting to violence. A nighttime raid?"

Samoset didn't answer, his gaze hardening. "Bad men,

Em. Take what is not theirs. Kill two braves."

"They will be tried for their crimes, Samoset. The settlers don't condone killing any more than the tribe does."

He shook his head. "Colonists not believe Samoset. Think I lie because tribe not like trappers on hunting lands."

So he'd talked to the magistrates already and they didn't believe him. This could lead to bloodshed. But I was still focused on the elders blaming me for all of it. "The spot I found for the village was safe for over a year. It isn't my fault that trappers arrived." But then it hit me. Maybe my traveling through time had changed history. My eyes welled as the terrible thought took root.

When Samoset saw my tears he reached for me, pulling me to him.

"What can I do?" I sobbed into his shoulder.

"Em live away from tribe. I come when can."

"You want me to live alone? Where?"

"I build house." He jumped down from the boulder and reached for my hand. I followed him on a zigzag path through the forest. It took us nearly an hour of fast walking before we arrived at a craggy hill, high mountains rising behind it. A small reed covered *wetu* partially obscured by trees stood next to the cliff. "Safe," he said, pushing the mat door back to reveal the inside. He had brought my beads, stones and feathers and grouped them together like a small shrine. Next to them were a pottery bowl and jug of water. A heavy deerskin blanket lay on a bed of pine needles, with a second one to use as a cover. My blue dress and a deerskin cape and skirt hung from a protruding stick, my extra moccasins on the mat floor below them.

I sat heavily on the blanket and stared at him. "But I'm your wife. How can they banish me?"

"They want baby, Em. Until baby no wife."

"We can't make a baby if I'm not with you."

"They say you are bad spirit. If good spirit would be baby by now."

"Do you believe them?" I willed him to say no but he only gazed at me sadly.

"Heart," he finally said, placing his hand on his chest, but the look in his eyes said something different.

"You aren't sure if I'm bad or not."

"Why no baby yet? Make love many times and still nothing in belly?"

"I don't know!" I shouted. "Maybe it's because I'm from the future. How can you not trust me, Samoset?" I was crying in earnest now. "I want a baby too!"

"I bring food," he said, turning to go.

I wanted to grab him and shake him. How could he think this of me? The tribe was my family too. Just because I hadn't gotten pregnant didn't mean I was some evil spirit. But the natives had their own beliefs, and from what I'd observed since I'd lived with them it was hard to change their minds—these ways of making sense of the world went back centuries. After watching him walk away and disappear into the dark forest I burst into tears, sobbing as though my heart was breaking. And in a way it was.

I waited for him all day. He never came back. I wondered if I'd ever see him again. I thought of the night before and how our bodies had connected, his kisses lingering and sweet. I'd felt his passion rise, that moment when we reached the pinnacle and fell panting together on the other side. That was not the behavior of a man ready to abandon his wife. I felt isolated and sick with a sorrow that left me hollow and shaking. He was my life, my world.

When night finally came I curled up under the blanket shivering with nerves and cold. I had no food and only a bit of water left in the jug. If he didn't come in the morning I would have to find a spring and forage for any fallen nuts the squirrels hadn't yet found. I was on my own.

I was dozing when I heard footfalls in the dry leaves on the ground, coming fully awake as adrenaline shot through my body. Trappers. But when the flap opened it was Samoset who crawled inside. He handed me a hunk of deer jerky, which I gnawed on hungrily. "Aunum will keep you safe," he said, pointing to the mastiff poking his head inside.

"Why didn't you come earlier? I've been so afraid all day—afraid I'd never see you again. I don't understand this, Samoset. How can you leave me out here? I don't want to stay here without you. I may as well go back to the future or live with Grandma."

Samoset moved closer, but when he reached for me I pulled back.

"I need you, Em. This is the only way. Tribe does not trust you."

"What do you need me for—sex? If I can't get pregnant what's the sense in that? It's too cold out here and I'll get too lonely. Does the tribe know what you've done—this house?"

"Tribe thinks you gone for good. Tribe has new woman for me."

I knew it. I knew this day was coming. "No, Samoset. You can't."

His eyes glittered with unshed tears. "I am sorry, Em. It is the only way we can be together."

My heart softened. When I took hold of his hand he pulled me close. A few moments later we were lying entwined on the bed, our clothes discarded. He loved me but he had to obey tribal law. I lay beneath him, my tears falling silently as we coupled. He cried too, and when it was over he dressed and left without saying another word.

The days went by in a blur, sorrow and depression taking me to such a dark place I wondered if I would ever return. Aunum slept beside me and hunted during the day. Samoset came sporadically to bring food and make love. I knew he hoped I would get pregnant so he could take me back. I didn't have the heart to ask if he had another woman yet, but his urgency when he was with me made me think that a new marriage hadn't yet taken place. Why couldn't I conceive?

"Have you found Numee?" I asked one very cold and drizzly afternoon after our usual hasty coupling.

He sat up and pulled his deerskin cape around his shoulders before pulling on his leggings, preparing to leave. He shook his head.

"Did you find the trappers?"

"No, Em. Trappers are gone." He produced the food he'd brought, placing the pouch next to the bed before standing.

"The trappers are gone—where?"

"Gone from forest. Tribe is angry."

"They blame me for this too?"

"No deer, no fish, tribe sick."

"I'm not there—how can they still blame me?"

He placed his hand on my lower belly. As though I could will a baby and have it be there.

"*Hobomock* very bad spirit, Em. Elders say my fault—I bring you into tribe."

I scoffed. "Maybe you should move out here with me."

"One moon, two moon," he ticked the months I'd been out here off with his fingers, gazing at me with narrowed eyes.

I could hardly believe it had been two entire moon cycles. I'd noticed how lately the coupling had turned into a sort of mechanical ritual, done thoroughly but without a lot of feeling on his part. I'd cried several times in the middle of it, hoping the old Samoset would reappear, but there was something missing, as though his connection to me was loosening. With the threat of another woman on the horizon Samoset had been testing me to see if I would get pregnant. Maybe he'd proved to himself that the tribe was right—I was a *Hobomock*.

"Don't bother coming out here again. It's obvious I can't get pregnant. I don't know why that is, Samoset, but if that's all you care about there's no point in being together. I kind of wish you'd told me about this tribal rule when we married."

He didn't respond as he finished dressing and left the hut. When he headed toward the forest he didn't look back.

After he was gone I dressed warmly and left the tiny *wetu*, my prison. I walked for a long time, keeping the cliff edge on my left and trying to stay under the trees to protect myself from the chill rain. It wouldn't do to get lost, especially with the temperature dropping. In the distance Aunum followed, a dark shadow watching over me. I let my mind wander, trying to form a plan. I couldn't go on like this, seeing Samoset every few days and not having a life. I had the feeling that his new marriage was imminent, a thought that filled me with dread. Grandma was a witch with herbal knowledge. Maybe she could help. But there was a part of me that didn't even care anymore, as though my love for Samoset had been crushed under the weight of his expectations.

I briefly wondered what Samoset would think when he came and I was gone. I hoped he cared enough to worry. I pictured Grandma's house, hoping I could move through the ether. It had been some time since I'd done anything but wait for Samoset's visits. I was weak, my muscles slack, my mind as empty as the flat gray sky. I crouched to say goodbye to Aunum, my tears landing in the ruff around his neck. "Go back and tell Samoset I love him," I whispered.

I pictured Grandma and a moment later the forest faded, rainbow colors whirling by my eyes.

Chapter Nine

"Emeline, why are you here again?"

I stared at her familiar face, tears filling my eyes. "I've been kicked out of the tribe. They think I'm some evil spirit called a *Hobomock.*"

Grandma actually laughed. "A hobomock? What silliness is that?"

"It isn't funny. They think I'm the cause of every bad thing that's happened since I've been living with them. And it's all because I haven't gotten pregnant yet."

Grandma grew serious, her eyes turning dark. "What does Samoset say?"

"They want him to remarry and he's going along with it."

"Are you still living with the tribe?"

I shook my head and looked down. "Samoset built a little house for me. He comes every couple of days and brings food. The tribe thinks I'm gone for good. But Samoset—he's changed. I don't think he loves me at all. Oh Grandma, what am I going to do?"

Grandma gazed into the distance, her brows furrowing. "First we need to discover why you aren't conceiving. Maybe there's some physical reason for it. There are doctors here who can examine you."

"Do you think it's the time traveling?"

She shook her head, dislodging her carefully constructed chignon. "As you know I came and went from the past many times. I had a child in the past and one in your timeline. I doubt that would cause this problem." She twisted up

her shoulder length hair again and stuck a handcrafted wooden hair stick in to hold it in place. "Sam made this," she said proudly, turning to show me the carved end in the shape of a rose.

"It's beautiful," I said, trying to keep my mind on the hair stick and not on my predicament. I let a moment tick by before I asked, "What about herbs, something I could take?"

"I do know of some," she said slowly, "but you need to be checked by a doctor before we go that route. You could have a deficiency of some kind. Perhaps it's Samoset who is at fault."

"I doubt it."

"In the meantime why don't we visit your real family? There are better doctors there."

"My real family as opposed to the parallel reality ones?"

Grandma snorted. "Yes, that's exactly what I meant. I'm sure they would be very happy to see you again."

I had a sudden flash of guilt. I hadn't been to see them for over a year. "Do they know about Samoset and me?"

"Yes, Emeline. I've told them all about where you are. They miss you."

"I'm willing to go as long as it's you who takes us there. I don't trust myself anymore."

"You made it here, didn't you? But if you'd rather, I'm fine with it. Just let me change out of these gardening clothes and let Sam know what we're up to."

A half an hour later Grandma grabbed my hand and we whirled away from Plymouth. I closed my eyes against the wind, holding on tight until I felt my feet touch down again. We were standing inside my parents' house and there wasn't a sound to be heard.

"Where is everyone?"

Grandma shrugged and looked around. "It seems they've been gone for some time," she said, pointing to the cobwebs in the corners. "Perhaps if I try and find *them* instead of the house we'd have better luck." She took hold of my hand and a moment later we were in the ether again.

I heard my mother's voice before I opened my eyes. "This has got to stop, Henry. We can't live out in the middle of nowhere forever!"

My parents and Jean were inside a small cabin. Through the picture window I could see a lake shining in the distance. When they saw us there was a general shout of surprise and then greetings and tears. "How did you find us?" Jean asked. "You must have found out about Danvers."

"What about Danvers?" I asked.

"There's a leak from the nuclear power plant. Everyone's been evacuated," Dad answered.

"Oh dear," Grandma said. "I wondered why the house seemed abandoned."

"We've been out here for nearly a month," Mom said. "I was just saying…"

"When will it be contained?" I asked.

Dad shook his head, dislodging his horn-rimmed glasses. "If they told us it was safe I wouldn't believe them. Too many odd goings on these days."

My mother let out an exasperated huff. "It's just too much. We pay taxes and our money goes to pay for weapons and chasing immigrants out of the country. What about our needs as citizens? And how did this power plant come to have a leak? I'm telling you, our country is falling apart!"

Uh oh. This sounded suspiciously like the parallel world. I glanced at Grandma who met my gaze before addressing Mom.

"It has always been this way, Theresa. Those in power do what they want with our tax dollars. You just don't happen to agree with the ones in charge at the moment."

I let out my held breath. "What about school, Jean?"

"It's break, you idiot," she quipped, making a face.

This was my sister all right. "What all's happening, Dad?"

He gave a shrug and pushed his glasses back up his nose. "They just got another very conservative judge on the supreme court, one who goes along with all that's bad for the country."

"According to you," Mom said. "I'm more of the 'wait and see' attitude."

Dad stared her down. "This new president could care less about any of us, Theresa. And without any representation in congress we're like sitting ducks waiting to be shot."

Grandma laughed. "I never knew you to be so melodramatic, Henry."

He turned to her, frowning. "You haven't seen what's happening, Rebecca. Perhaps you'd like to read a newspaper before you dismiss it so lightly."

"Why are you here, Emmy?" Mom asked worriedly. "You aren't sick, are you? I worry so about the past you live in with no antibiotics or proper hygiene."

"You'd be surprised at how clean things are with the tribe, Mom. They bathe regularly and they eat so much better than the settlers, with greens and..."

"She needs to have some tests run," Grandma interrupted.

Mom moved close, peering into my eyes. "What kind of tests?"

"I can't get pregnant," I answered, heat moving into my cheeks.

"Why would you want to?" Jean asked. "Having a baby sounds horrible to me."

"Samoset and I are married and we..."

"The tribe has kicked her out because she and Samoset have not yet conceived," Grandma interrupted bluntly. "They think she's an evil spirit."

"Oh my goodness," Mom said, her hand going to her mouth.

"What?" Jean let out a roar of laughter.

"It isn't funny," I said sharply. "I love him and he's about to marry some other woman."

"I thought you said you were married," Dad said, confused. "Is this some heathen thing where a man can have more than one wife?"

"No. The tribe thinks I'm gone."

"And so you are," Grandma supplied. "Where's the phone book? We need to locate the closest hospital and order some tests."

My mother's voice woke me early, bringing me up and out of a dream in which I was flying over a fantasy landscape of green and purple trees. I turned to Samoset but he wasn't next to me. And then I came fully awake, aware that I was in a cabin with my family and sleeping on the pullout couch. Grandma and Mom were making coffee in the small kitchenette. The smell of toast wafted toward me making me hungry.

"Emily! Thank goodness! I wondered if you would ever wake up. Your appointment is in an hour and it will take us forty minutes to get there. Henry!" she shouted before turning back to me. "Have some coffee and brush your teeth. There's an extra toothbrush in the cabinet over the sink. There's no time for anything else. We can eat later."

I moved off the couch and found my clothing.

Dad entered the room, rubbing the sleep from his eyes. His thick hair looked mussed and unruly. "For goodness sake, Henry. Comb you hair at least," Mom said. "And hurry up—we're leaving in five minutes."

"Why do I need to go?"

Mom just looked at him for a while and then seemed to come back to herself. "Well, I guess you don't. How about you, Jean? Are you coming with or staying?"

My sister glanced at me. "I think I'll keep Dad company, if it's all the same to you."

I smiled at my sister who I knew hated doctors and

hospitals as much as I did. But in this case I thought the tests might be a good idea. I had to find out if something was wrong with me. And if there were, what would I do? It wouldn't change the situation for me to go back and tell Samoset I couldn't have children. That would only make the tribe more determined to find him another wife. I was feeling very low when we exited the cabin and headed for the car.

"There is nothing physically wrong with you, young lady," the East Indian doctor in his forties told me. "You are a healthy woman in the best child-bearing years. As to why you haven't yet conceived, there could be other factors."

"Like what?"

"It could be your husband who is at fault. Perhaps he could come in for

tests? That way we can rule it out."

"That won't be possible, but I don't think he has a problem."

"Many men are too proud to take the blame for this, but if he has a low sperm count, say he's done drugs in the past, or..."

"He hasn't."

"Well, then I would caution you to take a look at your state of mind. Nerves can contribute to the problem."

I thought of the tiny hut and Samoset's recent behavior. "Thanks. I'll keep that in mind."

When he left the examining room I dressed, wondering what could be happening. It had to be about the time traveling.

"What did he say?" Mom asked when I walked into the waiting room.

"Nothing's wrong with me."

"I thought so, Emeline," Grandma said. "I have another theory to propose, but I'll wait until we're in the car."

By the time we were on our way back to the cabin I'd forgotten all about Grandma's statement. But when she brought it up again I leaned forward from my place in the back seat. "Tell me."

"Do you want a child, Emeline? Think hard on this and be honest with yourself."

I stared out the window visualizing holding a baby in my arms. Nerves fluttered in my belly and my breath stopped for a moment until I remembered to breathe. "I…I'm not really sure. Maybe not."

"Can you come up with a reason?"

"I'm afraid of the responsibility. I'm not ready. And right now I'm hurt and angry with him. He's been a jerk for the past couple of months sticking me out there alone and only coming by to…" I closed my mouth, aware I was saying too much.

But Grandma seemed unfazed by my outburst. "You and Samoset have only been together a little over a year. Your life has changed drastically. You may be overwhelmed by the idea of another big upheaval. Perhaps you want more time for the two of you. You're still practically in the honeymoon stage."

If this was the honeymoon stage I couldn't wait to have it be over. "But if I feel this way why would it have an affect on whether or not I get pregnant?"

"Because you're a witch. You can block conception."

"But...how am I doing that? I've been trying to get pregnant."

"You have shut yourself off from the part that doesn't want a baby. It is now unconscious and on the magical level."

Tears filled my eyes, guilt washing over me. "But it doesn't mean I never want a baby...I mean..."

"No, Emeline, it doesn't. Can you tell Samoset the truth?"

I thought of the new cold Samoset, the one who didn't stay long enough to ask how I felt and didn't seem to care how lonely I was. "I don't know. He's different now. I'm not sure he loves me anymore."

"Of course he loves you, Emeline. He's under tremendous pressure with the tribe after him to marry another and the need for a baby. Tell him you need more time with him alone. He can explain it to the rest of the tribe. They can be reasonable even if it's tradition to have a baby within the first year."

"If they think I've kept myself from conceiving it will be even more of the *Hobomock* theory. And I'm not sure that's all that's going on with the tribe. They've had a very bad year with strange illnesses and not enough game. It was a dry summer and the animals moved into the mountains. The illnesses seem to be flu related, not serious, but enough to make them believe I've cursed them. I've mentioned all this to Samoset but they'd rather blame me."

"They have medicine people with psychic abilities. They can't fault your gifts and project them onto some evil spirit."

"But that's exactly what they've done, Grandma."

"You and Samoset will have to speak to the elders. And, my dear, you can't completely rule out the possibility that he has a problem."

"I seriously doubt it, but if I overcome my fears and I still don't get pregnant, I'll drag him back here and make him get some tests."

"Good luck with that," Mom said, never taking her eyes off the road.

Grandma chuckled.

Once we reached the cabin Grandma took me aside. "How old are you now, Emeline?"

"Eighteen. Why?"

"Because there is something important you need to know. I should have mentioned it earlier but time got away from me."

I laughed. "Time got away from you? That's a good one, Grandma—so what is it?"

Her blue eyes penetrated into mine, a sinking feeling coming along with that serious stare. Uh oh.

Chapter Ten

I was on my way out the door when Jean came into the living room. "Where are you going?" she called.

"Library. Grandma gave me the name of a book I have to find. I'm taking the car and I should be back in a couple of hours."

"What? Why?"

I didn't answer, anxious to get this over with and find out that it was all a hoax meant to bring me out of my depression.

In the car I mulled over the crazy story Grandma told me. I was already dealing with Samoset and my inability to get pregnant. Why would I be interested in belonging to some ancient coven? But I had to admit that what she'd said had taken my mind off Samoset and my worries about our future. Maybe the book she told me to find would turn out to be filled with jokes or herbal remedies to help me with my current problem. Our conversation echoed in my ears as I drove down the street toward the library:

"A thousand years ago our ancestors formed a group,

one in which others of our kind met. They kept the world safe with spells and slight alterations in the timelines here and there."

"Kind of like the Hopi?"

She nodded. "The Hopi consider themselves the keepers of the earth. There are other tribes and ethnic groups who believe this about themselves as well. But look what's happened—the earth is nearly destroyed, people starving, animals dying off in greater and greater numbers. The planet has grown beyond anyone's ability to help."

"And yet you think *I* can?"

She ignored me, continuing. "The clan of our forbears still meet and you will be part of them. They come from all walks of life and all nations. You will have to forsake a portion of your life with Samoset to do what is asked of you, Emeline."

My stomach clenched when I heard those words. "Are you saying this is my destiny?" I'd asked. "I don't like the sound of that."

"This is what happens when members of our lineage turn eighteen. I went through it just as you will, and hopefully your sister, once she comes of age. I know it's a lot to foist upon you right now with everything you have going on, but it is necessary."

"What about you? Do you still belong?"

"Not in any really sense, no. I've grown old and let my eligibility card lapse I'm afraid."

"Eligibility card—what's that?"

At that point my mother came into the living room. "Find the book and we can talk further," Grandma had whispered, her smiling gaze on Mom.

Middleton was quiet but luckily the town had not been evacuated. However there was concern about the radiation leak. I ignored the headlines in the local paper of '**ARE WE SAFE?'** locating the library using the GPS on the phone Dad lent me.

The library was filled with muttering groups of people lurking around the science section. I heard partial conversations about the government and why they had allowed nuclear power plants to be built so close to towns if they weren't safe. I saw fear on several faces and worry on others.

I headed to the occult section and let my gaze run down the list of books. _Witches and Warlocks, Witches of Salem, A Witch in Time Saves Nine_…that last title must be fiction, I thought, glancing at it before moving on. Cool cover. And then I saw it: _Witches of the World_, an oversized leather bound book with gold lettering on the spine. I pulled it out. Published in 1624—what? I perused the frontispiece, noting the list of names of those involved with the writing of this book: Kalinda Legere, Canton Musir, Valir Goswell, Catalina Heidrig—who were these people? Did Grandma know them? Behind me I heard murmuring, turning to see three women probably in their early fifties standing at the end of the aisle. Their hair was wiry and mostly gray, their eyes bright with knowing. One was African American and another sort of a mocha color that seemed to indicate an island heritage, the third one white. They were dressed in what looked like costumes for Halloween, with lots of layers of chiffon-like material in purples, oranges and greens. They all glanced at me before turning away, moving to the next aisle. I heard them whispering and I had a feeling they knew about this book and were watching to see what I would do. I opened it to page thirteen and moved my finger down the paragraph, counting lines until I came to thirteen.

> *To Luxembourg where naked Luna lifts her arms to the moon,*
> *Shine down on this child who seeks your blessing.*
> *Take her truth and make her one,*
> *And bind her to us where she belongs.*

It didn't even rhyme. I read on, but the passage shifted and changed in front of my eyes, and when I went back to the lines I'd first read, they were gone. Surely Luxemburg was a large place—how was I to find this statue of Luna, the moon goddess? The word *bind* didn't sit well with me— I'd always thought of myself as a free spirit, not part of any group. And as far as belonging, I had no feeling about that either. When I went to the travel section and looked up Luxembourg I discovered a famous fountain with a statue of Luna as its centerpiece. It was in the historic part of the city of Luxembourg.

When I left the library I was sure I saw the same three women eyeing me from behind a pillar on the porch, but when I turned there was no one there. I hurried to the car.

"And why do you think it's necessary to travel to this place?" Mom asked when I got back, echoing my own thoughts.

"Because Grandma said…"

Mom turned her back to put the kettle on the cabin's ancient electric stove. "Your grandmother is not the end all and the be all, Emily. You need to think for yourself. What about the young man you left in the past? What must he be thinking right now?"

"Samoset is the reason I left, Mom. The tribe thinks I'm some evil spirit."

"But surely he…"

"He relegated me to a tiny hovel away from the tribe— he let them believe I was gone. He may be marrying some other woman as we speak. He's been treating me badly and I'm furious with him."

"Who knows what might have happened in your absence? Doesn't your time traveling affect things in strange ways?"

"Well…I guess it can. But Grandma was adamant about this. She insists it's my destiny."

Dad arrived from another room and placed his hand on Mom's shoulder. "Let her go, Theresa. She has to see this through."

I sighed and sat down on the lumpy couch, glancing up at Dad. "Frankly I wish I didn't, but something tells me I must. How long are you planning to stay in this cabin?"

"Until they give the green light for Danvers," Dad answered. "I've rented it for six months. Radioactive contamination is nothing to fool around with. Will we see you after this next escapade?"

I shrugged. "I have no idea. Where's Grandma? I was surprised she filled you in since she seemed so secretive."

"I'm not sure where she went. Your grandmother explained it all after you left, Emily. She knows how I feel about secrets. When will you go?" Mom asked, pouring hot water into the teapot.

I shook my head. At the moment I felt exhausted and overwhelmed, unsure why I was even considering it. "I suppose when the spirit moves me."

"Where's the book?" Jean asked, emerging from the bathroom with a towel wrapped around her hair.

"I left it at the library."

"Why? Seems like you'd need it."

"I only needed the lines I read, and they disappeared right after I read them."

Jean's mouth dropped open. "Cool! That sounds like Harry Potter magic."

I shook my head and rolled my eyes.

I spent the rest of the day thinking about Samoset and what I now knew about myself. Would he be willing to listen if I told him my feelings? Grandma didn't come back, and after dinner I fell asleep on the couch, my dreams taking me to Samoset and the tribe. Samoset was cold to me in the dream, his focus on a young Indian woman who seemed fixated on him. When I tried to get his attention he grew angry and told me I wasn't part of the tribe and had no right to be there.

I woke close to tears, the feeling of being utterly alone so strong I could barely stand it. I had to tell Samoset my news but I was afraid it might be too late for us. The recollection of that tiny hovel and his attitude toward me made me feel sick inside. The passage I read in the witch book seemed to indicate urgency. But how could I go without speaking to Samoset?

I suddenly realized that this was it for us. He'd taken things too far. Tears welled and spilled over, scalding my cheeks as I fought for control. The house was dark. Everyone had gone to bed. When I reached to put on my shoes I found a note tucked into the toe.

My dear girl,

Now that you know where to go, trust the process and take yourself to the coven as soon as you can. If you need help the witches there will come to your aid. As to Samoset, the problems between you can keep. He loves you and you love him and that's what matters in the long run. Maybe the time apart will do him some good.

As to the coven and your part in it, I sense a crisis brewing. You will need to be up to speed once it happens. You'll understand more once you get there. I'm heading back to Sam. If you need me you know where to find me. And do not worry—all is as it should be. Good luck, my sweet girl.

Love,
Grandma

I hoped her statements about Samoset were more than wishful thinking. I took in a deep breath and put my mind firmly in the present moment before I snuck into Jean's room, dressed in a long black skirt and a loose-fitting hip length sweater, and crept quietly out the front door. "Take me to the Luna fountain in Luxembourg," I asked the ether, hoping the coven would come to my aid. I didn't know what timeline I needed to be in. I hoped they did. *Trust*, I told myself. *Just trust the process.*

Chapter Eleven

Fingers touched my hair, hands on my arms. I was embraced, an enormous feeling of relief flooding my body. I was meant to be here.

"My dear, we worried so," a female voice murmured.

I turned to look at the petite Asian woman with the wide gray eyes. Her hair was loose around her pale heart shaped face. "Why? Was I supposed to do something I didn't?"

She smiled, placing a soft hand on my cheek. "Nothing like that. But we could see your hesitancy, the battle within your heart. This decision was not easy for you." She turned to the many others who crowded around, both men and women, mostly gray-haired as she was.

"I was supposed to come now—Grandma said..."

"Yes, yes, you were. Circumstances have been closing in on us. We need all our new witches. I am Lin Chen, and this is Valir Goswell." She pointed to a tall middle-eastern man dressed in a dark robe. His brown eyes reminded me of a hawk's eyes, far-seeing and rather hooded.

"I am Kalinda Legere," another woman told me, taking

hold of my arm. Her skin was the color of hazelnuts and shone as though from an inner light. Her eyes were pale green, the whites very white, and for a split second I saw her differently, as a larger than life goddess, silver hair rippling across her shoulders, a scepter held in her hand.

I greeted her, remembering the list of names in the front of *Witches of the World*, which was supposedly written in 1624. And she resembled one of the women I'd seen in the library that day. "I'm Emeline Chase. Are we in the sixteen-hundreds?"

There was a low murmur of laughter. "No, dear," a younger woman said, reaching for my hand. "I'm Catalina Heidrig and this is my husband, Canton Musir."

I stared at her round face, the tangle of brown curls that stood out from her head. Her husband looked East Indian, although I couldn't be sure.

"Glad to see someone so young," he said, leveling his gaze on me. "Most of our lot have grown old and gray," he laughed, looking around at the others crowding close.

"Wouldn't have happened if…" a female witch began, but she was cut off by Kalinda.

"Come now," Kalinda said, peering into the darkness. "There are things at work here that we would rather not disturb."

Instead of walking away as I'd expected, I felt myself taken into the ether, our trip swift and quiet. We landed in a large meadow where moonlight shone down on a dark house. It looked medieval, with leaded glass windows and stone turrets, several chimneys rising up from the slate roof. When Kalinda raised her hand lights came on inside the building, turning it from shadowy to welcoming, golden light spilling from every window. Warmth emanated from the structure as though it held out its arms to embrace us.

"This is our home, at least until we are forced to leave it," Kalinda said, taking the lead.

I wondered what could force us out, but I didn't dare ask. My excitement grew.

Pentagrams, constellations and several other magical symbols had been carved into the heavy wooden door, quarter moons in gold leaf shining out from each corner. When the first witch crossed the threshold all the stars lit up, twinkling as if to say, 'welcome home'. I was still staring at them when the housemaid appeared to take everyone's cloaks. She eyed me suspiciously before scurrying off.

"Don't worry about Geeta. She has an attitude," a dark haired man told me. "You have no cloak so she's wondering who you are. I'm Henry Osborne," he continued, holding out his hand.

I grasped his dry fingers in mine. "My father's name is Henry," I said meeting his direct gaze. All at once I was filled with nerves, aware of the many witches who crowded around. They whispered amongst themselves, glancing at me as though I was some exotic bird they'd just collected.

"All right everyone, listen up!"

I jumped and turned to the dark skinned witch with the piercing brown eyes, my jangled nerves ratcheting up.

"Emeline must be initiated immediately. We all know what might happen if we put this off until morning."

"What?" I muttered to myself.

"You don't want to know," a diminutive gray haired witch next to me answered. "Let's just say the creatures of darkness might have their way with you." She let out a cackle that sent a shiver down my spine.

There was a low murmur before all eyes turned to me. "Are you up to it, my dear?" Kalinda asked.

"I guess so, but I don't know what *it* means."

"The rite of passage, the way for you to become part of our coven, of course."

"Are there other covens?"

"Oh, my yes," a woman dressed in purple answered. "We are but one small group here in Luxembourg. There are many, many covens across the globe." She moved to take my hand in hers. "I'm Violet Lansing, but you can call me Vi. Everyone does."

Her eyes were lavender, her lashes thick and black. She reminded me of a witch in a children's book with her black velvet dress, dangling silver hoop earrings and long black hair. She looked to be around forty but it was hard to tell since all of them seemed to look old one minute and young the next. I felt dizzy for a second, vertigo making me stumble. Someone took hold of my elbow.

The witches stirred around me, going in and out of focus as I examined my surroundings. The front hall was enormous, with pillars holding up a balcony that jutted out from above—below it shadowy areas seemed full of unseen creatures; I was sure I saw yellow eyes peering out from the dark. Portraits lined the walls, some of the faces seeming to turn their heads to stare at me, but before I could get a good look at them the group began to move, taking me through double doors into another room.

An enormous hand carved table took up much of the space, medieval chairs with leather seats all around. Wall sconces held candles instead of light bulbs, flames licking at the wallpaper covered with the same symbols I'd seen on the front door. Four narrow mullioned windows looked out on darkness, images of mythological creatures and birds appearing and disappearing as the candlelight flickered in their opaque surfaces.

A woman smiled, coming up next to me. "I'm Carlotta Von Hapsburg, the only one here of noble blood."

I turned to the white haired crone with the bright blue eyes. She reminded me of Grandma. She took my hand, leading me to the head of the table. "You sit here," she said with a wink before pulling out a chair with a flourish.

Other witches came through the doors, ones I hadn't seen before. They filed in quietly and stood with their backs against the wall. I saw the other two from the library, trying to smile as their eyes met mine. Once the doors closed there had to have been close to sixty people in the room.

Once all were settled the man at the other end rapped sharply on the table with a silver hammer. "I am Denton Feiderhausen, head witch. We do not divide up witch and warlock as you modern people do. We are all witches here," he added, chuckling as though it was a big joke. "Now, Emeline, it is our understanding that you are here of your own free will?"

"Yes," I said, hoping the initiation wouldn't be a bunch of questions I couldn't answer. The room shimmered and pulsed around me, one minute looking larger and in the next smaller, as though it was all an elaborate hallucination.

He nodded. "Good. It is also our understanding that you know our purpose here. Is that correct?"

"Not really. Grandma said you're like the Hopi?"

He smiled and looked down for a moment. "Only in how we

view our purpose on earth. What we do is very different." His gaze went around the table at the assembled witches. "Is there anyone here who objects to Emeline Chase joining this coven?"

One woman raised her hand. She was young, maybe a few years older than I, her cheeks rosy, silky blonde hair piled on top of her head in a braided medieval-looking configuration. I took an immediate dislike to her.

"Yes, Helga?"

She stood, smoothing out her long silk skirt, her gaze going to me. "What can you possibly bring to this group?" she asked me in a challenging tone.

My dislike intensified. "I have no idea what I can bring. I don't even know what your mission is. I only know that my grandmother told me that this was my destiny, and now was the correct time for me to seek you out."

As Helga continued to hold me in her gaze, an ache started in my belly. I refused to look away despite knowing it was her spell that was causing the pain. The seconds ticked by while I struggled to keep from doubling over.

"Helga? What say you?" Denton finally asked.

When Helga frowned and turned to him, the pain immediately disappeared. I sucked in air, wondering if coming here was such a good idea.

"I do not think she is schooled enough to be of much use. She is untested and of the *modern* world. She will disrupt the balance."

I heard the disdain when she said the word modern. "Yes, but I've been living in the sixteen hundreds with a tribe of Wampanoag Indians for over a year," I responded. "I've learned their ways and have respect for the world around me."

"Well said," Denton complimented, smiling.

"What does a band of Indians in the 1600's know? They are still savages, killing and fighting for no real reason."

"They understand nature, which is being destroyed at the hands of *modern* man. They care for the earth. They've been on the earth for more than ten thousand years. How long have you been here?"

Helga glared at me and sat down, examining her hands.

"Emeline will be in classes with the other new witches, Helga," Denton told her. "She will learn, just as you did. Anyone else?" he asked, looking around.

There was silence.

"All right, then. Let us commence. Violet, extinguish the candles, please."

Violet raised her right hand and a moment later the room was plunged into darkness. My hands trembled where I held them tightly clasped in my lap.

"Emeline Chase, do you solemnly swear to uphold the covenants of who we are and what we do?"

"I don't know what the covenants are."

There was a short silence in which I heard several intakes of breath and a few chuckles.

"The covenants are as follows:

1. You will never use your gifts to do harm.
2. You will attend your classes and when assigned a task not deviate from what is laid out for you by this group.
3. You will regard everyone here with respect.
4. You will regard the world with respect.
5. You will never reveal what you are.
6. You will remain with us until we give you permission to leave."

"But what if I want to leave?"

"You will come to me and make your case for why, Emeline. Do you agree to what I've laid out?"

I thought about it for a few minutes, contemplating the idea of not being allowed to decide what was right and what was wrong. "But what if I need to make changes to a plan, either for my own safety or for someone else?"

Denton sighed. "It is not advised, but there have been cases…"

"Well, then, my answer is yes. I do agree to all the covenants you've mentioned."

All the candles lit at once, soft welcoming light suffusing the room. The seated witches stood, each one coming by to congratulate me while the ones against the wall filed silently out of the room—less seasoned, I figured. Out of the corner of my eye I saw Helga push back her chair, and when I turned her way she gave me a freezing look, a stab of pain entering my chest. A moment later she was gone. I shivered in the chill wind that wafted around me.

Chapter Twelve

I'd been with the coven for over a week, learning names and getting to know a few of them through my classes. I was becoming used to the shifting stairways, the lights that blinked off and on when I walked by, the whispering in corners that didn't seem to have any origin, and the witches who wafted about as though powered by air. My days were filled with lessons on spells and potions, which included herbal knowledge, how to contact spirits, concealment spells and lastly a class on witch ethics.

I would not be allowed to leave the coven for one month, a fact that disturbed me. I had hoped to take a trip to Salem and at least let Samoset know where I was. Also the matter of my lack of conception needed to be discussed with him. But when I brought it up to Violet she was adamant.

"It is imperative that you remain with us for one moon before you venture out on your own. You need to be acquainted with all the rules and be one of us before you leave the coven. This is for your own good, Emeline. I hope you can understand why."

I didn't understand but I decided not to say anything. Going against any of these formidable witches gave me a prickly feeling all over.

Our meals were taken together at the same long table where meetings were held. But even that was fraught with strange happenings, as plates appeared out of the ether, leaving in the same manner, witches grabbing them before they self-destructed against the walls. I saw several stains that indicated mishaps. Was everything here bewitched?

I had a room and a bathroom to myself high up within the attics where the roof sloped down. I didn't mind, enjoying the coo of pigeons on the windowsill and the view of Luxembourg City, and the Alzette and Petrusse rivers where they met in the distance. My narrow bed was comfortable enough, the chest of drawers empty one day and full of clothes the next, all of which fit. Even a toothbrush had appeared my first morning, a tube of my favorite toothpaste arriving next. It was as though my thoughts conjured what I needed.

"Emeline?"

My new best friend, Noisette, was standing in my doorway, a smile on her face. "Today we go to town," she announced. "'Tis high time you had a change of scenery, *n'est-ce-pas?*"

"*Oui,*" I answered, pulling her into my room. She was around my age, fair-haired with bright hazel eyes, her curiosity sometimes giving her a bird-like appearance. We sat together three days a week listening to Kalinda and Violet reciting coven history and spells we needed to learn. "Tell me what you see down there," I asked, pushing out my one casement window.

She peered over my shoulder. "I see the river, the city with its spires and towers, the Adolphe bridge…oh, *oui!*" she clapped her hands. "It is the circus!"

"I thought so. I've never been."

"We must go today after our shopping."

"Will they let us?"

She shrugged. "If we do not mention it, how will they know?"

I laughed at the look of glee on her face. I'd grown to like it here with all the unusual happenings, the witches who were happy to see me when I walked into a room. I still thought of Samoset and planned to seek him out once the one month restriction was over, but I no longer felt the hollow emptiness he'd caused when he took me away, the feeling that I was a pariah. My abilities were growing, my understanding of what I was, increasing with every day. I'd reclaimed my freedom here, glad to have one good friend my age. By now Noisette had heard all about Samoset, her questioning making me realize how much I'd put up with.

"If he loves you he will be there for you, Emeline. If tribal law comes first then he is not the one for you. It is good you did not become pregnant."

The structure that housed the coven was built in the fourteen hundreds by a man versed in black magic. Gregory Ravel and his wife dabbled in the dark arts, doing spells for people who wanted spouses dead or to do harm to others. Many an innocent man had been hung in the village square as a result of their magic. When the two of them came into town women ran from them, afraid of what they might do to them or their children. Children had disappeared never to be seen again, possibly used for the witches' own gratification or even for some ritualistic sacrifice. Gregory and his wife had died in this very house when the place burned to the ground, caused by some stronger magic that had decided to be rid of them.

The coven had rebuilt centuries ago, imbuing the place with good energy and magic meant to serve rather than to do harm. The new name for our home was Geistigehaus, the German word for spiritual. And so it felt—a temple that kept us safe from any outside influences that could do us harm.

I had my hand on the front door handle when I heard a sharp voice. "Where do you two think you're going?"

Noisette and I turned to see Violet standing with hands on hips. "Didn't you hear that we have a new mission? We have been summoned by the High Priestess."

"What about Denton Fiederhausen—isn't he head witch?" I whispered.

"Yes, he's head witch of Geistigehaus, but Saffron is above him in the hierarchy. This does not bode well." Noisette's normally rosy cheeks had turned pale, her hand trembling where it rested against my arm.

As soon as we entered the room I noticed the tension, a low murmur of whispers wafting around the room. Seated at the head of the table was a large boned woman, a tangle of flame red hair standing out from the dark skin of her face. She was dressed in green brocade, the fabric straining across her large breasts, an aura of absolute power shimmering all around her. Her head swiveled toward me as I entered. "I see we have a new witch in our midst. I hope she can live up to her promise." When her gaze moved to the group at large I let out my held breath, glancing at Noisette who seemed shell-shocked.

"As you all know my name is Saffron Valadia, and I have been tasked with keeping you up to date on your assignments. We have a situation brewing on our small planet that will take a concerted effort to quell. You," she said, pointing at me. "Do you know what it is?"

I was struck dumb for a moment. Of course I didn't know what it was—how could I? "I don't know."

She glared at me for a full minute before turning away. "Anyone?"

Violet stood up. "It's the violence, the killing."

She nodded and scanned the room. "Anyone else care to elaborate?"

I glanced at the sea of faces focused on Saffron. Some held rapt expressions others looked angry and annoyed. She was not well liked but most were intimidated. I was glad when Kalinda stood up, her spine straightening as she faced Saffron. For one second I saw another body, another face superimposed over hers, a larger than life goddess whose expression brooked no disagreement. Had Saffron seen it or was it all my imagination? But Saffron was looking down, her attention on the papers in front of her.

"The earth is warming, creating massive storms and killing off fish, birds and many other creatures. Humans were tasked as shepherds of the earth, but instead they've twisted this into taking everything the earth has to offer. The ones currently in charge, at least in the United States, refuse to acknowledge what is. Other countries are making some inroads, but the richest country in the world seems to have gone off the rails. Without their participation climate change will continue unabated. Added to this problem is the racism and hatred that is being encouraged by the people in power. This causes fear, which causes more violence and more hatred. We are all one human family living on a planet with finite resources, and until we admit this fact the ongoing problems between people and countries will continue.

We are tribal beings but we are also capable of rising above our baser qualities. Every human being on earth descended from a small tribe that began in Africa one to two million years ago. The earth itself is crying out for justice and we as witches must heed her call. We need to change hearts and minds—not an easy task, but definitely doable."

"Very good, Kalinda. You're lengthy explanation is good for all to hear, especially those new to the coven." She glanced at me. "Our current assignment is to educate within the one country that should know better. All our creative ideas will come into play as we use what we know as witches. People must be turned toward the light again if we as a species are to survive. Any questions?"

I raised my hand. "What timeline are we talking about?"

"Yours will be a special assignment, Emeline Chase. I had hesitated to include the newer witches, but Kalinda and Violet have both given their approval."

I gazed around the room, checking out the witches in my classes. Their faces all seemed whiter than usual, their eyes wide. "But I don't know any spells well enough yet, and as far as potions, I…"

Saffron pinned me with a scathing look. "You will do as you are told, Emeline."

Noisette put her hand on my arm, stopping me from asking another question. "Do not get on her bad side," she whispered.

"I think she's taken a dislike to me," I whispered back.

"Silence!" Saffron bellowed, glancing toward us. "In a few moments everyone will come up to receive assignments. Kalinda, you will be first."

Kalinda stood and walked to the head of the table, waiting while Saffron spoke to her in low tones. It took barely five minutes before the next person was up and heading toward Saffron.

My turn came too soon. I was trembling as I made my way toward where Saffron sat. Once I reached her she looked me up and down before examining the papers in front of her. She riffled though them. "You are able to time travel—do you have control of this gift?" she asked, looking up.

"Most of the time," I answered honestly.

"You will need to hone your skills to carry out the assignment I have in mind for you. I have heard from several sources that you attempted to save the witches in Salem Village, Massachusetts during the unfortunate events of the late sixteen hundreds."

I nodded. "I saved nine."

She paused, glancing down at her papers. "Since you are familiar with the area and the relationships between groups you will go to colonial America."

I stared at her. Did she know about Samoset? "I lived with the Wampanoag. I'm actually married to…"

She waved her hand in the air to stop me. "I do not care what your romantic liaisons have been. I am asking you to change history, Emeline, to stop the savagery that crept into the Americas once the settlers arrived. This particular timeline represents the beginnings of what poisoned this part of the world and aided in the destruction of the native peoples."

"But by 1694 they…"

"No quibbling about details. I understand your newness to all this and also that you are not as equipped as others, but you do have time travel, and you have learned several spells by now, correct?"She didn't wait for my answer before continuing. "This is your assignment and I expect you to carry it out to the best of your ability."

I glanced over my shoulder at Noisette. "Can I have a partner? I thought maybe…"

"Helga will be your partner. You will leave immediately."

I opened my mouth to protest but she was already pushing me on so that she could deal with the next witch in line.

I looked around for Helga, not surprised to see her staring at me with narrowed eyes. Reluctantly I headed toward her.

Chapter Thirteen

The acrid smell of smoke assaulted my senses as soon as Helga and I landed, a feeling of doom settling into my belly. The forest surrounded us, cool and dark, but something was off, and it wasn't just the odor from the recent fire. I glanced at Helga who was straightening her skirt, the fingers of her other hand in her hair to replace the stray ends. She looked completely out of place in this setting, like a hothouse flower plucked from a greenhouse.

After we explored we found out that Samoset's village was gone, every remnant of the tribe's life here destroyed by the fire. The drying racks had been smashed and lay disassembled in the dirt, a few beads scattered here and there. I found the remnants of a papoose ripped apart and pottery smashed and blackened. The fire pit rocks had been scattered as though someone had a fit of rage, charcoal and ashes spread across the pounded earth that served as our meeting place. But worst of all were the chicken carcasses, chickens I'd raised and tended who provided us with eggs and meat once they grew too old for laying. They'd been hacked and discarded, a waste for everyone. I was surprised scavengers hadn't been by to pick their bones clean.

When had this happened and why? Tears filled my eyes as I searched through the rubble.

"What is your problem?" Helga asked. "Focus, witch, or both of us will end up as these people obviously did. I should never have allowed you to take us into the ether. Your priorities are not what they should be."

"These were my people, Helga. One of them is my husband."

"Well, goody for you. But to be honest, I don't care. We are on assignment, and I for one, plan to do what is required. Why did you bring us here?"

"I don't know. I guess I thought it was a good place to start. We're trying to change the attitudes between the settlers and the natives, right?"

"You're partially correct in that assumption. We need to cull the troublemakers out of this part of the world—take them to another timeline where they can't do damage. We can leave the good ones behind."

"And how are we to decide who's good and who's bad?"

"Don't you know your history? It's really quite simple. From what I understood you've lived here and know what's going on."

"I did…I do. But who knows how people change? I can't be judge and jury. Didn't Saffron say change hearts and minds?"

"That was Kalinda, the do-gooder. History is not written in stone, especially with us around." She laughed and turned away, her attention on an empty quiver left behind. I watched her pick it up and examine the intricate beadwork before casting it aside.

It was dusk before we discovered the footprints left in the ash indicating men wearing boots. I racked my brain for historical events. This was not where I'd landed on my last trip back from Grandma's house. That time I'd ended up in a new longhouse, in a new village—the place where they moved *after* the trappers attacked. This scene of destruction was the earlier spot I'd chosen for them, where the trappers had come and killed two braves and stolen Numee.

When I picked this spot I'd assumed there was little reason for the settlers to covet an area with no tillable soil. But this fire was recent and the damage seemed more extensive than a couple of trappers could manage. This had to be the wrong timeline because I had no memory of anything this devastating happening here.

I wondered for an instant if my leaving and return had altered the trajectory of events. But here I was again, my assignment to amend history—how could that be a good thing? "We have to find out when this happened," I muttered. "When I left here the tribe was living in another place—this is their old site, the one I picked for them—the one that Samoset told me led to…"

"Led to what?"

I looked up. "Led to them thinking I was an evil spirit. Trappers came and killed several braves and kidnapped a young woman. After that happened Samoset and the elders found another site for their longhouses and they moved."

Helga laughed. "An evil spirit? So what you're saying is

either you've brought us to the wrong timeline or someone's been messing with time."

But I barely heard her, tears tracking down my cheeks as I thought of those last two months and Samoset's attitude toward me.

Helga noticed the tears, her eyes narrowing in annoyance. "You need to pull yourself together, witch. This is our job, not some sad little story for you to get caught up in."

I glared at her. "This is my story, Helga—these were my people. Do you have any empathy at all?"

She laughed. "Empathy? What's that?"

I turned away, wishing I had Noisette for a partner instead of this heartless bitch who seemed to hate me for no reason at all.

"It's easy enough to take the ones who did this out of here," I heard Helga say.

"How do we figure out who it was?"

"My tracking skills are unparalleled. Come on," she said, grabbing my hand.

But I managed to pull away before we moved into the ether. "Some tribe member might come back tonight. And besides it's getting dark. I say we spend the night and leave in the morning." Before she could argue I set out to check Samoset's traps, hoping for a squirrel or a rabbit to cook up for dinner.

The forest was filled with shadows, a feeling of sadness circling around as I followed the familiar trails. Lights flickered on and off in the dark tree branches. I spied them out of the corner of my eye, but when I tried to focus on them they were gone. They had to be the tree spirits Samoset had told me about. But why could I suddenly see them when I'd never been able to before?

There was a freshly dead rabbit in the first snare I came to. *Thank you*, I whispered, removing it gently. I cut it free and tied it to my belt.

Back in camp I set to work, skinning it to prepare for cooking. Helga watched me working with the knife, trying to hide her revulsion. I found pleasure in her discomfort as I made a fire using modern day matches I'd brought along. I waited until she was watching before I forced a stick through the carcass to roast it. She gagged and turned away. But once it was cooked she ate hungrily, gnawing on the bones once the meat was gone.

"I take it you're not a nature girl," I commented, glancing at her lightweight dress and the dainty Capezio style shoes on her feet.

She looked up, her chin jutting stubbornly. "I don't usually have to rough it."

"You didn't think that 1694 might be a little rough for that outfit?"

She frowned. "And who are you to talk, miss emotional? You aren't prepared at all for this assignment."

"At least my clothes aren't made of paper thin material—why didn't Saffron give us a checklist of things to bring along?"

"Maybe she thought since you lived here you might provide some directions. Would have been nice to have some real food."

"You treated me like a pariah—if I suggested anything you would have bitten my head off. If it wasn't for Samoset's traps we would have gone hungry tonight."

"Whatever. And FYI, I'm pretty much impervious to cold."

"Good for you," I muttered, adding a few larger pieces of wood to the fire and poking it with a stick. "How can we figure out the timeline? Nothing like this happened while I lived here."

She scoffed and showed me the watch she wore around her wrist. The face was round and covered in numbers and tiny dials that looked intricate. "What is that?"

"This is a chronoscope given to me by…never mind. From what I can tell it's fall 1694, just as it should be."

"No exact date?"

She let out an exasperated sigh. "I'm not quite up to speed with reading it yet."

"So it could be September, October or November."

"Look around, Emeline. Are the trees completely bare yet? No. The leaves have turned and some have fallen. If I had to guess I'd say it's late October—is that close enough for your majesty? You're the one who brought us here—how did you pick the time?"

"I thought of the tribe."

"Did you picture the new longhouses or the former village?"

"I don't know, Helga. I made a mistake, okay?"

"Maybe you didn't make a mistake—maybe there's something dark at work here."

When our eyes met I realized she wasn't kidding. A chill ran down my spine. "What do you mean?"

"I'm just saying there might be magic—some dark force that wants to screw with us."

I stared at her. "What kind of magic? Are you saying other witches, or some kind of evil force, or what?"

"I don't know, Emeline. I'm just trying to come up with

an explanation for the timeline mix-up. We'll know soon enough."

Would we? The fire crackled and spit, shadows folding into shapes under the trees. I heard rustling and small moans. I chanted my newly learned spell for protection, hoping my fear wouldn't stop it from binding us in safety. I curled up next to the fire, but as the long hours rolled by sleep eluded me, my mind conjuring scenes of magical creatures with sharp claws and small pointed teeth. By morning I was bleary-eyed and even more worried about what had happened here, as well as angry with myself for not being more exact when I took us into the ether.

I rose and covered the fire with dirt, pressing my toe into Helga's ribs to wake her. "Time to rise and shine."

Her eyes narrowed as she sat up. "You're a bitch."

"So are you," I said, turning to go.

"What do you think you're doing? We don't have to travel on foot."

"How else can we follow their trail?"

She smirked at me. "We aren't following your precious tribe's trail, we're going after the bastards that did this. I can track through the ether—can't you?"

"I never have," I admitted. "Shouldn't we talk about this first? I don't want to make things worse than they already are."

"I know what I'm doing," she said, grabbing me none too gently by the shoulder. "I'm not a newbie like you."

A moment later we whirled away.

We landed on well-trampled ground that held evidence of blood. I saw a few feathers, a broken tomahawk and an arrow embedded in the base of a tree.

"They were here," Helga announced with a smug expression.

I walked the surrounding area, checking for evidence of the tribe. I felt them close like an ache in my chest. When I reached another small clearing I followed very obvious drag marks to where they disappeared under the cedar trees. My heart was now in my throat, sure I would come upon some horrible scene of blood and mayhem.

I was calling on my witch powers when I heard a shriek, running back to where I'd left Helga.

"What is *that* doing here?" she pointed to the black cat that walked toward me to rub against my legs.

"Lucifer, is that you?" I hadn't seen this creature since the day he helped us all escape the hanging tree. At the time he'd been in his other shape, Lucifer, the being of light, his magnificence beyond anything I'd ever witnessed. He'd enfolded us all within his enormous wings and transported us out of danger. The cat looked up at me before setting off under the trees. I followed him.

"Wait! Where are you going?" Helga yelled.

I turned. "He just answered my call. We need to follow him."

Helga jogged after me. "What call—why? He's just a creepy animal."

"Creepy animal? Are you sure you're a witch? This is Lucifer in his cat form. I thought you would recognize him since he's an angelic being of light."

"A familiar?"

"That and a lot more. He sort of belonged to my grandmother—maybe he's decided to hang around me now. Haven't you been around animals?"

She made a face. "I never liked them much."

"I thought our task was to rid the world of haters. How can you do your job if you don't love what lives on the earth?"

She was silent after that, her lips pressed into a thin line.

The sun had gone down before Lucifer turned his bright green eyes on me, his expression cat-like and inscrutable. We were in a part of the forest I didn't recognize, far from any of the many places I'd been with Samoset and the tribe.

"Are we stopping for the night? I hope so because my feet are sore and I'm starving—any ideas for dinner, oh high and mighty angelic one?" Helga asked derisively.

For a fleeting second the cat began to transform, wings sprouting behind a frowning and yet angelic visage as he rose up from the ground.

"What's he doing?" Helga shrieked, hiding behind a tree.

"I told you who he is—didn't you believe me?" I turned to the cat. "Sorry, Lucifer." The cat peered at me and then trotted off.

When Helga emerged again her hair had come loose, sticks and leaves tangled within it. "He…he scared me."

I smiled, feeling sympathy for the first time. "He's an angel, Helga. And if you saw him in his other form you'd be in awe, believe me. He doesn't take well to being ridiculed."

She tried to re-do her hair, giving up when she realized her pins had disappeared. "What do we do now?"

"We follow him."

Helga was leaning against a tree dozing, her exhaustion plain in the shadows beneath her closed eyes. Her silk dress was torn, her shoes muddy. Streaks of dirt lined her pale cheeks and her hair looked as though she'd been through a windstorm. I felt for my braid, glad it was still intact. I'd worn sensible shoes and a pair of loose fitting wool pants with a sweater over them. The cat had brought us even deeper into the forest where we waited for some sign of why we were here. It was then that I heard the voices.

"Helga," I hissed.

Her eyes flew open. "What?"

"Listen."

She cocked her head, her eyes going wide. "Who is it?"

"Not the ones we're after."

"How do you know?"

"They aren't speaking English."

She pushed herself to standing. "Why are we here, Emeline? Are you searching for your long lost love?"

"We followed the cat, remember?"

She glanced at Lucifer. "The cat doesn't know what he's doing. I suggest…"

"Shh," I said, creeping forward through the brush and low hanging branches. I could hear her behind me, her breath coming in gasps. She was seriously out of shape. A few minutes later I came upon several tribe members sitting around a fire. But when I called out and hurried toward them I found myself alone in another part of the forest.

Helga was right behind me, the expression on her face as bewildered as mine. "What's going on?"

"I think they're in another timeline."

"Oh, for god's sake," she said, grabbing my arm. I felt the whoosh as we entered the ether, but when we landed nothing had changed.

She glared at me as if it was my fault. "What did you do?" she demanded.

"What did *I* do? Nothing. But whatever you did, didn't work, did it?"

"You are a real bitch, you know that?"

"So you've said. I'm sorry, Helga, but whatever's going on here doesn't have anything to do with me."

She stared at the people sitting not ten feet away from us. "Why can't we reach them?"

"How do I know?"

Her eyes narrowed as she glanced down at the cat. "He did it."

The cat seemed nonplussed, his gaze bland, and then he seemed to shrug, an action I'd never seen a cat do.

When Helga kicked him he disappeared.

"You just kicked Lucifer—do you realize what happens if you piss off a god-like being?"

"I don't give a care, Emeline. Now let's get out of here and look for whoever caused this mess."

I stared into the clearing where my tribe sat around a fire talking. Samoset was not among them, but I did see several people I recognized as well as Aunum, the mastiff who was my constant companion when I first arrived in 1692. The tribe talked in low tones, their complicated language eluding me. All I knew for sure was something had happened to upset them.

When I called his name Aunum barked frantically,

running toward me, but as soon as he got to the invisible wall between us he disappeared. A moment later he was back, looking confused. Weetamoo called to him, her gaze going to where I stood. She couldn't see me. Aunum moved to her side but his eyes stayed riveted on me, his ears pricked forward. When he whined she rubbed his ears, murmuring something in Algonquian to soothe him. "Weetamoo!" I shouted, but she couldn't hear me either.

"What's with the dog?" Helga asked.

"He belonged to me and Samoset."

"I think he can see you."

"I do too, but the timelines are just enough off that…"

"We're wasting time here." She grabbed my arm and before I could protest we moved into darkness.

A second later we landed in a clearing next to a stream. Several men were seated next to a fire, and in the distance I could hear crying. "Shut yer trap!" one of the men yelled.

Helga glanced at me and moved forward, but just as before, we were not quite in their timeline. "What the hell," she muttered. She turned to me, irritation marring her perfect features. "Why is this happening? I've never had trouble like this."

I shrugged, peering into the shadows and trying to see who might be crying. It was Numee. Her hands were tied behind her back, her ankles too. She had red scratches down one cheek and her deerskin dress had been torn, exposing one breast. Her hair was filled with sticks and leaves, her eyes red from crying. She looked terrified. "That's my friend," I murmured.

Helga came to stand next to me. "They've either raped her already or they're planning on it."

My mouth opened in shock. "How do you know that?"

She made a face and stared at me. "Open your eyes, Emeline."

When I looked again I knew she was right. The men were drinking and casting glances at Numee, their eyes glittering. "What can we do?"

She shook her head.

At some point I fell asleep, my head lolling against the trunk of a wide oak tree, moss softening the ground under me as I slid down. Everything was damp from recent rains and colder than I was used to. I slept fitfully and woke shivering to a gray dawn, my gaze immediately going to the men on the other side of that impossible veil. They were gone. I glanced at Helga who stared blankly into the distance. "When did they leave?"

She looked over, her eyes red-rimmed. "A while ago. I've been sitting here trying to figure out how to get into that timeline." Her blood shot eyes met mine. "They raped her, Emeline, and I watched and couldn't do one thing about it." She burst into tears.

Chapter Fourteen

Helga's eyes were narrowed in hatred, her hands balled into fists. "I swear to god I'll kill them when we catch up to them."

"If we can get into their timeline," I muttered, not disagreeing.

Helga rose and paced, an intense expression appearing on her even features. "I've never done this particular spell before but I've heard it works."

"What spell? I know next to nothing about spells."

"Where did you go to school before you came to Geistigehaus?"

"I didn't."

Her eyes went wide. "You didn't go to witch school? How did you come to be there?"

"My grandmother sent me."

"Who is your grandmother?"

"Rebecca Chase."

She stared. "I know that name—she's famous."

"She is? What did she do?"

"She was very powerful in her day. I heard she stopped some kind of rebellion back in 1200's England. She's featured in our history books. The peasants revolt I think it was. If it hadn't been for her most of them would have been executed."

"Really? She never said."

Helga ran agitated fingers through her tangled hair and brushed off the back of her dress. "Repeat these words after me and I think we'll be able to get into their timeline." She closed her eyes, the words appearing in the air as she spoke them before they dissolved like sugar in water.

'We move from fourth to fifth dimension as our cells take on a higher vibration. Time is but a construct, not real. We break into a million light filled particles; we move where and when we please. Darkness to light, solid to liquid, liquid to air…bring us to where we need to be."

I repeated the words as she said them, a strange feeling steeling over me. My body no longer felt corporeal, instead I saw myself as pixels, as though I was merely sunlight sparkling across the ocean. A moment later I heard a sonic boom, as though we'd crossed the sound barrier. My eyes flew open. "Where are we?"

"We're exactly where we were, except now we're in the same timeline as those bastards. Let's go."

We found them an hour later, a stink of sweat and filth wafting toward us. When Helga lurched toward them I held her back. "We can't just go and kill them."

"Why not? You didn't see what they did to that young Indian woman."

I didn't see it but the thought of it made my blood boil. "Let's take them to another place and time—some parallel reality."

Helga's eyes lit up. "Do you know how to get to one?"

I shook my head. "Every time I end up in one, it's a mistake."

She stared into the distance thinking. "Have you studied the spells for dislocation?"

I shook my head. "We've just barely scratched the surface of spells for protection."

But Helga wasn't listening, her fingers dancing in the air, her mouth moving as she muttered incantations. "Follow my lead," she said a few moments later.

We stormed the camp, both of us yelling at the top of our lungs. The men were drunk and out of it, our arrival such a shock that one of them fell backward off the stump he was sitting on. Helga grabbed one and I grabbed another, Helga creating a mystical lasso of light around the others. "Dislocate!" she yelled.

We landed on a flat plain, the sky filled with malevolent dark clouds that moved and shifted like something alive. The place was desolate, with no trees or bushes to break up the ominous monotony. I heard a strange whining sound as though an enormous hive of bees were coming toward us. Sure enough a black mass of something was bearing down on us fast, its intent clear. We had to get out of here before the horrible things reached us. The men saw it too, their eyes wide with terror. They turned in a circle trying to decide where to run, but there was nowhere to go. I suddenly felt sympathy for them—what a horrible way to die. I was about to renege on our entire idea when Helga grabbed my hand. The last thing I saw was the buzzing swarm covering the men, their high-pitched screams dying away as we moved into the ether.

When Helga took us back to their camp I couldn't hide my horrified tears.

"What now? Don't tell me you feel sorry for those bastards."

"I would have felt better if we'd dropped them off somewhere to fend for themselves. That death could not have been pleasant, Helga."

"If you'd seen…" She shook her head, her lips pressed together. "Believe me, they deserved every horrible second of it."

I looked around the camp. "Where did Numee go?"

She shrugged. "I don't know but if I had to guess I'd say she was searching for the rest of her people. She'll find them now that the trappers are out of the way."

"Where was that horrible place you took them?"

She shrugged. "It's a world where people like that belong."

"But how did you find it? Was it the spell or did you know about it?"

She glanced away. "I asked for a suitable place to leave rapists. That's where the spell took us."

"I'm not sure I want to learn that spell."

Helga's eyes clouded. "You won't learn that in your studies. I found out from…well, never mind that. It's done and that's what counts." She turned away.

"Who taught you?"

"Don't worry about it. Right now we have larger issues to deal with. Remember why we're here? We're supposed to stop the violence between the colonists and the natives."

"Well…we just removed several creepy men from this place. I didn't like it, but it does give me a few ideas of how to handle the rest of them. There must be other worlds that don't have a mass of stinging bugs."

Helga smiled a nasty smile. "I like how you think." She grabbed my arm.

A few seconds later sixteen hundreds Salem materialized, the familiar sounds of horses clattering down the road, a hatchet hacking into wood, hammering, as well as the lilt of archaic English. "We need to be more careful, Helga," I whispered, glancing around at the townspeople moving along the road. "If someone sees us arrive out of thin air…"

She waved one hand in the air. "I always cast a spell of amnesia when I do this, Emeline."

Sure enough, the people wandering about barely glanced at us despite our strange clothing and abrupt arrival. In the distance I was sure I spotted Samoset heading toward the town meetinghouse. I hurried toward him.

"Where are you going?" Helga asked, grabbing hold of my arm. Her gaze went to Samoset disappearing into the building. "Is that your Indian?"

I nodded, my eyes welling.

She pinched my arm painfully. "You have to focus, Emeline. We have our own job to do."

I twisted out of her grasp, my fingers going to the welt forming on my upper arm. "I have to talk to him, Helga. He doesn't know what happened to me."

She shook her head, frowning. "The only way I'll let you talk to him is if he's part of our mission. Otherwise he's off limits. Do you remember what you swore to the day you were initiated?"

"Yes, but it didn't say anything about…"

"You will obey the task that is laid out for you and you will abide by the instructions given. Taking time out for this man is not part of our job."

"And neither was leaving those men to die."

She gazed at me. "They were horrible men and that was a suitable punishment for their crime. Now come on—we need to find out what's going on so we can work an angle or two."

We skulked around the meetinghouse, peeking through windows and trying to hear the mumbled conversations. Several natives, including Samoset, were inside, speaking with the darkly dressed magistrates. Townspeople sat on benches observing. By their hand gestures they seemed to be negotiating something. "He *is* part of our mission," I hissed, turning to Helga. "He can tell us what's going on."

Helga sighed. "Maybe you're right. When he comes out corner him."

I watched and waited, things I wanted to tell him whirling through my brain. When Samoset emerged a half hour later I was already in motion, closing the distance between us.

Just before I reached him he turned, his eyes narrowing. "You go," he said, his gaze wary.

"Do you mean you want me to leave or are you reminding me of when I took off? You left me out in the wilderness. What did you expect?"

He frowned, confusion appearing for a moment before he said, "Tribe is not happy. Tribe go hungry—many bad things happen now."

"Are you still blaming that on me?"

"Elders say bad medicine—say you curse tribe. No more game."

"The game is sparse because of how dry it's been—you know that."

His gaze softened for a moment. "No understand, Em. No understand you leave."

"I left because I missed you. The tribe was my home."

"Day you leave tribe, elders find new wife."

"You're with another woman?"

He didn't answer, his gaze going to Helga.

I grabbed his arm. "Look at me! Are you with another woman?"

"Ceremony soon. First business with magistrates."

"I don't understand. You took me away and left me out in that hut. Isn't that enough? I'm sorry about the baby thing—I have to talk to you about that."

"What hut? You leave with sister. Tribe sure you gone for good."

I stared at him. "You don't remember building a little shelter for me?"

Samoset shook his head, frowning. "You abandon me, abandon tribe. Is why elders want new wife for Samoset."

"If you still love me you can't marry another woman. You have to…"

"Get on with it, witch," Helga called. "We don't have time for this."

Samoset looked from Helga to me. "Why are you here?"

"I'm working with a group of witches. We came to sort out the problems between the Indians and the settlers. Why were you in the meetinghouse?"

"Tribe move soon to praying towns. Puritans come and take children away."

I'd read all about these so-called praying towns, how the Indians were still considered second-class citizens—just like minorities everywhere. And in the end the land they'd been given was taken away. The Indians weren't used to the impersonal English society. Tribal life was based on relationships and reciprocity. They would never survive it.

"You can't give in to them; you'll be miserable without your culture!"

He shook his head and sighed. "Too many white man, not enough Indian."

"Samoset, please. Don't give up. I love you. I want to be with you. Don't let them marry you off."

He took hold of my arm. "Come now and talk with elders. When they see you maybe they…"

"Emeline," Helga said, impatiently.

"I can't."

His eyes went dark. "Will be too late," he said, watching me. A moment later he walked away.

Running after him wouldn't do any good. Helga would never let me take time to talk with the elders. Apparently we were in the timeline that happened before he took me out to the hut—but how was that possible?

"At least you didn't run after him like a meek little wife," Helga muttered. "So what was the meeting about?"

"The tribe is moving into the praying towns," I said, still watching Samoset.

"Praying towns, what's that?"

"Basically the first reservations, Helga. The Indians are supposed to give up their culture and take on the white man's ways, including Christianity. You must know the history of this place—how the mostly middle to upper class Puritans, who followed the teachings of John Calvin, fled England? They're Protestants who take the bible literally. They want a theocracy. The pilgrims, on the other hand, are from all walks of life, mostly poor and uneducated. They came to the new world for a new life."

"I knew all that," she snapped. "As to the praying towns, we can stop it."

I could barely react. Samoset was about to marry someone else.

"Snap out of it, witch. We're powerful and we can put an end to this before it happens."

"How?"

"Would you use your brain for once? We'll find the ones advocating for these praying towns and remove them from Salem."

"I have a feeling it's most of them, Helga. The Puritans probably outnumber the pilgrims twenty to one or more. If we start moving them there won't be anyone left. They already persecuted the Quakers, what's to stop them from doing the same to the Indians?"

She smiled an evil smile. "They can go live with the trappers."

I pictured John Hathorne and Cotton Mather running for their lives. "This is the wrong timeline, Helga. Samoset doesn't remember anything about the house he built for me, or…" I stopped talking when the stern men dressed in black appeared from within the meetinghouse. They examined us with frowns on their faces.

"I suggest we get out of here before we're rounded up

and burned at the stake," Helga hissed.

"The witches here were hanged."

"Whatever. Follow my lead and get ready to move."

My chest ached and I couldn't seem to take in a deep breath. Samoset had no memory of what he'd put me through—the little hut and his nasty attitude. He was still the man he'd been when I left with Jean, the man who loved me and didn't want me to go. My leaving had caused this anomaly, I was sure of it. Jean had been from another reality—maybe that's what started it all.

A second later we were in the ether and a moment after that we were back in the woods.

Chapter Fifteen

We camped in the woods, arguing about what to do next. I was determined to help the tribe but Helga would have none of it. The birds sang in their sweetest tones, the sun shone down through the branches of the firs and hardwoods while the last midges of the season flew around our heads. But instead of either of us reveling in the last warm days of the season Helga psychically slapped me around while I floundered in an emotional quagmire.

Not only was Samoset oblivious of taking me to the hut he also didn't yet know what I'd discovered from my visit to the doctor. The tribe still blamed me for everything bad happening to them. I couldn't believe Samoset was considering going along with their plan to marry him off.

"If you don't get yourself together I'm taking you back to face the Queen of darkness. I'll tell her you're hopeless and see what she decides."

"I guess you're referring to Saffron?"

Her eyes narrowed. "I'm serious, Emeline. You're screwing up our entire assignment."

"I don't see how we can change history without suffering a bunch of consequences," I said. "Especially since the timelines are completely screwed up already—any more insight into that? What if we're related to one of these men you want to send to another planet?"

"And what about those trappers? You were fine with that. One of them could be your great great great..."

I held my hand up to stop her. "I wasn't fine with that but I went along with it."

She made a face and continued. "And besides, Saffron knows exactly, and I mean *exactly*, what's going on."

"How is she so powerful? Is she the daughter of Zeus, the muse of history? You're telling me that if we remove someone who shouldn't be removed...what? He or she shoots right back in?"

Helga's eyes narrowed even further. "I don't know," she hissed. "I only know that Saffron is in touch with things that we're not privy to, all right?"

"Have you ever had an assignment like this?"

Helga scowled. "No. I've had to cast spells, and remove certain important people from dangerous situations."

"Being in the wrong timeline seems dangerous to me. I hope I don't run into my other self and create a paradox or something."

"Stop trying to pull me into your world of doubt! So what if it's the wrong timeline? It doesn't really matter since the issues are the same. I have no idea what happens if there are two of you—I suppose that could cause a problem. That's why I suggest we get on with things and get the hell out of here."

"Maybe we should re-locate the tribe instead of getting

rid of the Puritan settlers. There are less of them."

"I can't imagine you want to take your precious tribe to that nasty place."

"Maybe there's a better one. I'm sure you didn't ask for a pleasant place to take those trappers."

"You're right about that." Her forehead scrunched in thought. "There have to be hundreds of parallel realities, right?"

I thought of the times I'd ended up in them accidentally. I sincerely hoped she had more control that I did.

"Historically white skinned peoples have an air of superiority, sure that they are more intelligent than those of color," she continued. "Slavery is the perfect example. And look at Nazi Germany. Even the German philosopher, Schopenhauer, talks about it."

"True, but maybe there's a world where things didn't develop the same way. Why did Saffron give us this impossible assignment? There's no way we can fix things here."

Helga stared into the distance. "I think you may be right. If we move people to a parallel world we won't be following the rules. We need to go back and discuss it with Saffron before we start messing about."

"I'm glad to hear you say that. Will we fess up about what we did with the trappers?"

Helga scoffed. "Of course not. But maybe she can give us some tips. If she were here it would be done by now."

"Maybe she should come back and do it then," I snapped.

Helga gazed at me blandly, a little smile playing at the corner of her mouth. She loved it when I lost my cool.

Saffron shifted in her seat, her eyes dark with annoyance. "No parallel worlds. We're trying to fix this one! I sent you two to figure this out on your own. Why are you here?"

"Because we can't come up with a solution," I answered. "And the timelines are screwed up."

Her gaze turned to me. "How do you know that? Perhaps you sent yourself to the wrong one, Emeline. From what I've seen so far of your skills they are sadly lacking. I know you've not had the schooling that Helga has, but I thought pairing you two would give you the opportunity to combine your talents. Was I wrong?"

I glanced at Helga who seemed more subdued than usual. "Every scenario we come up with seems wrong. We've already sent..."

"We've already spoken with the tribe," Helga interrupted, rolling her eyes at me. "We'll figure it out—won't we, Emeline?" She stared at me, her eyes widening further.

"Yes, we will," I answered quickly, anxious to get out from under Saffron's scrutiny.

"Okay, then. Get on with it," Saffron said, turning back to the stack of papers on her desk.

Helga grabbed my arm and a moment later we were back in Salem standing in the middle of the town square.

"That went well."

She scoffed. "I had a feeling this would happen. We'll have to come up with our own solution whether it goes against the rules or not."

"I was afraid you'd say that," I muttered as we walked along the road toward the market in the center of Salem.

For once we'd been provided with a few antique coins for purchasing food. "What timeline are we in now?"

"I visualized where to bring us—probably the same as the one before. Maybe I should have let you do it?"

"I think we should be more precise, that's all. I'm still worrying about my other self. Too bad there isn't a newspaper around to show us the date."

"You mean like this?" She pushed up her sleeve and looked at her weird watch.

"So what's the date?"

She frowned. "I'm still figuring out how to read it."

"So it's useless."

She pushed her chin out and hurried away.

As we drew closer to the tables set up with vegetables, meat, eggs and cheese, I felt a buzzing in my ears—as though the energy was off. Women hurried past with their heads down, men stood in groups talking in low tones. "What's happening?"

"There's been an Indian uprising," Helga whispered.

I stopped to stare at her. "How do you know that?"

"Didn't I tell you about my ears? I have extrasensory hearing."

I thought she was kidding until I saw the expression on her face. "Why didn't you say?"

She shrugged. "Not important."

I heard a shout, turning to see several men hurrying toward us yelling something about witches. We took off running, heading toward the woods, but they were faster, closing the gap between us until I could almost feel their hot breath on my neck. They had nearly caught up with us when I turned and raised my arm. A pulsing green ball of energy appeared in my hand and I was nearly as surprised as they were when I hurled it toward them.

The ball expanded in size until a fog separated us from the men. They shouted and swore on the other side of the thick greenish haze, struggling to get through it. I grabbed Helga's hand and a moment later we were in the ether.

I must have been thinking of Samoset and the small house he'd built for me because that's where we ended up. In my absence it had been damaged by weather, with several rushes gone from the roof, the reeds dark from rain.

"What *was* that?" Helga asked me, her eyes wide.

"I have no idea—I've never done that before."

She laughed. "Seems there's more to you than meets the eye, Emeline."

Her silk dress was now ripped in several places and covered with burrs and twigs, her silky blonde hair a rat's nest of dreadlocks and tangles, her cheeks streaked with mud. Her shoes were gone, her white stockings shredded. My pants were ripped, my hair had come out of its neat braid. One side of my sweater was torn and the other side was covered in mud and moss. "Look at us. No wonder they chased us—we look like witches."

Helga doubled up with laughter. I giggled and then lost it, the two of us falling in a heap and rolling around as we tried to get control of our giddy hysteria. But when I felt the first cold flakes I stopped laughing, suddenly aware of the change in the weather. I pushed myself to my feet. "We're in a different timeline." The sky was the flat gray that portends a major snowstorm, the trees leafless and stark in the muted light. When I hurried to the *wetu* Helga followed, both of us glad to get out of the snow that now fell thickly, already coating the ground in a layer of white.

"This is the hut I was telling you about."

Her green eyes turned dark inside the *wetu*, a frown between her pale eyebrows. "The one that didn't exist in the last timeline? How did you manage to move us here?"

I shrugged, as surprised as she was. "Is the uprising you heard them talking about in this timeline or the one we just left?"

Confusion moved across her features. "How can we figure that out without another trip into Salem?"

"If we go I think we should walk this time. That way we'll know for sure where we are."

"In this weather?" Helga gave a huff of annoyance. "How far is Salem from here?"

I let out a sigh. "A long way."

Helga's eyes narrowed in thought. "That uprising may mean that your tribe decided they didn't want to become white men—maybe they balked about the praying town."

I thought of Samoset then and the Samoset who had left me alone in this hut. I liked the other one better. "I guess it could but I'm still confused about the timelines."

"But this place is what you remember from your last time here, right? I mean before we arrived from Luxembourg."

I looked around the interior that smelled of damp and mold. "Yes, but the *wetu* has obviously been weathered for at least a month since I was here. And it's snowing and the trees don't have leaves."

"True." She stared at the chronoscope for a while before her eyes lit up. "I think I figured it out! If I'm right this is October thirty-first."

We stared at each other, both of us wondering what that might mean. Spirits roamed the earth on this night, and because we were witches we were well tuned to them. We huddled together as the light waned and darkness fell. "We're witches," Helga said mostly to herself. "We have spells of protection."

"If you know one please cast it, Helga. I can already hear something moving around outside."

When I glanced out the doorway I was sure I saw ghost-like figures wafting through the trees. When something moaned I grabbed hold of Helga's arm. "Did you hear that?"

The whites of her eyes glowed as she turned to me. "Come on, Emeline. Time to face our fears."

She dragged me from the *wetu*, heading on a zigzag path into the forest. The wind whistled through the branches, sending snow eddying around us. I saw lights in the upper branches of the trees, heard the scrabble of claws. "What's that?" I hissed, pointing to a translucent figure walking toward us.

Helga stared for a long moment. "It's my brother," she whispered. "He's been dead for four years."

We waited as the figure drew close, a long bloodless face finally appearing out of the dark. "What do you want?" Helga asked, backing into me.

His eyes were black holes in the pale face, his lips thin and sad. He paused and turned to his sister, his translucent hands raised in a pleading gesture. "Why?" he asked, his reedy boy's voice echoing.

"You know why!" she hissed. He watched her for another second before he slowly dissipated, turning into so many strands of cobwebby white. A moment later he was gone.

"What was that about?"

Helga shook her head, looking at the ground. "He blames me for his death."

"What happened, Helga? I didn't even know you had a brother."

"I can't talk about it," she said, heading back to the *wetu*. The press of her mouth let me know there was no point in questioning her further.

At some point during our long vigil we both fell asleep, exhausted from the stress of our situation. *Tomorrow*, I told myself. *Tomorrow we'll figure something out and come up with a plan.*

"Em?"

I woke with a start, surprised to see Samoset peering at me from the opening. I scrambled to my knees and joined him outside. It was very early dawn and it had stopped snowing, leaving three inches of fluffy white behind. Our breath came out in white clouds in the gray-blue air. "What are you doing here?"

"I come take *wetu* down."

"Why?"

He regarded me solemnly. "You gone long time, Em. I give up on you. And now tribe is angry with magistrates. We fight to keep our ways."

"Do you remember me telling you that a day or two ago?"

He frowned and shook his head. "Elders decide not good for future to live in praying towns."

The last time I'd seen him the tribe had been preparing to move. Had they decided not to go? How far in the future were we? But right now I had more pressing things on my mind. "Samoset, we have to talk."

He waited while I pulled my thoughts together. When I folded my arms across my chest he took off his deerskin cape and put it around my shoulders.

"I know why I never got pregnant."

He looked away, as though this subject was too painful to discuss.

"I'm a witch and I've been keeping myself from conceiving."

He turned. "Why you do this?"

"Because I wasn't ready. I didn't know I was doing it. I wanted more time for the two of us. Taking care of an infant seemed too overwhelming. I'm part of another tribe now—a witches coven. There are others like me there."

"What about our life?"

"You brought me out here, away from everyone. Do you remember how awful you were? I don't think you love me anymore."

He shook his head, his eyes turning dark. "Tribe turn my thoughts dark—make me believe in *Hobomock*. But since you leave many bad things happen."

"So maybe my leaving is what caused the *Hobomock* to come?" I asked hopefully.

I could feel the heat from his body and smell the pinesap that he always seemed to get in his hair. The snow began again, tiny flakes that stuck to us and turned his hair salt and pepper. He blinked away the flakes on his eyelashes before taking one step toward me. When he reached for me

I moved into the circle of his arms. Our lips met and clung, our bodies pressing close. He glanced at the *wetu* and then pulled me away into the forest, finding a bed of pine needles under a cedar where we were protected from the snow. He pressed me back and kissed me again before his hand went inside the waistband of my wool pants. He slid them down, exposing my skin to the chill air. "I miss Em," he murmured, nuzzling my neck. "No want other wife, but elders say…"

"Don't talk," I said, pulling him to me. I wanted to savor this moment. It had been months since we'd made love and I'd been sure we were finished. The cold disappeared as my body warmed up beneath him, our low moans like the sounds of the earth moving in its orbit. We touched and explored as though it was our very first time together, our bodies like magnets that couldn't remain apart. It wasn't long before our breath raced, the scene around us disappearing into pure sensation. It was always like this with him, as though at that critical moment we traveled to another galaxy. When it was over we lay close together on our sides, our eyes locked.

"Em," he said, his hand on my cheek. I guess I was crying because he wiped tears away with his fingers. "Elders have wife picked out."

"But I'm your wife, Samoset—how can you marry someone else?"

"It is tribe way. Sachem must have baby."

"I told you why I didn't get pregnant. Maybe now things will be different."

"You part of new tribe, Em. No longer my wife."

"But I am your wife. I can do both."

"With baby?" He shook his head. "If baby come must stay with tribe. Sachem must raise boy."

I laughed. "What if it's a girl?"

His expression remained serious as he watched me. "Life different now."

"I know you still love me."

He nodded. "Heart does not matter—sachem must do what is right for tribe."

I tugged my wool pants on and pulled down my sweater, beginning to shiver. "I don't want you to do this. Maybe I'll be pregnant. What if I am and you're with this other woman?"

He shook his head and pulled on his leggings, his gaze moving into the distance. "Marriage in seven days." He counted them out. "Must go through with ceremony. If baby we talk again. But..." he looked skeptical.

"I know—it hasn't happened in all the many months we've been trying." I pulled my gaze from his, thinking about how much I liked the coven and my new life. Was I being forced to make a choice between Samoset and being a witch?

"Much confusion now. War with settlers come." He watched me for another moment before he stood and pulled me to my feet. He pressed his lips to my forehead and nodded, as though that was enough to quell my worry. A moment later he was walking away.

"Please be careful. The men in town have guns. If you go to war you could all be killed," I called out.

"I know this, Em. Tribe have guns now too." He glanced at me over his shoulder before disappearing into the shadowy snow covered conifers.

I straightened my clothes and followed our path back to the *wetu*.

"Was that Samoset?" Helga crouched in the opening watching me brush the snow off the back of my pants. I knew what I must look like.

"He loves me, Helga. And the tribe is planning war with the settlers. It's going to be a bloodbath. In a week he's marrying another woman." I burst into tears.

Helga let me cry it out, offering no comfort. "Did you actually screw out there under the trees in the middle of a snow storm? You're crazy. Having sex doesn't mean the man loves you. Maybe he's just horny. And besides, you can still see him even if he's with someone else."

"No, Helga. That isn't who he is. He's loyal to a fault."

"Doesn't sound like it if he's abandoning you. And from what I saw yesterday you have a larger purpose than being the squaw of some Indian chief and having his babies."

I glared at her even though I knew she was right. That green sphere had changed things.

"You may love him but it won't do much good. He has his destiny and you have yours. In the meantime we need to find a solution to the problem we're supposed to solve."

She began to pace in the snow, her arms folded across her chest. I handed her the deerskin cape and went back inside the *wetu*. I tried hard to focus on Saffron's assignment, but all I could see was Samoset with another woman in his arms, a tiny newborn lying close beside them.

Chapter Sixteen

I was dozing when Helga came back inside. "Did you ask him about Numee or tell him what we did with those rapists?"

I sat up. "I didn't get a chance."

She scoffed and rolled her eyes. "No, I guess not, what with rolling around in the snow like a couple of rutting…"

"I did tell him about the timeline mix-up," I interrupted. "He said I'd been gone a long time."

"What does a long time mean? Does he know about weeks and months?"

"Yes, he knows how we measure time, Helga. I figured a long time for him meant at least a month, maybe more."

"Imprecise, Emeline. You're surmising."

"I know how his mind works—it may be simplistic but it's how we communicate."

"We need to get to town."

"Are you willing to walk?" I asked, looking at her bare feet.

"Didn't you say we had to walk?"

"Yes, but you usually don't listen to what I say."

I struck out ahead of Helga, but her voice followed me. She seemed bound and determined to lecture me about all my shortcomings.

She caught up to me, continuing in a parental tone. "You have to speak up for yourself—don't let him take over! Just because he's a man doesn't mean he gets to be in charge. You shouldn't have let him have his way with you, Emeline. Playing hard to get once in a while won't kill you. And if you care for him you can't let him marry this other woman."

I stopped to face her. "And how am I supposed to do that? He's sachem, Helga. And his culture is not like ours. I can't suddenly foist my modern mores on him."

She shut up for a while after that, only cursing occasionally as she tripped over a root or stubbed her toes.

It was just before we reached the outskirts of town that I had a vision of my grandmother. She was at her house in Salem and I felt a burning need to see her. When I headed away from the main road Helga grabbed me. "Where are you going? I want to use our money to buy some food. I'm starving."

"I had a vision of Grandma—she's here in her house. I'm sure she can feed us, Helga."

Helga stared at me for a long moment. "Okay, if you think she's really here. I hope it isn't just wishful thinking on your part."

"I did tell you I have visions, right? You can trust me."

I set off along the side street, listening to Helga huffing behind me. I hoped she didn't have frostbite.

Once we reached the familiar house I lifted the lion's head knocker and let it drop, the sound echoing inside. A moment later Grandma opened the door. "Why Emeline and Helga, what a nice surprise!" She ushered us in and closed the door behind us.

Instead of hugging me she embraced Helga, pulling her close.

Helga quickly pulled away. "Why are we here?" Helga asked me.

"Rude," I mouthed, widening my eyes. When I reached to give Grandma a peck on the cheek, her shoulders tightened. I was about to ask what was wrong when she turned toward the kitchen.

"I'll just make tea," she called.

"Why are you being so rude?" I hissed as Helga and I followed her.

"That woman is not your grandmother."

"What? She may be a little distracted but seems fine to me."

Helga shook her head. "How did she know my name? You want her to be your grandmother but she's not. Tell me the vision again?"

"Are you two planning to join me?" Grandma called.

"It was only her face and I knew she was here…"

Grandma appeared in the doorway. "What are you two whispering about?"

"Nothing," Helga said, moving into the kitchen. I followed.

A fire was burning, sending welcome warmth into the

narrow room. When I looked around everything was as it had been the last time I was here. I let Helga's warning go, concentrating on Grandma. "Do you have anything to eat, Grandma? We're starving."

"Yes, of course." She went to the cold room and brought out the remains of a chicken and a loaf of bread. "Feast away," she said, handing us two plates and two forks.

We did.

"Where is Jonathon Corwin?" I asked, looking around for signs of her husband, the magistrate who assisted Hathorne with the hangings. Last time I'd been here he'd been puking his guts out and bellowing for the maid. I smiled, remembering the voodoo doll under his bed with the pins stuck in the stomach. Why Grandma had married him was still a mystery.

Grandma seemed startled for a moment her eyes flicking up and to the right. "He left me to be with his ailing sister."

"How is Sam?"

"Sam...well...I suppose he's fine." Her hand fluttered to her neck to straighten her collar. "But I came to Salem because of you, my dear. I knew you needed help. It takes an older more seasoned witch to solve a dilemma of this magnitude."

I glanced at Helga who had a funny look on her face before turning back to Grandma. "How did you know about our mission?"

"Saffron contacted me."

She did? "Saffron...she..."

"We stay in contact," she added quickly. "I may not be a

part of the coven anymore but I'm still listed as a consultant."

I wondered why she'd never told me this.

Helga shifted on her seat. "Do you have a plan?"

When I glanced at her she was staring intensely at Grandma.

Instead of answering Grandma rose and poured tea with her back to us. When she returned with two full mugs her face looked different somehow, her features slightly off kilter as though she might be having a stroke. I was about to grab her arm to help, when her features rearranged themselves.

"I do have a plan. But I am not at all sure it will work," she answered.

"Did you discuss it with Saffron?"

She shook her head, loosening a tendril of gray hair from the twisted chignon. She pushed it back behind her ear instead of re-pinning it. "That is forbidden. Once a task has been set all witches must figure things out for themselves. You two broke the rules."

"We went back for her advice, though," I said.

"And yet you did not mention what you did with those men."

How did she know about that?

"Or your utter confusion with the timelines. Really, girls—these sorts of things belong in Witch 101." Grandma sat down, her gaze on her tea mug. When she looked up again her eye color had changed to midnight blue, as dark as the sea.

"We thought we might be expelled," I answered, uneasy for the first time. "But those men were really terrible men, Grandma. Maybe they deserved it."

Grandma's gaze narrowed. "Is that decision up to you?"

Helga began to cough, her hand going to her throat. She stared at the teacup. "What did you do?" she asked hoarsely.

Grandma smiled and it was a smile I did not recognize. "I should have known you'd see through me," she said.

I watched her features shift and change, the gray hair turning darker, her lips plumping, the lines around her mouth disappearing. A moment later she looked surprisingly like me. I gasped and stood up. "Who are you?"

Helga grabbed my hand. "She's dangerous," she hissed, pulling me with her into the ether.

When we landed back in the woods Helga's face was chalk white. "What's going on?" I asked her, worried.

"We aren't safe. That woman masquerading as your grandmother is a very powerful witch. There is no place we can go where she can't find us."

"She's a shifter?"

"Yes."

She was about to say something else, but instead of listening I envisioned Grandma's house and entered the ether. I had to see for sure.

A stranger wearing a pristine white cap answered, her wary gaze going to my clothing. "Who are ye, child, and what would ye be wantin'?"

"Is my grandmother in? Rebecca Chase, or possibly she goes by Rebecca Corwin."

The woman frowned. "There is no such person livin' here."

Before I could respond she slammed the door in my

face. I stood there for several moments trying to calm myself. Helga was right. But who was she?

"So?" Helga asked when I appeared out of the ether. She pushed herself away from the tree, her hands cupping her blue toes, trying to rub some warmth into them.

"Grandma wasn't there, and according to the woman who answered the door, she doesn't live there."

"Why didn't you believe me? You saw how she was. Why do you have to question everything I tell you?"

"I wanted to believe it was her. The vision was so real. I was sure she was here to help us. I *needed* her to be here to help us. How did this other witch manage that?"

"Did I mention she's the most powerful witch I've ever known?"

"No, you didn't. She sent the vision?"

She ignored my question, her eyes faraway and worried. "We need all the magic we can conjure to keep ourselves safe; there's bound to be more trouble."

"Who is she, Helga? And how do you know her? She looked like me. Did
she do that on purpose?"

"Lourie was the darling of the entire coven—until…"

"Until what?"

Helga turned to me with an expression I'd never seen on her face. She looked seriously freaked. "It was about a year ago when she didn't get the assignment she wanted. Something snapped and she set Geistigehaus on fire. Several witches died because of it. If it hadn't been for Valir and Catalina, more would have died. They found her and bound her in a spell until Saffron could be summoned.

After that she was banished. Today is the first time I've seen her."

"Tell me about your relationship with her."

Helga looked near tears, her face turning red. She didn't speak for a long time. "I loved her. We were lovers, Emeline." She stared at me defiantly.

"If you think I'm going to condemn you for being a lesbian, you're wrong. I had lesbian friends at school."

"Remember how I was when we first met? How hateful?"

I scoffed. "I'm glad you got over whatever *that* was."

"It's because you look so much like her. You could be sisters. The first time I saw you I thought you were her playing a trick on me."

"How would she know about me and my grandmother?"

Helga made a face. "Are you kidding? She's a time traveler and has dark magic to work with. She'll stop at nothing to get what she wants."

"So way more powerful than we are."

Helga made a derisive sound. "If you ever got over your fear you'd know what powers you have; remember that fireball you threw? You act like you're normal, Emeline, but you're not. I hope one of these days you'll recognize this fact, because without it we won't get very far. To go up against Lourie we'll have to be very clever, believe me."

"I haven't had much cause to discover my talents—except with those magistrates. Is she a lot more powerful than us?"

"As I said, she uses dark magic. She can call on the underworld. We are not allowed to do that."

I shivered. "And I'm glad of it. Good can win over evil."

Helga made a face. "You are unbelievably naïve. Lourie will chew you up and spit you out if you don't get with the program. You have to know and understand what you are if you want to have any clout at all. I can't believe they actually let you in the coven without giving you a crash course."

I let out a long sigh. "I can travel through time and I know now that I have some energy orb at my disposal—not sure what all it can do yet...and I get visions and know things before they happen."

"That's all well and good, Emeline, but your mind is wide open. It's how Lourie planted that vision. You must learn how to close it. As for me, I'm a time traveler and I know at least a hundred spells. I have exceptional ears and I'm clairvoyant. And I do not let my emotions get the best of me," she added sharply.

"You almost cried just a minute ago—don't give me that."

"But I don't let it incapacitate me the way you do. This thing with Samoset for instance—you have to let him go. You're on a different path now, and so is he."

"We're married."

She pressed her lips together in irritation. "No you're not—if you were he wouldn't be about to marry another woman and you wouldn't be working for the coven."

I glared at her. "I thought we could figure this out if I told him why I hadn't gotten pregnant, but it didn't make any difference. I guess the tribe has decided his fate. But he did say if it turns out I'm pregnant to come and talk to him."

"How magnanimous of him. You are really too much, you know that?"

I didn't answer, Samoset's statement sounding lame even to me.

Helga began to pace, a sure sign she was getting bored with conversation and ready for action. "We need to safeguard ourselves from Lourie and then get on with our job."

The next hour was filled with Helga reminding me of spells of protection and new ones to keep my mind from being invaded, her shrill voice drilling them into me like an army sergeant.

When I balked and said I couldn't absorb the information that quickly she said, "They'll come to you when you need them." But I wasn't at all convinced. These sorts of spells needed to be practiced for months to get them fully integrated. The coven shouldn't have sent me out here without them. But then again, they didn't know Lourie would be thwarting everything we tried to do.

Chapter Seventeen

Two days had gone by with no more sign of the dark witch, but our mission had stalled as we waited for her to show herself. Helga acted like a nervous cat, jumping at every sound and moaning in her sleep. We'd made a permanent camp in a hollow next to a circle of trees where we were protected from the weather, but the damp cold seemed to seep into my bones. By now Samoset had taken down the *wetu* and was planning the ceremony—all trace of our relationship gone as though it had never been. My stomach clenched as I stared out at the gray morning light, sick of everything.

I brewed water over the fire in the iron pot we'd purchased with the last of our money, adding a few tealeaves. "We should probably replenish supplies," I said, huddling close to the meager fire.

Helga held her shaking hands toward the flames. "I need warmer clothes but we don't have any money left."

I handed her Samoset's cape, which we now used as our blanket. "Wear this, Helga. You seem like you may be coming down with something."

She did look sick, her face pinched and white, her lips blue. She was too thin, and despite her boasting about being impervious to the cold, she had visibly deteriorated during the past week. I traced it back, realizing it began with the appearance of her dead brother and grew worse after Lourie. "I have a few more coins in my pocket. Stay here and I'll buy us as much cheese and bread as I can."

When she pulled off the cape to hand to me I shook my head. "You need it more than I do. Keep the fire going and I'll be back as soon as possible."

"Use that spell I taught you—the one to deflect focus. That way they won't pay attention to how you're dressed."

In town I got a few stares but was able to surround myself with an aura of belonging, heading directly to the open market in the town center. Everything seemed normal as the townspeople purchased their supplies and chatted amongst themselves. Above the town the clouds darkened and spit out sleet, threatening something worse as I hurried to make my purchases and get back.

Helga was asleep when I got back, her face ashen. I built up the fire and sat next to it, my mood as dark as the weather.

"Maybe Lourie's decided to do something else," I said the next morning, more worried than ever about Helga. I was sure she was running a fever.

"Whatever she's up to has to do with us and this place. She's not one to get off track, and her focus right now is on me and what I did to her."

"You didn't do anything to her."

Helga shrugged. "She doesn't think like normal people, Emeline. In her mind I betrayed her."

Sometime later I decided to take a walk into town—I'd been awake since before dawn worried about what might be happening. It was time to find out.

"Just be careful," Helga said hoarsely. A moment later she had a coughing fit.

"Will you be okay?"

She waved me away and curled up by the fire.

I'd been right to be worried. The calm of the day before had been replaced with an air of unease. The market was closed and windows along the street had all been boarded up.

"What's going on?" I asked the one man I saw. When he turned to me his skin was florid, anger wafting off him in sickening waves.

"We had warnin' that the savages are not planning to keep their promise," he hissed. "Just like 'em if ye ask me. If they do not keep their word there will be war—and there is no question who will win."

Unfortunately I knew he was right—the tribe didn't stand a chance against the muskets and the vast numbers of militia the colonists could muster.

When I got back I told Helga what I'd heard, waiting for her coughing fit to subside. She was seriously ill, her face blotchy and red.

"I suppose we should get on with things before all hell breaks loose. You do realize that all that confusion with the timelines is Lourie's doing, right?"

"That means she's been here for a while. Why would she mess with the timelines? Why not just confront us head on?"

"She wants me to fail. She would like nothing better than to see me kicked out of Geistigehaus."

"Do you think we should consult Saffron? If we tell her that Lourie's here and she's mixing up the timelines, maybe…"

Helga shook her head and looked away. "There's danger everywhere. We already talked to Saffron and I'm sure she would not be happy to see us again."

"But there's no way to save this place now—not unless we take the Indians into another timeline in the distant past."

"And as I said before the same thing will happen all over again. Think out of the box, Emeline. We can't eradicate white supremacy. It's part of the world's history." She wheezed and had a coughing fit, bending at the waist to suck in air.

"Will it? If the Indians are gone how could it happen again?"

"There are thousands of tribes in the New World. If not the Wampanoag than another will come along. And if not Indians they'll find someone else to oppress. The Europeans are conquerors and conquerors always need someone or something to lord it over."

"But that's exactly what Saffron tasked us with, Helga. If it isn't possible shouldn't we tell her so?"

"It has to be possible. We just haven't come up with the solution yet."

Several coughing fits later I finally said, "I need to find some willow. I'm sure you have a fever."

Instead of denying it she looked up, here eyes watery and red. "I could just go back to Luxembourg and get some aspirin."

I shrugged. "If you think that's best."

She sighed. "All I want to do is go to sleep."

"Put up a spell of protection and then nap. I'll find the willow." I pulled a pack of zinc lozenges out of my pocket. "I forgot I had these. Suck on a couple until I get back." I handed them over before heading off. White willow grew close to water. I knew exactly where to go.

On my trek through the woods I encountered several members of the tribe, red and black war paint slashed across their faces, bows and arrows slung over their shoulders. They ignored me as they ran by. They were scouting, planning their attack. My adrenaline raced.

Once I reached the inlet and the willow trees I used my knife to strip off the bark, stuffing as much as I could into my pocket. The bark was the part that contained salicin, the active ingredient that helped bring down fever. The tribe had known about it forever.

When I got back to our little camp Helga was sound asleep, the fire cold. I banked it up and added twigs and bigger branches, using dried leaves to get it started. Thank goodness for the matches. Once the fire began to spark she woke, wiping the sleep from her red eyes as she sat up. "The zinc helped," she wheezed.

I pulled the willow out of my pocket and handed it over. "Chew some of this."

She stuck a wad of it in her mouth and did as I asked, her glazed eyes going to the middle distance. "While you were gone I was thinking about our conversation. Our only

job is to stop the hate in this small corner of early America."
She coughed and spat, clearing her throat. "Other witches
have the same job in different parts of the world. It isn't
only the Indians who are being affected, you know."

"I know that, Helga. Racism and hatred touches all
minorities, including women. But we were sent to this timeline
for a reason. I still vote for a past world where the Indians can
live in peace. Lucifer could help if you hadn't kicked him."

She glared at me. "All I did was touch him with my toe."

"Then why haven't we seen him since?"

"How do I know? And good luck getting Samoset to
agree. He seems pretty set in his ways."

She was right. It could be a problem, especially with his
upcoming marriage and the war starting over the proposed
relocation.

"This plan of yours will mean confronting your precious
Samoset, who I think is a complete bastard, and get him to
convince the rest of the tribe," she continued.

"He isn't a bastard, Helga, he's just sachem and has to
act like one."

"And you're a witch and need to act like one. Once I'm
up to it can you take us to Samoset and talk to him about
this?"

I nodded. "I hope you're better soon, because I noticed
several scouts while I was gathering willow. My guess is
they will attack in the next few days."

Helga didn't answer as she curled on her side and closed
her eyes. I covered her with the deerskin cape and built up
the fire.

It was several hours later when she woke again. "I feel
better—I guess that willow must have done something."

I reached over to feel her forehead. "Fever's down. But are you up for a trip through the woods?"

She looked down at her feet. "Can I borrow your boots?"

I nodded, pulling them off. I had on heavy wool socks that would save me from the worst of it, at least for what I had in mind.

"Follow me."

Helga huffed behind me, occasionally swearing as she got tangled in a briar bush or tripped. "Why didn't you just take us through the ether?"

I glanced back. "Why do you think? I'm not giving that witch the chance to screw this timeline up again. And we can get moccasins and deerskin robes from the tribe. That is if they haven't already attacked."

"I'm sure we'd hear shouting and gunshots if they had. But if you think our not traveling through the ether can stop Lourie from changing timelines, you're wrong."

I had a sinking sensation wondering if we'd suddenly find ourselves in some future reality where the tribe didn't even exist—either that or some horrible past with sabre toothed tigers chasing us.

The lackluster sun was disappearing under a layer of dark cloud when we reached the outskirts of the Wampanoag village. The place seemed deserted, houses pulled apart and various contraptions for carrying things sitting here and there. When Samoset saw us he frowned and raised his fist. "Why you here again!" he shouted.

I stepped back, surprised by his anger. "I need to talk to you. We've come up with a plan to save the tribe."

His eyes turned dark and menacing. "Tribe not need saving. You make tribe angry. Elders say you *Hobomock!*"

"I know all that, Samoset. You told me when we met in the woods. Why are you so angry all of a sudden?"

He moved toward me, his fist still in the air. "Go. You not belong here." He turned to help a young Indian woman with a large basket of clothing and household items.

When the young woman saw me she backed away like I was a rabid animal. Samoset looked from her to me, moving toward her protectively. His anger exploded. "You hurt Aimee! Why you do this?"

"What are you talking about? This is the first time I've seen you since we met in the woods by the *wetu*. I've never seen this woman before."

He shook his head. "What you say is not truth. I see you, Em. See what you do to Samoset and to Aimee. Tribe see you." He glanced back at the woman. "Aimee new wife." He took her arm and the two of them picked up the baskets and headed off together, leaving me stunned and confused.

Helga touched my arm. "What was all that about?"

"He accused me of hurting Aimee. I don't get it."

"I do," she said, her narrowed eyes glittering dangerously. "It was your doppelganger Lourie who probably tried to have sex with him in front of her. It's typical Lourie behavior."

"How would she know about Samoset? And why would she want to turn him against me?"

"Did I mention she's the most powerful witch I've ever met? This seems like a simple way to keep us from getting our job done. And if we fail we could be expelled. Lourie would love that."

I stared at the place where Samoset and Aimee had been a moment before. I felt his anger even now, white-hot energy pouring over me. What had the witch done? But the more important question was how to convince Samoset that it wasn't me. "What do we do now?"

"We follow them. And on the way you concentrate on your undiscovered powers. Saffron would never have sent you here if you didn't have more to offer."

More to offer. The words rang in my head. So far I'd failed at just about everything, including talking with Samoset. After what we'd experienced in the woods his coldness was like a slap in the face. I wondered if the timelines had been changed again.

As we followed at a safe distance I conjured the sphere. It shimmered with an inner light, reminding me of a tiny planet filled with life. It grew larger when I threw it, enveloping several small trees in its eerie mist. When the mist dissipated the trees were gone. "Did you see that?" I shouted.

Helga did not seem impressed. "Yes, but where did they go?"

I gave a little cry of exasperation. "I don't know where they went—isn't it enough that they went somewhere?"

Helga just stared at me. "Are you for real? Disappearing things is a simple parlor trick, Emeline. What were you thinking when you threw it?"

"I was thinking several things at once—Samoset and his new wife and that bitch witch, Lourie, who's trying to screw up my life…"

"You were angry. Does it only work when you're angry? And you need to determine where those trees went. Once you figure out those two things you'll be one step closer to understanding your power."

"But how?"

"That's the question, isn't it?"

It was an hour before Samoset and Aimee reached the outskirts of the new Wampanoag village. Helga and I stayed in the shadows, watching what was happening. The colonists expected the tribe to move into the praying towns but here they were safe against a hillside in a wide clearing, a stream running along one side of where they worked. They'd found the perfect place.

It made me glad until I noticed Samoset and Aimee speaking with Weetamoo. Samoset's mother was obviously delighted with Samoset's choice of wife, her fingers going to Aimee's long hair, holding it back from her oval face. She leaned toward Samoset as though to get his opinion on the subject. Samoset stepped back and cocked his head, contemplating. I knew what they were doing—they were planning the headdress. They were planning the wedding. I felt like someone had punched me in the stomach.

They spoke together for another minute or two before Samoset and Aimee headed toward a longhouse that stood apart from the others. This was the most important structure, the heart of the village, where winter meetings took place and ceremonies were held. It was where the elders lived.

When Aimee stumbled over an exposed root Samoset's arm came round her waist to steady her. Bile rose into my throat and I almost retched, turning away for a moment to breathe.

153

"Don't let them see you," Helga hissed, pulling me back under the trees.

But I was riveted in horror, watching Samoset and Aimee speaking to an elder who ushered them inside the partially constructed longhouse. "They're discussing the ceremony," I muttered, feeling sick again.

"Look over there," Helga whispered, pointing.

I turned to see an array of weapons laid out in neat rows, ready when the time was right. As soon as the tribe was settled here they would attack. I knew the signs. I turned to go.

"Where are you going?" Helga hissed. "I thought you were planning to relocate them."

Helga's hair was covered with snow, her white-knuckled hands clasped in front of her shivering body. I hadn't even noticed the leaden sky above the trees or the sudden drop in temperature. I realized suddenly that my teeth were chattering from nerves and cold. "You didn't seem to think that was a good idea, Helga. And now there's no way I can talk it over with Samoset." I glanced at her. "And you need warmer clothes. I know a place where we can steal a couple of capes. Maybe some boots too."

"In this weather? And I thought you could use that sphere to do something. What's the point of it if you can't use it for magic?"

"I haven't played around with it long enough to understand it. I can't send the Indians off in a green mist without knowing where they went." I took hold of her arm. "Let's discuss this after we have warmer clothes." I willed Samoset and Aimee out of my mind as we whirled into the ether, wondering again how this could happen so quickly.

We'd been together so recently, his love for me beyond question. It had to be Lourie.

We landed in the wealthier section of Salem where large colonial houses sat back from the road. Some had diamond shaped leaded glass windows set evenly within the two stories made of wood, other houses had chimneys on either end and two six over six windows on either side of a wide recessed front door. Others had a center chimney and the same window pattern. The gardens were well-tended, bare rose bushes and fruit trees pruned and ready for spring.

The Parris house had seen better days, shutters hanging askew from the front windows and paint peeling. The center chimney was leaning a bit to one side. This was where I'd first met Tituba, the African slave who worked for Reverend Samuel Parris. It seemed that Betty, his daughter, and Abigail Williams, her friend, had begun the rumors about witches that first implicated Tituba. It was old history for me now. Tituba was long gone and the girls were older and perhaps living elsewhere.

I put the terrible time out of my mind and headed around the house to the backyard. Sure enough three heavy capes hung from the line, a light covering of snow clinging to the thick wool. I hurried over and grabbed a red one and a black one before beating it back under the trees to hide.

When I peeked out between the snow-laden limbs Helga was standing on the back porch talking to a dark-haired man. From his stance he seemed very taken with her, his eyes on her body under the thin silk. He disappeared and a moment later re-appeared with a blue dress and another cape. He handed them over.

I heard her mumbled 'thank you', and watched him watching her as she pulled the cape on and headed toward where I hid.

She moved under the trees, her expression serene. "Like taking candy from a baby," she said, smiling.

"You put a spell on him?"

"I didn't have to. The poor man is so horny he would have done anything I asked."

I did have to laugh at that. "What about shoes?"

She lifted the blue dress revealing a pair of brown boots underneath. "I told him savages had stripped me bare, leaving me with only my shift."

"That gives the Indians a bad name, Helga."

"Don't they already have one? It was the only way I could explain the silk. He said the town is readying for the fight. Everyone is armed to the teeth. He hates the savages and thinks they all need to be exterminated. He said if the Indians don't come to the praying towns by Friday it will be outright war."

I felt sick imagining what was to come.

Helga handed me my boots and slipped off her silk dress, exposing her stick thin body to the cold. I was shocked to see her ribs protruding, her flat chest and hips so narrow they could have belonged to a girl of fourteen.

Once she had on the dress and boots and the new cape I pulled on the black one, trying to think what to say to her. I couldn't mention anorexia or ask why she'd allowed herself to get so thin. I wondered about the dark witch's affect on Helga. Lourie could very well have put a spell on her. They'd been lovers in the past, making her vulnerable to Lourie whether she knew it or not.

Before we left I threw the extra cape back over the line, hurrying away before someone could see us. When we got to town I was glad to see how closely we resembled other sixteen hundreds women going about their daily business.

"We need to find out the latest news," Helga whispered as we came into the main part of town.

Before I could respond she'd stepped up to a woman walking in the other direction.

"When do the Indians move to the praying town?"

The light-haired Puritan woman with the pristine cap and dark clothes looked startled, her hand going to her chest. "I've been told it will happen in two days time. But there has been some unrest regarding this move." She looked us over. "You two should not be on your own. Where are your menfolk?"

"I'm meeting my brother in the square," Helga lied, smiling sweetly.

The woman nodded, adjusted the basket on her arm and hurried on her way.

"Let's test that ball of yours," Helga said, glancing at me as we walked along with our heads down. "You can move the tribe before the unrest happens."

"I told you already, Helga—I need to figure out what it does first."

"We have to move fast, Emeline. This thing is about to start." She pointed to the barricades set up, the men marching in formation. There was an air of tension that hadn't been here the day before.

"Let's say I can figure out how—we haven't found a safe place for them yet."

Helga stopped and frowned. "We really need to find that stupid cat. Didn't you say Lucifer could help us?"

"In 1692 he took us forward in time when we were about to be hanged, but…"

"If we don't get a move on we'll be sending dead bodies to this 'safe' other reality. I say use your mist and hope for the best."

"I'm not testing it on humans."

"Give me another solution then." A second later Helga had another coughing fit.

"You're still sick. You need to rest."

"Test the ball on me."

"On you? What if I kill you?"

She scoffed. "It won't kill me, Emeline. You're a good witch not a dark witch—now in Lourie's hands who knows what it might do?"

"I think we need to find an abandoned shed or something where you can get warm. I'm worried about you."

She frowned, looking up at the sky. "The snow stopped and the cloak is warming me up. We simply don't have time to rest right now with the Indians and the colonists about to go to war."

I let out a long sigh. "I guess if worse comes to worse we can go back to Geistigehaus and get you some antibiotics."

"I'll let you know if it comes to that."

"Will you?"

"Stop worrying and send me into the mist."

"What should I think about?"

"Visualize where you want to send me. But not where we sent the trappers, okay?"

We moved off the road into the woods where we wouldn't be seen. I decided to send her back to the *wetu*—still in this timeline, but not far away.

I backed away from her and held my arm up, conjuring the ball, but when I threw it, it veered off course and set a tree on fire.

Helga laughed. "What were you thinking about?"

"I was thinking about how exasperating you are."

"What else?"

"A thought crept in about the dark witch and the fire she set at Geistigehaus."

"Ah ha. The ball didn't know what you wanted. This is good information. Try again, and this time focus your thoughts."

I visualized Helga standing in front of the *wetu* and conjured the sphere. When I threw it toward her she was enveloped in the green mist. And when it cleared she was gone. I had a moment of panic, sure that I'd killed her. But when she appeared out of the ether thirty seconds later my racing pulse slowed.

"See? I told you it would be all right."

"Where did you end up?"

"I don't know. It seemed like someplace way in the past. There was a herd of wooly mammoths in the distance and I could smell meat cooking."

My mouth fell open. "Oh no. I have no control at all."

Helga let out a huge belly laugh followed by a coughing fit. "Just kidding. I ended up in front of your hut. Is that what you intended?"

"That's exactly where I wanted you to go. You are such a bitch."

"And so are you. Now we're even."

"What did *I* do?"

"You blame me for why your cat's gone, you keep telling me how wrong I am about every idea I have…you…"

I put up my hand. "You've been doing the exact same thing. I feel like an idiot when I'm around you."

Helga smiled, lighting up her green eyes. She came toward me and a moment later we were in an embrace. We'd become friends.

"Now," she said, pulling back, "we know that the green ball can relocate humans and trees and start fires. What else do you think it can do?"

"I don't know, but I'm ready to find out."

For the next couple of hours I practiced with the energy sphere, moving rocks and downed tree branches from one place to another, and creating a veil of impenetrable mist between Helga and me. At one point I enveloped her and floated her in the air—that is until she let out a bloodcurdling shriek.

She glared at me. "That was not fun at all—my powers were gone!"

"You couldn't get out? Maybe I could use it on Lourie."

"Possibly, but I have a feeling it wouldn't have much of an effect on her." She held a finger to her lips. "Hear that? The militia is gearing up."

Five ceremonial gunshots went off in rapid succession. A moment later I heard the kind of rally call done before a football game and then another volley of gunshots. Deep in the forest drumming could be heard, dark rhythms alerting us to the tribe's intentions.

"We have to do this soon," Helga said.

"I agree but where do I send them?"

"Somewhere safe."

I shook my head. "There is no place safe for them, unless...

"Unless what?"

"Unless I send them way into the past—the past before the settlers arrive."

"And before they were ever born. Let's go," she said, setting off toward the drumming.

I hurried after her. "I hate to test it out on something this momentous. What if I screw up?"

"You won't screw it up, Emeline. You need to have more confidence in yourself."

Famous last words.

Chapter Eighteen

We hid in the shadows of the forest, watching the war preparation ceremony. It was beautiful and frightening, all the braves dressed up, their eyes masked in black, red streaks down their cheeks. They chanted and danced, bending at the waist and straightening again, their hands wielding tomahawks festooned with feathers as they worked themselves into frenzy. I knew all about this, had seen it in the past, but the ceremonies I witnessed had all been for show. This one was real.

Samoset danced along with them, his oiled body gleaming, masked eyes scaring me as I watched him. Outside the circle of dancers the women watched, including the beautiful Aimee whose eyes were glued to Samoset in all his finery. I had one horrible moment when I thought I might be sick.

"Do it," Helga hissed. "It's the perfect time."

I conjured the ball, concentrating hard on the tenth of December in the year 1407. That would take the tribe back one hundred years before any colonists arrived on these shores—I had a sinking feeling there was something I was forgetting from my history lessons but there was nothing I could do about it now. If I wanted to save them this seemed the safest way to manage it. Their hunting grounds would be full of game with no encroachment from any settlers. What could possibly go wrong?

"Emeline, what are you waiting for?" Helga whispered, grabbing my free arm. "The ceremony is winding down."

At that moment Samoset saw us, his face turning purple in anger. When he rushed toward us, his tomahawk held high, the sphere accidentally flew out of my hand, covering him in mist. By the time it cleared he was gone and other braves were hurtling our way. I conjured another sphere and threw it up in the air, letting the mist envelop Helga and me. The scene around us changed and changed again, my heart in my throat as we whirled through season upon season. We finally came to a stop in the same place, but now there was no forest, no tribe—nothing but a desolation of tree stumps and dirt spreading into the distance. The wind whistled around us, icy fingers that worked their way under our clothes.

Helga shivered, her arms around her body. "Where are we?" she asked, looking down at her chronoscope. When she looked up again her eyes were wide with horror. "This is Salem in 2160. How did you do that?"

"I don't know—I don't know what was on my mind when I sent us away. I wasn't thinking anything. I thought the ball would know better."

"The ball? The ball is yours to command, Emeline. Do you think the sphere is an entity with a mind of its own?"

But I wasn't listening, my thoughts on Samoset's face

when the mist enclosed him. Where had I sent him? He certainly wasn't here. "I can take us back," I muttered, hoping it was true. "But what about Samoset? That ball slipped off my hand—I never meant to throw it. He could be anywhere."

"Forget Samoset. Take us back. I don't like the feeling I'm getting from this place."

I gazed around at the unrelenting landscape, aware of the stench of something chemical. "This might be the end result of what began back in Danvers 2017. There was a leak in a power plant—maybe it led to a nuclear meltdown." I thought of my parents and my sister. Did I need to go back and warn them?

"And that means radiation. It hasn't been long enough to clear it out."

When she took hold of my arm I tried to conjure another ball, but it fizzled in my hand and disappeared.

"We're stuck here?" she shrieked. "We're going to die!"

I grabbed her by the shoulders. "What is wrong with you? We can both travel through time with or without my orb."

She took in a deep breath and let it out. "I'm sorry—this is just too close to another time when I…never mind."

"Do you want me to take us back, or do you want to do the honors?" I asked.

"You'd better do it—I'm still too shaken."

We whirled away a moment later, landing safely in the woods close to where the ceremony had been going on. But now the place was abandoned.

"What the heck now?"

Helga shrugged but I could see the relief in her eyes. "Maybe they're attacking the colonists."

"And that doesn't bother you?"

"Not as much as 2160, no. If we can make it back to town before they're all slaughtered maybe you can use your ball and…"

"Not sure the ball works anymore."

"It didn't work there because of the radiation. Test it here."

I conjured the sphere, relieved when it didn't fizzle out in my hand. Why radiation would affect it was beyond me. "Okay. Let's get to Salem before they all kill each other." And then I remembered Samoset.

"What's wrong? Why aren't you moving?"

I stared at Helga but didn't see her. "Samoset. I don't have any idea where he is."

"Can't you just visualize him and take yourself there?"

I thought about that for a moment. "I probably should try that before we go to Salem. He's sachem."

She scoffed. "As if that makes any difference to how you feel. Go. I'll wait here." She glanced at me staring at her. "Don't worry—I've already cast a spell of protection around myself."

After picturing Samoset exactly as he'd been when I sent him away in the mist I landed in the bustling Wampanoag village—the same one I'd been living in before I took off with Jean. There was a good chance there was another me here, I realized, looking around furtively. And two of Samoset, I thought, watching Samoset skulking around one of the longhouses. He was the one I'd sent here, his face still painted, the tomahawk now hanging on his belt. When he saw me his eyes narrowed. "Why you send me here?" he shouted.

A moment later the other Samoset walked out of the forest carrying his bow, a couple of dead rabbits hanging from his belt. He looked at me before his gaze swiveled to the other Samoset. "Em?"

Tomahawk Samoset froze, watching us as I moved forward to embrace former Samoset. "In a year from now things turn into a major mess," I told him. "I'm trying to fix it."

My old Samoset hadn't yet been told of the *Hobomock* theory, love shining from his eyes as his arms went around me. I wanted to stay here forever and never go back to the future where Lourie had wrecked things so thoroughly. But other Samoset watched me, shaking his head in anger, his fist in the air.

"Em hurt Samoset!" he shouted.

"What does he mean?"

"He's talking about a dark witch, Samoset. She's destroying timelines. She can make herself look like me—she fooled him."

Samoset let me go and turned. "Em never hurt Samoset," he said clearly, facing his other self.

When Lourie appeared out of the ether I shrank away from her, horrified at what I'd done. My coming here had left an energy trail and now I'd made everyone in the past vulnerable to Lourie's dark magic.

"Easy to track you, witch," she said, smiling. "You should have taken more care." Her features shifted and changed as she watched me, even her clothing becoming like mine. Now there were two of Samoset in the same place, as well as my doppelganger—but it wasn't until my other self appeared from within one of the longhouses that my body began to tingle, a buzzing starting in my ears. This was not at all good.

"Okay," other me said, stopping in her tracks. "I know if this is happening that something dire has taken place in the future. And who are you?" she asked, staring at Lourie.

"She's a dark witch," I answered, moving closer to past Samoset. "And a shifter."

"Well, that's obvious," other me said. "I think you and Samoset should go back to wherever you came from before something extremely weird happens. My body tingles all over."

Lourie grinned and moved toward the other Samoset, the one with the tomahawk. "Not sure which one you are, but for my purposes it doesn't really matter." When she moved closer he backed up, his eyes darting from me to other me, and back again. At that moment I decided to take my other self's advice, my right hand moving to Samoset's shoulder before I conjured my ball. I threw it up in the air, letting the mist settle around us as I said, "Take us back to where I started," hoping that this time I wouldn't end up in some horrible dystopian future.

As we whirled away I heard other me shout," Where are you taking my Samoset?"

When we landed Helga was still there, her shocked expression nearly making me laugh. "Who...?"

"This is the past Samoset, the one who still loves me," I said, smiling up at him.

"And where's the other one?"

"In the past."

Samoset frowned, a look of worry on his face. "Em, not

good plan. Other Samoset not right for past. Have memory of future."

And then it hit me. This was why the timelines were all screwed up. It wasn't Lourie's doing, it was mine. "Oh my god. You're right. What do I do now?" I asked, staring at Helga.

She raised her eyebrows and shook her head. "I have absolutely no idea."

But the situation was resolved in the next moment when Lourie arrived with future Samoset. She dropped him off and grabbed the other one, both of them disappearing before I could catch my breath.

This Samoset glared at me for a moment before his eyes softened. "Understand now, Em." And then he turned and ran, melting into the woods.

"Holy crap," Helga muttered. "What in hell is going on?"

I brushed tears from my cheeks. "It was my doing, Helga. I'm the one who messed up the timelines because of what I just did. I gave the past Samoset knowledge of the future."

"No, Emeline. If that were true everything would have settled down by now. But instead Lourie has past Samoset and god knows what's happened to past you. This is really bad."

"But how can it be so bad? Now past me and past Samoset are aware of the future, or at least a part of it, and this Samoset knows I didn't do anything bad to him and Aimee…"

"Yes, but a war is about to begin and Lourie has past Samoset. She is capable of removing any memory of your former time together."

"My memories too?"

"Past you, yes. And past you will affect current you. It will be like you and Samoset were never together."

I tried to wrap my mind around that. "Why would she do that?"

"Because she can? I don't know—she enjoys chaos."

"Is there anything we can do?"

"Short of killing her?"

I stared at Helga, the horror of what could happen taking away my breath for a second. I felt dizzy. "Maybe it won't occur to her."

Helga scoffed and looked down. "Oh, she'll think of it all right. I know how her mind works and this is exactly the kind of scenario she loves."

Chapter Nineteen

My feet felt heavy as I lifted them, as though they didn't want to be making this trip. I heard sounds and noticed the pinprick brightness of woodland spirits floating in the air. They were trying to tell me something but I couldn't stop my overactive mind long enough to catch their message. Dark shapes appeared out of the dark and shrank back again as I walked by. Spirits of the dead— I thought of Helga's brother, wondering what she hadn't told me.

Salem was quiet, as though the war plans had subsided. Had the Indians acquiesced after all? After everything that had happened in the past twenty-four hours I couldn't be sure of anything. Helga hadn't said a word since early morning, her one statement that things were about to change whirling through my brain. So far I remembered everything of my life, including my recent idiocy in traveling to the past. I still had hope.

It seemed like a long time before we reached the north of town and the makeshift houses set up for the tribe. I heard the soft murmur of Algonquin before I noticed the native men sitting around the fire. Samoset was one of them. He looked up, his eyes meeting mine briefly before he continued his conversation with the others.

"Samoset," I hissed, gesturing for him to come over to the fence. He frowned, watching me, finally rising and heading my way.

"He doesn't remember you," Helga whispered. "Look at his face."

He did seem to have an uncomprehending expression, his brows furrowed. "Why you summon Samoset?" he asked, staring at me.

"I…I thought you were planning to fight. But now you're living here? Helga and I are still trying to find you a safe place to be."

He shook his head, gazing around. "How you know this? Who are you?"

My mouth opened and closed. "I'm your wife."

"Wife? No wife. Ceremony tomorrow. Make plans now."

"You're getting married tomorrow? And I'm supposed to just leave you alone—is that it?"

He looked me over, seeming to come to a decision. "Tribe have plan. We attack once ceremony is over and women and children safe in woods."

When he made his way back to where he'd been sitting several tribe members gave me hostile looks. After that they were deep in conversation again. They were planning a sneak attack. Maybe it would go well for them, but from what I'd seen of the militia, I doubted it. The manpower alone outnumbered the natives at least four to one.

"He didn't know you, Emeline," Helga said as we walked away. "Lourie did this."

"How come I remember him?"

She shrugged and threw up her hands. "The timelines just moved around again too. That attack he was just talking about was supposed to happen yesterday."

"But he was happy to tell me his plans."

"Probably thought it was the best way to get rid of you." She glanced at me, her gaze going from my tangled hair to my mud streaked face. "You don't look like much of a threat."

I felt muddled and confused as I followed her back to our former camp in the woods. She made the fire this time while I stared into space, my mind unraveling as I tried to make sense of things. I looked up from my slumped position against a tree trunk. "How can I still remember if he doesn't?"

"I told you, Lourie's good with spells. She's bewitched him in some way—or maybe she didn't have to. Maybe she's done something in the past that changed things."

"Like what—removing me from the equation?"

"Possibly."

"But then I wouldn't be here, would I? If I die in the past I'm dead for all time." I curled up close to the fire and tried not to think about my life ending. I wanted Samoset to know about the dark witch, wanted him to understand and remember our love. This clash between the tribe and the militia couldn't be allowed to happen, but I didn't know how to stop it.

Weak sunlight streamed through the thick branches of the firs, sending shadows scurrying. I pushed myself up and looked around. No Helga.

I was becoming worried when I heard her crashing through the forest. She arrived carrying cardboard cups and a paper sack.

"Lattes," she said handing me one. "And croissants. Thought you needed some cheering up."

"Did you go to Luxembourg?"

She nodded. "I also got some antibiotics. One dose later and I'm already feeling like my old self."

"Did you tell anyone what's going on?"

"I told Kalinda. Saffron isn't there. Kalinda already completed her assignment. All she had to do was get a few journalists in the future to write one positive article a day." She took a sip of coffee. "Oh, and a few spells."

"Lucky her," I groused, taking a sip of coffee laced with foam. "So the articles are about…?"

"The dangers of hate and racism and why we need to embrace our common humanity."

I let out a humorless laugh. "It must be the spells that did the trick. No one changes that fast."

Helga smirked. "That's exactly what I said, but she said if people hear something often enough they tend to believe it."

"What did she say about the timelines and Samoset?"

"I didn't go into detail about all that. But she did say that Saffron had a thing for Lourie."

"Saffron? I'm surprised."

"You'd be even more surprised if you knew how many witches are bi-sexual."

I ignored her. "Is Saffron on our side or not?"

"I'd say not."

An idea was forming but it needed my full attention. I

got up and walked away, pacing as I contemplated. I idly conjured my ball and threw it, watching it catch a tree on fire. Yes, I was angry and upset. I doused the fire with my thoughts. *Okay that was new.* "I just used my thoughts to put a fire out. That's helpful, right? And I just had an idea. Instead of sending the tribe into the distant past how about arranging it so the timelines are just slightly off—like when we first got here? That way we won't disobey our orders but they also won't be able to fight. The hate will just go away."

"Will it? For one thing what's to keep them from fighting the ones who are in the new timeline? Just a minute or two off doesn't solve anything. And it doesn't solve the problems of their hunting grounds either."

I let out a long sigh. "At this point I'm desperate, Helga. I have a strong suspicion that sending them into the distant past could cause a major anomaly—the Indians living then are the ones these are descended from. It's probably a good thing I screwed it up."

Helga frowned. "You think moving the tribe will get us off the hook with Saffron?"

"Does she want us to succeed or is she in league with Lourie now?"

She huffed and shook her head. "If Saffron and Lourie are working together it doesn't matter what we try—the combination of those two could end the world as we know it."

"We need to talk to someone who knows the truth, like Kalinda. She can advise us. Maybe we just don't understand time well enough."

But just as we were preparing to head to Geistigehaus,

Lourie appeared out of the ether. "You two are both idiots," she hissed, her gaze fastened on Helga.

Helga's face went white. "What do you want?"

"I heard your conversation and wanted to put in my two cents. Saffron has been an invaluable asset to our cause, Helga. You could too if you came to your senses. Why fiddle around with this stupid assignment when you could join us and have more power than you could possibly imagine?"

"Forget it, Lourie. I'm not like you. How did you get Saffron on your side?"

Lourie pushed agitated fingers through her brown hair. "You used to be like me—we had plans, or have you chosen to forget all that? After you turned against me, Saffron came to my aid. How do you think I got away?"

"What have you done to Samoset?" I asked, taking her attention from Helga.

She smiled. "He doesn't remember you, does he? It won't be long before you won't remember him either." She turned back to Helga. "I miss you, Helga. I never felt for Saffron what I feel for you."

"If you hadn't killed people I might still care for you, but…"

"I did it for you!"

Helga's gaze flicked to me. "Don't remind me."

"You know that fire was an accident. I dropped that damned oil lamp and then all hell broke loose. Where were you? You told me you'd meet me…"

"Why didn't you put the fire out?" Helga interrupted. "You're certainly strong enough."

I looked down at the glowing orb for one second before

I hurled it. It caught Lourie unawares, holding her fast in its mist. Her features contorted into ugliness as she twisted, trying to get free.

"What shall we do with her?" I asked Helga.

"Let's send her to the alternate world with the two rapists," she answered, watching Lourie. "It will serve her right."

"Are you sure?"

Helga nodded. "You throw the ball and I'll give the directions."

She lifted her arms and chanted while I threw another ball, watching as it enveloped the first one, swirling around Lourie. Her struggling turned frantic, her eyes widening in fear. As soon as Helga dropped her arms, the mist and Lourie disappeared.

"Shall we assume it worked?"

Helga was very pale. "I've cast this spell before, but as I've said…."

"Yes, I know…she's the most powerful witch and all that. Funny that she arrived just when we decided to speak with Kalinda. And what was she talking about, Helga? Were you involved with the fire?"

Helga stared at the ground. "I told you already about our relationship. She wanted us to leave Geistigehaus and go off on our own to be witches together. That last day is kind of a blur. I told her no but I'm not sure she heard me. And then after the fire I kind of forgot all about it." Her face crumpled, tears welling as she fought for control.

"Forgot about it? That doesn't sound plausible."

Her tear-filled eyes met mine. "You can either choose to believe me or not, Emeline. I refuse to defend myself to you."

We were both silent for a good long while after that. I wanted to believe her—she was my friend. But something didn't add up. Why hadn't she mentioned any of this before? She'd told me that Lourie wanted to hurt her, when in reality Lourie still loved her. "What should we do now?" I finally asked, breaking the uncomfortable silence. "Should we go back and talk with Kalinda?"

"If we decide to move the tribe into some other timeline will you tell Samoset first?"

"He doesn't know me and the last time I was there he nearly bit my head off."

But before I'd finished my thought Helga was gone, disappearing into the ether. After their conversation I seriously wondered about her connection with the dark witch. This had all the makings of a double-cross.

I was staring into space trying to find a solution to all the madness when Helga arrived with Samoset. His frown of anger was followed by an expletive in Algonquin as he took in his surroundings.

I stared at him, trying not to cry when I saw the ceremonial loincloth and beaded breeches on his legs. He wore the beaded cuffs I remembered around his upper arms, his loose hair held with a wide band, an eagle feather secured in back. His face was painted with the same swirls as the day we said our vows. He was gorgeous and I could barely stand to look at him.

"Why you bring Samoset here?" he shouted looking around. "Bad medicine," he said, narrowing his eyes. "Must complete ceremony. Elders angry now and war plans off because of timing."

I moved close and put my hand on his arm. "Just listen for a second. We…"

Samoset hardened his gaze as he shook off my hand and walked away.

I ran after him. "We're going to relocate the tribe," I said jogging next to him. "We don't know exactly *when* we're sending you yet—first we thought a couple of minutes out of synch but realized that wouldn't work—now we have to rethink it, but whatever we do will keep you from having to fight or move into the praying town."

He stopped and turned. "Sound crazy. Tribe will blame *Hobomock*."

The *Hobomock* again—I should have known it would come up. "They'll think it's the *Hobomock* that saves you from going to war? What about *Nikommo*—the good spirit?"

We came out of the forest and he headed across the square and up the road. "Too much magic."

"Once I've moved you I promise I'll leave you alone. But I don't want you to fight. If you do you'll lose."

He stopped again, his dark eyes meeting mine. "Vision show tribe win."

"I'm sure that vision was planted by the dark witch, the one…"

But he was already striding away and didn't hear what I said. I ran after him. "Do you believe me about the dark witch? She took your memories, Samoset, and planted others."

He didn't answer, his focus on the road ahead.

"Can I move the tribe? If I can come up with the right timeline I have the means to do it. I don't care if they blame me."

This time when I grabbed his arm he backhanded me, knocking me down. "Must do what elders say."

I watched him go, each step he made tugging at my insides until I thought I might scream. He walked up the hill and disappeared over the other side. I lay where I'd fallen, feeling like my world had just ended. He was about to marry Aimee and I'd promised to leave him alone—how could I keep that promise?

Chapter Twenty

"What is going on with you? Just *do* something."

We were in the forest again, the scream of wind in the high branches grating on my already overwrought nerves. I wanted to shut everything out and sleep for a year. "Where do I send them, Helga? Anything I come up with just doesn't work. Our only chance is to send them away from here, otherwise there will always be settlers who will harass them."

Helga frowned. "I get what you're saying, but another country won't work because of their ancestors. Tell me again why the out of synch thing won't work?"

"Because there are settlers in all the timelines, that's why. Think about it—if I go two minutes ahead does that mean I won't see any settlers? No. It only means I've moved myself forward in time. I wish I could keep the settlers from sailing here in the first place."

"And then we wouldn't have been born."

I stared at her as a thought formed. "Maybe the sphere could protect them within its mist."

"You mean like a veil that separates them from the settlers? You'd better figure it out soon, Emeline. The war is about to begin."

"Yeah, but they trade with the settlers and…"

"So what?"

I stared into the distance, watching limbs bend and sway, the crack as branches broke under the strain. "He doesn't want me to use magic to save them but…first I have to figure out if it will work. How do I test it?"

"Forget about what Samoset does or doesn't want. He wouldn't know magic if it stared him in the face. If we don't do this we will not have fulfilled our task. Has that realization hit you yet, or are you so caught up in helping the tribe that you've forgotten about your own future?"

"I still think we should talk to Kalinda. This Saffron thing is really disturbing. If she's gone to the dark side why are we even trying to complete our assignment?"

"We aren't positive about Saffron. Lourie could be lying. And think about it—wouldn't you like to keep the tribe safe?"

I covered my face with my hands. "All I can think about is Samoset. I love him, Helga. How can I fix this so he remembers me?"

"I doubt you can, especially after he's married. And if I know Lourie your memory will be wiped soon as well. Maybe that will make it less painful for you."

"Shut up, Helga—that's a horrible thing to say. If that happens you'd better fix it for me, or I'll…"

She laughed nastily. "But you won't remember to hold me to it. Make up your mind. Do we test your ball and help the tribe or rush back to Kalinda to tattle to her about a rumor we heard?"

I thought about the tribe fighting the militia. I didn't care what his vision showed; there was no way the tribe could win. And if they lived in that shantytown, the children would be deprived of their language, their culture. No more hunting or fishing or gathering berries, mushrooms and greens for the stew. They would have no more freedom. I pulled up the hood on my cape as a gust of wind whirled around my face making my eyes water. "Does this wind seem normal to you?"

Helga glanced around at the swaying trees, her eyes widening. "I don't know—maybe not. If it isn't we need to get on with things and get out of here.

I'll be your guinea pig—send me into the protective mist."

I ignored the gusts and the falling limbs as I conjured the glowing orb. "I want you to form a protection around Helga," I whispered. "She will be able to move freely wherever she needs to go but no one will be able to get inside and hurt her." I threw the ball up and moved backward letting the fractured light particles shower down on her. The mist wafted and then seemed to disperse, revealing Helga and the landscape of trees and bushes. "Can you see me?"

But Helga was looking around, her focus elsewhere. And then she moved away and disappeared into the background. "Helga!" I shouted.

"What?"

I turned to see her standing next to me. "What did you do?"

"I used the ether to come back—what do you think?"

I let out an exasperated sigh. "But did it work? Could you see me? What was it like in there? You didn't test it out long enough."

She shrugged. "It was just like here except I couldn't see you."

"Did it seem like your world was small, like there was some kind of barrier between us?"

She shook her head. "I moved around—I didn't see anything odd or out of place."

"Wow. So maybe this will work." A second after that statement a limb sailed past, nearly hitting us before it crashed to the ground and splintered into several pieces. "Let's get out of here."

We took off running, heading toward Salem and away from the eerie wind that seemed to follow us, howling around our heels.

Once we came out from under the trees we slowed out pace, both of us wheezing to catch our breath. "Did you notice that there's no wind out here? There was something very odd going on in those woods."

Helga pushed her hood back. "I agree. It must have been Lourie, but it's not like her to work in the background like that."

I tried not to think about what it could mean as I hurried toward the north end of town.

When we arrived at the praying town there was an aura of upset, tribe members talking in small groups and women gathering up the children and taking them into houses. A few settlers were there talking to the elders. I didn't see Samoset.

"Don't even think about it," Helga hissed when I began to climb the fence. "Whatever is going on will be better once they're out in the woods again."

"But what about those men?" I asked, pointing to two severe looking individuals dressed in black. "And where's Samoset?" But then I saw him, his face pinched with worry and upset. He was still dressed in his wedding regalia but Aimee was nowhere to be seen. I watched him search for something in the dirt before being summoned by an elder. He disappeared into one of the houses.

"The houses will come too," I said, turning to Helga. "We don't want that."

"They can burn them down or use them. What difference does it make?"

I took in a long breath and let it out slowly before conjuring the ball. I pictured the tribe in the woods—*safe from the Puritans and any others who would want to harm them and in their own world filled with game and fresh water and everything they need to survive.*

Samoset looked up as the mist rushed toward them, his eyes widening when he saw me. I heard his bellow of rage just before the fog enclosed the entire area, buildings and all. I heard screaming and shouting, the sound of a baby crying. And then it all disappeared.

"Well done," Helga said, patting my shoulder. "Now let's get the hell out of here."

"Don't I have to check on them?"

"The only way to check is to go there. We don't have time for that now."

I felt a stab of fear. "What if I can't go there? Oh my god—what have I done?"

"Calm yourself, Emeline. I'm sure you can send yourself there. But now is not the time to do it."

But I wasn't so sure she was right. I'd thought *protection* when I sent that mist. What would it take to put myself inside it?

But Helga had already grabbed my hand and a second later we whirled away into space and time.

"I am not pleased with this outcome," Saffron said, watching the two of us. "It seems you have gone beyond the parameters of the assignment, and in so doing you have violated at least one of the covenants. I will have to take this up with the board and get back to you." She flicked her hand, giving us the signal that it was time to leave her presence. We left, closing the door behind us.

"Great. Now what? If she's in cahoots with Lourie we're done for. I wish we'd sought out Kalinda instead of Saffron."

"Kalinda isn't here right now—we had to talk to somebody." Helga stared into the distance as we walked down the dark hallway. "I can't figure out which covenant she thinks we violated."

"Deviating from the task, I suspect. But I can't remember what our task was other than stopping the hatred and racism. I have a feeling that whatever we did wouldn't be right. Do you think the board will decide to kick us out?"

"I seriously doubt it. We're powerful witches and time travelers too. Not everyone is. I think Saffron is jealous of your sphere, Emeline. And I don't remember her telling us not to use magic."

We both giggled, disturbing one of the witches working in the library we were walking past. He shot us an irritated glance through the open door, shaking his head as he pressed his forefinger to his lips. "Who is that?" I whispered as we walked away.

"Torent McCall. He's on the board."

I lifted my eyebrows. "Hope he has bad eyesight."

Dinner that night was quiet, most of the witches around the table studiously ignoring us. Saffron was still among us, staying until the board convened to decide our fate. I wondered again about her connection to the dark witch.

"What did you two do?" Noisette whispered, sitting next to me.

"We made the only decision we could, Noisette. "What have you heard?"

"Only that the dark witch was involved. This is very bad, Emeline. I hope you understand what it could mean."

"Lourie wasn't helping us, if that's what you heard. She was there to thwart our purpose and to…"

When Canton walked by I stopped talking.

"To what?" she asked.

"To hurt me."

"But why? You weren't even here when she attended."

I shrugged. "I'm not sure why, but for whatever reason she seems to have taken a dislike to me. Maybe it's because Helga and I are so close?"

Noisette's mouth fell open. "Are you…?"

"No. I'm not a lesbian, but Helga and I are good friends. Do you think that would bother Lourie?"

"Yes. Yes I do. She's vengeful and cruel and her methods

got her kicked out of here. The fire she set killed two older witches and injured a dozen more."

"We sent her to an alternate world."

Noisette cast a glance around the table. "You must know she's no longer there."

"Why not?"

Noisette shook her head, making her curls bounce. "Because she is part of the dark coven. You are new and not anywhere near her level. Now you will be on her radar for sure. Steer clear of dark places."

Chapter Twenty-one

Beware of darkness. The words floated up from some deep recess of my brain, waking me with a start. The sun had risen, filtered light shining through the open casement window. I rose to look out, not surprised when two pigeons flapped away. They'd left a feather behind. But when I looked closer I saw that it wasn't from a pigeon, it was an eagle feather. I craned my neck to look up at the sky. There was nothing there but wispy clouds and blue. I didn't see any large birds in the sky or roosting in the trees. I picked it up, examining the familiar markings—Samoset's feather—the one he wore for ceremonies. Was this a trick or could this be a message? Someone knocked on the door, startling me.

"Emeline?"

"Come in, Helga." When she came inside I held out the feather. "Look at this."

She looked it over and handed it back. "Some kind of hawk feather."

"It isn't a hawk feather, it's an eagle feather. I'm sure it's the one Samoset uses in his ceremonies. For some reason he used an owl feather when we married, but usually he…"

"An owl feather brings healing and keeps evil spirits away. Magical happenings are commonplace around here. I doubt it means anything."

"This is an eagle feather, Samoset's feather, on my window sill. How did it get here and why?"

Hegla's gaze went to the window, her eyes clouding. She turned to me, her lips pressing into a thin line. "Lourie could have sent it as a warning."

"Warning? About what?"

"You sent her to a very nasty place. She wants you to know she has control over Samoset."

"But he's in the protective mist now. She can't reach him."

Helga sighed. "The mist will only keep out those without magic, Emeline."

"Why didn't you tell me that? What should I do now?"

"We need to talk with Kalinda," she answered, grabbing my arm and dragging me toward the door.

"Wait! I'm still in my PJ's!"

"This can't wait," she said, hanging on to me as she took the stairs down two at a time.

I stumbled after her, trying not to fall headlong down the narrow stairwell.

Kalinda looked me over with a frown, pulling her sage green dressing gown around her body. "This is highly irregular," she said, "especially before breakfast. But if you must, I will listen to what you have to say."

Helga glanced at me and began. "We think Lourie is

interfering with our recent assignment."

"Not only interfering but threatening harm to a person I love."

Kalinda glanced at me before turning to Helga. "Yes, you mentioned her presence when we spoke earlier."

"She left her calling card,"Helga continued, "meant to terrify Emeline."

"And what exactly was her calling card this time?"

"An eagle feather like the one Samoset wears during ceremonies."

"Ah yes. We do not have many eagles around these parts. What exactly happened with Lourie?"

Helga slanted a glance at me. "We sent her to an alternate reality."

Kalinda shrugged and raised her hands. "And why is that a bad thing?"

"It was not a very appealing place."

"I see," she said, trying not to smile.

"Saffron seems to think we disobeyed one of the covenants. I hope this attitude about us won't prevent her from taking this seriously."

Kalinda looked skeptical. "Saffron was severely compromised by the dark witch. The coven has been planning to meet about Saffron's dismissal but we are also afraid she might have spies among us."

I glanced at Helga before turning back to Kalinda. "According to Lourie Saffron is working with her."

Kalinda nodded. "Could be lies, but...most of the witches worry that this is true. As you are aware, Saffron is very powerful. Without full cooperation from the coven our hands are tied. She must expose her connection to the dark witch before any of us has the authority to remove her."

"Can't she be threatened with exposure?"

"There is no one here willing to do that until we have all our ducks in a row. If she has any inkling that we're on to her there will be hell to pay. And believe me, you do not want to be on the receiving end of her wrath. Unfortunately it is Saffron who I must speak to regarding the Lourie situation. We will wait to see what she has to say before drawing more conclusions. If I need you two to corroborate your findings I will let you know," she added as we left her apartments. "Do not speak of this with anyone else."

Helga walked me back to my room where I paused by my door. "I hope something happens soon. I'm terrified she's hurt Samoset."

Helga shook her head. "She would rather bed him than hurt him."

"But he doesn't remember me now, and…"

"Try not to imagine the worst, Emeline. We'll get it sorted. See you at breakfast."

When I went down for breakfast Helga was not there and no one had seen her. After I'd eaten I noticed Kalinda heading off with Saffron, a knot forming in my stomach.

"What's so interesting?" Noisette asked, following my gaze.

"I'm thinking about the dark witch," I answered, watching Saffron lean down to hear what petite Kalinda had to say. They left the dining room.

"I saw Lourie in the hall early this morning."

I stared at her. "Are you sure? I thought she was banned."

"She is, but that doesn't mean anything to her. She has obviously escaped from where you sent her."

"Did you report it?"

"And get on that witch's bad side?" Oh *mon dieu, non*!"

"What do you think she's doing here?"

She raised her pale eyebrows. "Perhaps she has a lover? *Je ne sais pas.*"

If she and Saffron were still carrying on, that meant I would get nothing from the High Priestess. In the meantime I had to find out if Samoset was safe.

I had on my cape and was heading for the front door when Helga appeared out of the shadows. With only two high windows in the front wall the hall was cavernous and murky, the portraits of former witches barely visible in the gloom. "Why weren't you at breakfast?" I asked her.

Her gaze flicked away. "I had something to take care of."

"And you're not going to share it with me after all we've been through?"

She let out an exasperated sigh. "If you must know I've taken a lover."

"One of the witches here?"

"No. It's the groundskeeper's son. He's quite delicious."

"So who is this guy?"

"I already told you. But please don't mention it to anyone. Fraternizing with the help is strictly forbidden."

I thought of the lack of attractive, age appropriate men in the coven. "I haven't seen any young male witches here. Why is that?"

She smirked. "Most of them can't make the grade. They usually leave in their first year. Men lack intuition and a certain convoluted way of thinking, and most just want to use power."

When I laughed and turned to go she grabbed my arm. "You're headed off on some wild goose chase to make sure your Indian is safe, aren't you?"

I didn't answer.

"I came to tell you that we have an appointment with the Queen of Darkness in fifteen minutes."

"Crap." I pulled off my wool cape and slung it over my arm.

Saffron rolled the feather over in her hands. "Whatever this feather means to you is not its true significance. You are too unschooled to understand magic, Emeline. You jump to conclusions and think you know things, but you do not."

Saffron's eyes swirled and changed color as she spoke. I couldn't stop staring at them. "But the feather is the one he uses," I argued.

"How could you possibly know that? There must be thousands of nearly identical feathers. This one has been bewitched and I have no idea of the harm it might have done." She sat back and placed the feather on the desk, her hands moving over it as she placed it under some sort of spell. "As to this other matter, the board is meeting tomorrow morning. Until then you both are to remain in this house. Do you understand?"

Helga and I exchanged a glance before we nodded.

"And you, my dear," she said, eyeing Helga. "Don't think I don't know what you've been up to. I highly suggest self-control. It is the best way to avoid these sorts of sordid liaisons."

Helga's mouth dropped opened in surprise.

"Now go. I will see you both back here in the morning at nine o'clock sharp."

"How did she find out?" Helga whispered as we headed upstairs. "I cast a invisibility spell when I left the house and another when Tin and I were together in the potting shed."

"Tin? That's his name?"

"Yes. Why?'

"Unusual."

"It's short for Trentin." She grabbed my hand. "Come to my room for a minute."

Her room on a lower floor was twice the size of mine, with several large windows that looked out over the grounds. Before I could take a look at the pictures of her family, she pushed the rug back and pried up a floorboard, producing a bottle.

"Rum," she announced removing the cap. "But not just any rum. This one has been enhanced with magic. It won't make you drunk but you'll be able to see things the way they really are. I think it's time you looked at the truth, don't you?"

"Isn't it against the rules to drink alcohol?"

"What do you think? According to her majesty, drinking dulls our senses, rendering us helpless in the face of pretty much anything. I beg to differ." She grabbed two cut crystal glasses from the shelf and poured amber liquid into them. "Drink up, witch, and tell me what you see," she said, handing me a glass.

I stared into the swirling liquid that looked like some kind of potion. *Eye of newt, toe of frog, wool of bat and tongue of dog.* I sniffed, picking up an herbal aroma and some kind of spice.

"I got this from a cold weather witch before I arrived here." She tipped the glass up and drained it.

"A cold weather witch? What is that?"

"She lives in the mountains where it snows all the time. She's at least a hundred and fifty years old. I'd take you to meet her if I could." Her expression turned sad for a moment before she brightened and refilled her glass. "So far no matter how much I drink this bottle stays full."

I took a tentative sip, expecting the raw medicinal taste of hard alcohol, but this rum was smooth and almost sweet. Almost immediately I felt something shift behind my eyes. Colors swirled in front of me, the room spinning.

"Don't worry, the dizziness will go away in a minute."

I lowered to the couch and took another sip, watching Helga dance around the room. Liquid ribbons of turquoise, orange, and green streamed behind her as she moved, her arms lifting as she twirled. "Come on, Emeline, dance with me."

The distant sound of tinny music came to my ears as she pulled me to my feet. I put my glass down, the melody drifting through my mind like an ancient memory. I was a dolphin swimming in the watery deep, my body smooth and swift. A moment later I was the ocean, liquid and full of light, colors bursting like opalescent bubbles before disappearing. My body was liquid and light, separate from my mind. Helga had hold of my arms as we spun, liquid ribbons trailing behind us.

The room disappeared as we moved upward, through the ceiling and into a star-filled sky. Helga's head was thrown back, tiny stars of laughter spilling from her open mouth. Twinkling fairy lights lit up our faces, our bodies translucent. Our feet touched nothing solid as we rose higher, until we were enveloped in starlight. I laughed, but the sound I made was more like an underwater creature taking a breath of air for the first time. I was drunk with it as we flew and flew, our hands clasped, our bodies in perfect synchronicity as the music wafted around us.

And then I saw it—the reason for the commotion at the praying town village just before I enveloped it all in the green mist. Lourie, dressed in black and looking so much like me it made me gasp, interrupted the ceremony, arriving just as Samoset and Aimee were about to begin their vows. She whirled in through the ether and grabbed Aimee and whirled out again. The wind we'd experienced had been her doing too, meant to put us off our plan.

What I'd seen later was Samoset searching for the blue beads—the same ones I'd worn around my neck on our wedding day. During the confusion they'd fallen off Aimee's neck. And worse than all that were Samoset's thoughts that were as clear to me as my own. He loved Aimee and wanted a life with her. He had no memory of us—none at all.

All of it disappeared as my mind went blank, cold and empty darkness welcoming me like a long lost friend.

Chapter Twenty-two

"Emeline—wake up!"

When I opened my eyes I was lying on Helga's floor. I tried to push myself up but Helga pressed me back. "Not so fast. You have a nasty bump on the back of your head."

I reached around to feel. "OW!"

"I told you." She reached for my hand and hauled me to sitting. "How do you feel?"

"Strange, disoriented. What happened?"

"You went someplace dark. I didn't follow you."

I saw a face like mine as though reflected in a mirror. "Lourie."

"Did you see her?"

"I saw what she did. Remember how upset Samoset seemed before I sent them off in the mist? It's because Lourie took Aimee away."

"Before they got married?"

I nodded, a headache brewing in the back of my neck.

She handed me a glass of water. "I wouldn't have given you the rum if I'd known."

"Known what?"

"That you and the dark witch are so connected. Remember what Saffron said? That feather in your room was bewitched. You picked it up and now the two of you are linked. You won't be able to hide your thoughts from her."

"But didn't Saffron put it under a spell?"

"I wouldn't count on it, especially with her connection to Lourie."

"What about Aimee?"

"Aimee is the least of your problems. Knowing Lourie as I do she's probably bewitched her too."

"That's a horrible thought but I guess it's better than killing her."

"Once she grows tired of the game who knows what she might do? But right now we have to concentrate on you. If you don't have protections in place Lourie could kill you. She'll want to get back at you for what you did with the mist. At her best she's a sex fiend and at her worst she's a nasty vengeful devil. Believe me, I know."

"Who can help me?"

"With Saffron against us Kalinda is our best bet. She's very powerful, Emeline."

I nodded, trying not to start the headache up again. "She's the goddess of time."

"What?"

"Never mind." I downed my glass of water and rose from the floor. "I guess your truth juice worked, didn't it?"

Helga took hold of my arm and forced me to sit on the couch. "If I had known…"

I waved her off. "I'm glad to know what happened,

Helga. I just wish I knew whether the tribe is at least safe from the militia in Salem."

Helga stared at me, her green eyes very round. "Not with Lourie around they aren't."

"But you said the protective mist worked—you went there."

"And Lourie is…"

"Don't even say it."

We stood in front of the board. Ten feet in front of us seven chairs were placed in a row. Saffron was seated in the middle, brocade robes parted at her décolletage to show off the deep V between her breasts. Her eyes were heavily lined in kohl, her lips blood red. Kalinda wore pale yellow, her skin golden in the candlelight, pale pink lips parted to reveal very white teeth. When our eyes met she smiled reassuringly. Denton sat next to her and Torent McCall and three other witches I'd never seen before filled in the rest of the seats.

A witch came out of the shadows and placed two chairs behind us.

"You may be seated," Saffron said, pulling her robes closer. Her wild hair was up today, a seething pile of red that defied gravity and reminded me of coiled snakes. She looked around at her companions before her gaze came to rest on us. "There have been some interesting discoveries made regarding your decisions," she began. "For one thing your timeline changes have led to several chaotic occurrences."

Our timeline changes? "But…"

She raised her hand. "No talking please. You will have

your chance to put forward your defense once we reach the end of the evidence."

I glanced at Helga who sat impassively with her hands clasped in her lap.

"As I was saying. There is evidence of a battle, a very serious one that has caused great damage and taken many lives."

I opened my mouth to explain how this was impossible since the tribe was protected, when Torent began to speak.

"Whatever you two thought you did, did not work. And it brought a relatively peaceful alliance to an abrupt halt. The war is called King Philips war and is responsible for killing hundreds of people on both sides."

I thought of the war I'd read about begun by Metacom, a man also known derisively by the colonists as King Philip, because of the king-like way he conducted himself. He had rebelled against the colonists for plying the tribe with alcohol and then obtaining signatures on documents to give their land away. When three Wampanoag were hanged Metacom had enough, launching an attack on the colonists. But the incident was long past. "But that war happened back in 1675!"

Torent went on. "The entire historical trajectory has been compromised by what you did. Timelines are tangled and people lost. At this time there are so few Wampanoag left as to render the tribe non-existent."

A hard knot formed in my belly. "What happened to them? When we left they…"

"The few who were left were sold into slavery in Bermuda or the West Indies."

"That can't be true!" I shouted, rising from my chair.

"Sit down, Emeline!" Saffron called out sharply.

"You need to be aware of the colonists reasons for how they behaved," Trenton continued. "It seems you have a very skewed idea regarding the English. They are also human beings who bravely traveled to a new country and were greeted with what they considered dangerous primitive peoples."

"They could have cooperated with the natives instead of trying to…"

Saffron stood up and glared at me. "If there are any more outburst of this nature there will be consequences."

I closed my mouth and sat back, slanting a glance at Helga who hadn't uttered one word.

"You have embraced one side of a time period and refused to see what happened in historical context. As time travelers you have a responsibility to look at things objectively. Just because you fell in love with a Wampanoag Indian doesn't give you the right to denigrate every settler who arrived in America. I understand and applaud your actions during the witch trials, but this latest behavior will cost you, Emeline. The praying towns you so clearly were against may have led to a better understanding between the two groups. Instead you moved the tribe, against their wishes I might add, and plunged history into utter chaos."

"We thought it was the only solution," Helga said, coming to my defense.

"And it's a direct violation of the parameters of your assignment," Saffron said angrily.

Torent was right about my sentiments, but in my future many Native Americans had been reduced to alcoholism and drug addiction, their lives cut off from nature and everything that made them who they were. Human trafficking was rampant across the world and the jails were filled with black men and other minorities. How was that any different? Slavery had only taken a different form.

Kalinda stood up. "I have a question, Emeline. Did you tell Samoset about this assignment?"

"I told him I wanted to help him."

"But he didn't like the idea you came up with," Denton said.

"No, I guess he didn't."

"He was about to be married and led the tribe willingly to Salem. Is that correct?"

I glanced at Denton, trying to ignore the feeling of being under a microscope. "Yes, but they were planning an attack later that same day. If I hadn't done what I did they'd be dead at the hands of the militia."

"You do not know that, Emeline," Denton said.

"And you did not want him to marry?" another witch asked.

"Of course not. He was married to me. But that isn't the only thing. Lourie was there and had a hand in what happened. She took his memories, she's the one who…"

"Stop right there!" Saffron bellowed, raising her hand. I was thrown back in my chair, the breath knocked from my body.

Silence descended, ominous and filled with tension. A few long minutes went by before Saffron stood, gathering her brocade robes around her. "You two may go now. We will discuss what we've heard and decide on a suitable punishment. Do not leave the grounds."

The same witch who had brought the chairs escorted us out, the door closing solidly behind us. Tears filled my eyes.

"That was awful. They blame me for everything that Lourie did."

Helga stared at me. "You shouldn't have mentioned her. You know how Saffron feels. Why did you bring up her name?"

"They needed to know, Helga. From what they said things have changed since we left. They were planning an attack but there was no war going on when I sent that mist. Lourie is directly responsible for all of it."

"How do you know? Remember the uprising they were talking about? That could have been the beginning of it."

"That war Torent mentioned happened in 1675, Helga! What I want to know is how Lourie managed to move it up to 1694."

Helga glared at me. "We have bigger problems. Do you know what happens to disobedient witches? I just hope they realize that most of this is your doing. I was there but you made all the decisions."

"Who was it that insisted I do something even though I hadn't fully tested it out? This seems like a set-up to me. Saffron knew before she sent us that what she asked of us was impossible."

"I'm not going to be kicked out or stripped of my powers because of your stupidity. I tried many times to get through to you, but your obsession with Samoset turned your thinking to mush. I will appeal if I have to."

"And throw me to the wolves?"

"You'd better hope that's the worst of it," she said, hurrying away.

I stood in the dark hallway, tears sliding down my cheeks. Was Samoset still alive? Had he been sold into slavery? What could I do?

"Emeline, *mon dieu*. What is wrong?" Noisette peered into my face.

"I...I may be kicked out. And the love of my life might be dead."

She pulled me close and let me cry, her gentle fingers smoothing my hair. "*Ça ira.*"

It was a good long while before I was able to control my tears. My face felt swollen and hot, my eyes burning.

Noisette gazed at me worriedly. "What is this all about?"

"And Helga blames you?" she asked after I filled her in. "Seems it is the dark witch who is to blame."

I nodded. "Saffron didn't like me saying that."

She frowned. "I worry when they put you two together. Helga...she is trouble."

"I liked her until this happened. We had fun...until..."

"Until she turned on you? Helga takes care of Helga, no one else. Her connection with dark witch is strong. I steer clear of her."

"She told me they were lovers, but she also told me how horrible Lourie is."

"All I can say is be careful. Helga is very tricky. I would not be surprised to hear that it is Helga who is responsible for this chaos you have told me about. I hope you find the man you love."

"It can't be Helga—it has to be Lourie."

"Are you very sure they are not still involved? They were very close when Lourie was here."

I shrugged. "I don't know anymore," I muttered, heading upstairs to my room. I'd forgotten to ask if she'd seen Lourie again. I hoped not.

Chapter Twenty-three

I spent the next few days avoiding Helga, which was not hard since she seemed to be avoiding me. Several times I noticed her talking with Kalinda and Denton, my stomach contracting as I imagined what she might be telling them. I remembered our argument just before I enveloped the tribe, her insistence to get on with it. I hadn't tested it properly, only going by what she said after spending around two minutes within its protections. No matter—it had all been for nothing anyway.

I was thinking about Samoset when I heard the knock on my door.

"You are to go to the meeting room immediately," the young witch told me, turning away before I could reply.

I clattered down the stairwell, my footfalls echoing as I descended. On the way there I scanned for Helga but there was no sign of her. At one point the hallway decided to close off one section, the walls grinding as they sealed shut.

Another hall appeared and I took it, not sure it led in the right direction. When I came to a corner I was sure I saw Lourie staring at me, her dark eyes lit up in a sardonic smile. When I hurried after her she disappeared in a puff of smoke.

When I finally reached the closed door to the meeting room I stopped, my heart pounding. But before I could run away, it opened, revealing Saffron dressed in a sky blue silk robe. Her loose hair flowed down her back in undulating waves. "Come in, Emeline."

I followed her inside, surprised to see only one chair placed in front of the board members. I sat and waited as my judge and jury arranged themselves to face me.

Saffron began. "We have thought long and hard about this, Emeline. We understand you were trying to do your best, but your best is not always enough in circumstances like these. It is your relationship with the Wampanoag Indian that caused nearly all the problems. In light of this war, and what will more than likely become of him, we have decided to be lenient. You will be banned from the coven for one month. And when you return you will study with Kalinda until you've come to terms with the rules and are able to conduct yourself in a proper manner. From what Helga has told us your infatuation with this Samoset has clouded your judgment on many occasions. That is a situation headed for disaster from the get-go." She paused to slant a glance at me. "Kali has spoken up for you on numerous occasions. She will be your mentor from this point forward. Is that understood?"

Kali? I nodded.

"You may leave today, but please do not get mixed up

in what is happening in the sixteen hundreds. There are trained witches working to untangle the timelines and bring things back into order. As to your Indian, if he is still alive he will go on as though he'd never met you. I know this is hard, but in the long run you will thank me."

I stood up and headed unsteadily toward the door before turning to ask one more question. "Where is Helga?"

"Helga has left the coven."

"But…why?"

"Not your concern. Now please gather your things and be gone before the dinner hour tonight."

The words rang in my head repeating over and over. *As though he'd never met you.* When the tears came I gave into them, curling up in the fetal position on my bed. He didn't know me now, but hearing it spoken out that way, in plain English, had made it real.

A bang on my window woke me sometime later. Afraid it was a pigeon knocking himself out on the glass I rose to take a look. Helga was on the grass below me, another rock in her hand ready to hurl upward. I wanted to strangle her with my bare hands. How could she betray me like this? I pushed the window open and leaned out, but before I could shout something mean she put her finger to her lips and gestured for me to come down, pointing toward the small copse of firs to the right of the house. I finished packing and hurried down the stairs, carrying my small bag over my arm. I left the house quickly, hurrying to where Helga hid amongst the trees.

"What did you say?" I hissed. "They think all of this happened because of me and Samoset."

She smiled a crooked smile. "I fixed it for you."

"You did not. They forbid me to go back and worse than that they told me Samoset wouldn't remember me. How could you, Helga! You know how I feel about him."

"I said what I thought would help. If I'd told them the truth about Lourie, Saffron would have come down on us like a ton of bricks." Helga reached into her pocket and pulled out the eagle feather. "I stole this for you."

I took it out of her hands, feeling a vibration coming from it. "Why? Won't Lourie be able to connect with me now?"

"Do you have any sense at all? I know you've learned how to void magic spells by now. Undo it."

I held the feather, scanning back to my spell class. As soon as I mumbled the incantation the vibration was gone.

Helga smirked. "I knew you could manage it. As far as what Saffron said about Samoset why do you care? He already doesn't remember you."

"He doesn't remember me because of what Lourie did. Spells and enchantments can be undone. What Saffron was talking about is something else— something this coven is responsible for in their haste to bring the timelines back in order. I have to go back and find him before they permanently erase his memories."

"Kalinda knows what's going on. It's why you got off so easily. She threatened Saffron."

"And you got kicked out."

"I'm not really kicked out—I'm on special assignment to find Lourie and bring her in before she does any more damage. Want to help?"

"Who put you on special assignment—surely not Saffron."

"Of course not Saffron, you ninny. Kalinda asked me."

"But if Lourie has Saffron on her side, she…"

"Kalinda is keeping a close eye on Saffron. In the meantime I'm supposed to…"

There was a loud shout and two people came running out of the house. I recognized the small witch from the inquisition who was followed by Denton, his coat tails flapping as he chased her. I tensed.

"Don't worry yourself, Emeline," Helga said, placing a restraining hand on my arm. "Denton's a horn-dog and he plays these games with the younger witches."

"They enjoy being chased?"

Her eyebrows rose. "In a stuffy priggish place like this? I'd say they enjoy it quite a lot, especially what happens after he catches them."

Stuffy and priggish was not how I'd describe Geistigehaus, with its moving walls, plates sailing through the air under their own volition, and paintings that looked back at you.

Denton ran by, a smile playing around his lips. His long legs pumped as he hurtled under the trees on the other side of the woods. I heard a little shriek, a high-pitched giggle and then silence.

"See?"

When Helga headed into the deeper woods behind the house I followed. "So what's your plan?"

"Two things," she said, ticking them off on her fingers. "Take down Lourie and find your man."

"If he doesn't remember me it won't do much good. And what about Aimee?"

"They exaggerated when they told you nearly all the

tribe is gone. Their sources were mistaken."

"Who are the sources?"

"People who have skin in the game, like historians and descendants of the settlers. Never is good to piss off an historian—they don't want the extra work."

"I guess you mean rewrite everything; wouldn't it already be written up the way it currently happened?" I asked, remembering the changing history in the Danvers library encyclopedia after one of my first trips into the past.

"Not necessarily." She handed me a cloak and grabbed my arm, pulling me with her into the ether.

An eerie silence greeted us, the skeletal branches of the hardwoods dark in the gloom. Sodden leaves slipped under my feet. "This looks like where the Wampanoag village was, but..." I gazed around, trying to remember. Everything was overgrown, bushes and trees in places where dwellings had been.

Helga caught my eye. "Let's go to Salem first. We can find out what's happened and then backtrack."

"What if we run into one of the witches they sent to untangle the mess?"

"We won't see them, Emeline. They work in the background—their magic is done off site, so to speak."

When we came out from under the trees it was just as I'd feared. The scene reminded me of the dystopian future, with still smoldering buildings, bodies lying in the road where they fell. There was a silence here that had no peace within it, the nasty smell of gunpowder and fear assaulting my senses. I caught movement out of the corner of my eye, turning to see Lucifer heading toward us.

"Lucifer's here," we both said at the exact same moment. We exchanged a glance before she ran and scooped him up. "My poor baby," she crooned.

"I doubt he enjoys that," I muttered, searching through the rubble as she rocked the cat.

Most of the houses in Salem Town had burned, arrows strewn everywhere. Bodies littered the ground. I examined each one, glad when I didn't recognize a member of the tribe. "Is this from the 1675 war or something else? I thought the tribe was safe when I sent them off. Maybe it didn't work," I said, turning to Helga.

Helga shrugged, pushing up her sleeve to look at her chronoscope. "It's December something or other, 1694. The mixed up war is definitely Lourie's doing."

"Why would she do that?"

"How many times do I have to tell you? She enjoys upheaval and she thrives on chaos. I wouldn't be at all surprised if she's taken up with Samoset."

"I don't get the reason for that since he doesn't remember me."

"Maybe she bewitched him after she removed Aimee from the scene."

"Are you *trying* to upset me? Supposedly there are seasoned witches here trying to fix things. That doesn't really square with Lourie being involved with Samoset."

When Helga said nothing I thought of Noisette's warning. I had to block Helga from my thoughts and put up a protection spell. My fingers itched for my green ball. I did not trust her.

The stench of death followed us from one horrific scene

to another. But this war was not of this time. History had taken a step backward, a war fought eighteen years ago in 1675 moved up to 1694. How did Lourie have the power to do this? I had a stab of guilt as I realized my own part in it all. If only I hadn't led Lourie into the past none of this would have happened. A moment later I was running, my feet flying across the ground toward the praying town.

When I reached the north end of town all I found was a broken down fence and the burnt remains of a few rustic dwellings. They were still smoldering. But I'd sent everything into the woods and the surrounding mist—how was any of this here? Samoset's ceremonial loincloth, his headband and painted deerskin cape were burned nearly beyond recognition, discarded in a pile of ash. Everything I knew to be true had changed because of the dark witch. When I found his eagle feather in the dust I collapsed and let out a piercing shriek. He was dead.

I was still there when the sun began to set, rousing myself from the dark abyss I'd fallen into when I heard footsteps. I looked up to see Helga, her hair tangled and filled with moss and sticks. There were oozing scratches on her face and forearms. "What happened to you?"

"The cat got pissed off."

I made a sound that I hoped she didn't hear.

"What are you doing, Emeline?"

"I don't know. I think I fell asleep. I found Samoset's things burned…and…"

"And you fell apart…again? You know what's going on."

I pushed myself to standing. "No, I don't. I thought they

were safe. You said you'd help me find him, Helga."

"I am, but your sniveling isn't going to get us anywhere. If witches are working on this, everything's changed now. Didn't Saffron forbid you to come back here? She knew you'd do exactly what you're doing—meddle and try to figure out what's going on. I suggest we wait until the timelines are back in order before we search for Samoset."

I glared at her, anger rising into my throat. It was everything I could do not to scream at the top of my lungs. I took a deep breath and let it out before modulating my tone. "It was you who convinced me to come back here, Helga."

"Oh really? Are you going to tell me you wouldn't have come on your own?"

I was just about to shout something horrible when the rhythmic sound of boots took my attention. A moment later the militia marched toward us along the road. We slunk back behind the trees and watched them head by us, muskets over their shoulders and knives in their belts. They wore the familiar three-sided hats and long red coats. Behind them were several shackled Wampanoag braves. They looked exhausted and dejected, bleeding wounds on their arms and legs. I strained to see if Samoset was among them.

"He's not there," Helga whispered. "I think they're headed toward the harbor."

They're selling them as slaves."

She nodded. "Let's follow them."

"I thought you said…"

But she was already sneaking away, moving behind trees.

The ship sat like a great black blight, its decks covered with restrained natives, many of who were Wampanoag. When I moved toward the ship Helga grabbed me back. "Don't let them see you!"

"I want to check for Samoset."

"We can go once it gets dark." Helga lowered to the ground and leaned against an oak tree. "I suggest getting some sleep," she said, closing her eyes.

I joined her, wondering about her sudden change of heart. Something was up and I didn't like it—not one bit.

It was as black as pitch when we crept out of our hiding place—it was a moonless night, stars obscured by cloud cover. We crept like shadows toward the ship. Even in the dark I could make out the golden letters on her side. *Cradle of Liberty.* "This is the first slave ship, Helga—and look what they named her."

Helga glanced at the name before her eyes met mine. She shrugged. "How do we get on board?"

"There's a gangplank over there." I hurried away assuming she was following me, but when I turned she'd disappeared. I crept up the gangplank and onto the deck, trying to see in the gloom. "Samoset?" I hissed. There was no answer from the shackled groups aside from moans of pain. I moved among them, the sound of crying and sniffling disturbing as I made my way along the deck. I did not find Samoset. Before I left the deck I used a spell to release their shackles, happy when they crept away in the dark.

Where was Helga?

I was in the forest searching for Helga when I heard voices. Staying in the shadows I moved toward them.

"Yes, but you always were her favorite."

There was a low humorless laugh. "I'm not now."

"And what about this other witch? How do you plan to deal with her?"

"She thinks we're on a mission to save her precious Indian. He's probably halfway to Bermuda by now."

Lourie laughed. "She's kind of gullible, isn't she?"

"You could say that. She believes practically everything that comes out of my mouth."

Lourie swept her long hair over one shoulder before scanning the area. "I should go before she comes back. I'll find you again when it's safe." She leaned forward and kissed Helga on the mouth before disappearing into the ether.

I waited a suitable length of time before making a bunch of noise. "Helga?" I called out.

She appeared next to me. "Be quiet," she hissed. "I don't want to get caught."

"Sorry," I whispered. "Where did you go?"

"I was searching in the warehouses for other Indians. I figured both of us didn't need to board the ship. Did you find him?"

I shook my head. "I'm glad he wasn't there, but now I'm not sure what to do. In the meantime should we deal with Lourie?"

Helga's expression went blank. "Since we're here let's work on finding Samoset before we tackle the dark witch."

"Whatever you say," I agreed, following her through the woods. On the way I worked my spells, weaving a tangle around my thoughts so thick she would never get in.

Chapter Twenty-four

Despite the safety of the cave we found along the trail I didn't sleep, my distrust building as the hours went by. How long had Helga been working with the dark witch? Helga snored away, making me want to knife her in her sleep. But I didn't have a knife, and even if I had I wouldn't have been able to kill her.

I had a fire going when she woke, the fake smile on her face making me clench my teeth. She stretched and yawned.

"I slept like a baby," she said, gazing at me. "Doesn't seem like you did," she added, frowning.

Nothing got past her. "I was too worried to sleep."

"He has to be around, Emeline. He's too smart to get caught by those bastards."

I shrugged. "There were a lot of natives on board."

"Seems like this war took its toll on the Indian population."

"You don't say."

She pulled her fingers through her tangle. "You don't have to be snide about it."

I was just about to blurt out what I'd seen when Lucifer strolled into the cave. His savvy green eyes met mine.

"That damn cat again," Helga said, her hand going to the scratches on her face. "He's a turncoat."

"What do you mean?" I asked innocently, rubbing him behind the ears.

"He attacked me yesterday."

"He doesn't like being held," I said, picking him up.

"We have nothing to eat," Helga said, ignoring me.

"True. Why didn't I think of that?"

She glanced at me, eyeing the cat in my arms. "You're acting really weird, Emeline."

"I suggest you come clean, Helga. I know you aren't here to help me."

"What are you talking about?"

Our eyes locked. "I'm talking about the dark witch."

Her face paled. "You saw us, right? It's all part of my plan."

"Really? Down to the kiss?" Helga turned away, fiddling with the necklace around her neck. "Did she give you that?" I asked, moving closer.

"It's just a hexagram," she muttered, pushing it inside her sweater. A moment later a virtual hurricane whirled through the trees. I backed into the cave, trying to escape the wind and watching Helga who stood with arms raised, pale hair streaming behind her like a flag. Her lips moved and a second later she was gone.

I was still in the cave a half hour later when the words arrived in my mind, beautiful golden letters in intricate script that turned to dust once I'd seen them, falling away into the recesses of my mind. There was no way Lourie had placed them there. *People of the first light*, the literal meaning of the word *Wampanoag*. My mind went to the hill where Samoset and I watched the sunrise. He'd taken me there in his canoe. It was where we'd kissed for the first time—an act that confused him since the Wampanoag didn't kiss. I smiled at the memory of sixteen year old me trying to teach him how to kiss—the blind leading the blind. I grabbed my cape and threw dirt on the fire. Whatever was going on with Helga would have to wait.

When I climbed the hill I was surprised to see no sign of recent footprints, sure that he'd be here waiting for me. I thought of his blanket, the talismans he'd kept here, the voodoo doll he'd carved for me when we were trying to help the people accused of witchcraft. But that was before.

Something caught my eye—a feather, identical to the one on my windowsill. But Samoset was not a witch nor was he versed in magic. There must be a reason I was here, a reason for the feather. I closed my eyes, waiting and hoping against hope this wasn't the dark witch's doing.

It took a long while before a whisper of wind ruffled my hair. There were no words, only images of rippling water, shadows on the forest floor, the lap of wavelets against the wood of his canoe. I ran down the hill expecting to see his canoe in the reeds, but there was nothing there. Lucifer meowed, startling me. And then I knew what was wrong. Samoset and I were in two different timelines. But before I could follow this new train of thought I heard a whoosh and the dark witch appeared.

"You followed my clues," she said. "That native man of

yours is mighty cute. I might just keep him for myself."

I lunged for her but she disappeared, reappearing two seconds later, her lips parted in a sneer.

"What have you done with him?"

"What haven't I done with him? He is now completely under my spell."

"Why? Why are you doing this?"

"Because I can?" Her hand went to her chin, her head cocked to the side. "Let's just say I've taken a dislike to you." She watched me, her face taking on more and more of my likeness until I felt like I was staring into a mirror. "It's amazing what a few simple spells can do." She frowned. "As to you, I want you to go away and never come back." She flicked her hand and I lifted into the air, whirling backward and crashing into a tree. My head spun, pain shooting through my spine.

I heard her laughing and then Helga appeared. "Don't hurt her, Lourie."

"Why not? You don't care about her. If she's gone for good I can come back to Geistigehaus. I have her face and her mannerisms down now."

"Yes, I guess you do," Helga answered. "But this Samoset thing…"

"You're jealous."

"Maybe I am."

"He's only a dalliance, a way to pass the time until we can go back."

I heard a sigh and then their voices faded as they walked away. I stayed there, dizzy and sick, nearly retching as I pictured Lourie and Samoset. But until he remembered me I had no chance. How would I ever get him back?

I was still lying there when night fell, darkness filling in the spaces under the trees. I was unable to think, my mind like a vast empty space as I tried to make sense of things. The dark witch had stolen my reasoning along with the man I loved. I set another spell, this time using blackthorn for the impenetrable tangle around my thoughts—she would not get in again—would not be able to follow my energy trail.

The spirits were back, the whisper of wings whirring around me. *Use your magic,* I heard them whisper before I fell into a deep sleep.

I dreamed of Samoset and Lourie, their naked bodies moving together and apart in a liquid rhythm, their skin slick with sweat. I woke heaving, my empty stomach bringing up nothing but bile. I remained there until the sun had reached its zenith and then forced myself up. The cat was with me, the worlds within his eyes reminding me of who he really was. I had the sphere. The spirits were on my side. I would not give up.

I munched on hazelnuts and shriveled blueberries, leaving the mushrooms I found for later. After my meager meal I followed Lourie and Helga's energy trail through the woods until it disappeared. They'd moved into the ether but I couldn't get a proper bead on it. "Where did they go?" I asked the cat.

He only stared at me.

The ball was in my hands before I knew I'd conjured it. The sphere shimmered and pulsed with an internal fire. I pictured Helga before I threw it upwards into the air, letting it come down on me. The mist drifted around my body, splintering fragments of light moving within it as the scene changed. When the mist cleared I was in a new part of the forest and Helga was standing in front of me.

"I hoped you'd find me," she said, gazing around furtively. "I have to talk to you."

"I don't trust you."

She put her hand on my arm. "Please listen. That entire thing with Lourie was…" she looked around again, "done to gain her trust. If I can't get her to trust me I may as well hang it up—she's too strong to defeat any other way."

I said nothing, watching her eyes for signs of deceit.

"I know what you're thinking, Emeline. I'm sorry I didn't tell you what I had planned. I had to conjure that wind—I knew Lourie was watching me."

"So…what now? You'll take her back to Geistigehaus disguised as me and turn her over?"

"Pretty much." She glanced around again.

"Where is Samoset?"

She shook her head. "I don't know."

My hands balled into fists. "I'll only go along with this if you help me find Samoset. Otherwise I'm telling Kalinda that you and Lourie are plotting together."

"Kalinda already knows how I work. She won't believe you."

"What do you want from me?"

"Just go along with my charade, okay?"

"That's it?"

"I'll try to find out where she's keeping Samoset."

"Keeping him—what do you mean?"

Helga shrugged. "I don't know what's going on with the

tribe—she won't talk about it."

"Well, get her to talk about it and tell me what she says."

Helga nodded. "Have to go." A half second later she disappeared.

It was only a few moments later that Lourie appeared. Before I could take a breath her hand was raised, her fingers up as she made a shoving motion in my direction. I whirled away, rolling over and over, tumbling into the ether. I slammed into the trunk of a tree, every part of me shrieking in pain. Unable to sit up I closed my eyes against the light filtering through the upper branches, wondering if I was about to pass out. She'd followed Helga's energy signal, not mine, which meant Helga had led her directly to me. I felt a burning rage but I was in too much pain to do anything but lie there.

When the ground began to shake I thought *earthquake*. But it wasn't an earthquake, and in the next moment the earth opened up and I was sucked downward. I swallowed mud and tree roots, coughing and choking as rocks and wet dirt closed over my head.

Chapter Twenty-five

If it hadn't been for my orb I would have been dead. I don't remember conjuring it, but the mist provided a shell that protected my body from the crush of dirt and rocks. I had no recollection of how I worked myself back to the surface—perhaps the ball brought me there. Every muscle in my body ached.

It was too cold to bathe in the river so I had to put up with the dirt and mud that clung to my hair and clothes and even my eyelashes. Shivering and filthy I wandered aimlessly, my brain as empty as a sieve. When I found myself in Salem Town I headed to the harbor, hoping I might discover Samoset, but *Cradle of Liberty* was gone.

"What are ye on about?" I heard a male voice ask. "Are ye daft, lass?" He examined me from head to toe, his expression shocked.

"I fell in a muddy ravine."

He shook his head and turned away, obviously getting ready for the next shipment of goods coming in. "Looks like nearly the entire town is dead," I said.

"Nay, lass. The townsfolk have left, 'tis all. Now if its Indians yer lookin' for, most of 'em are either dead or on the ship that departed the harbor early this mornin'."

"But all the houses...."

"Aye, 'tis the work of the savages." He grimaced. "They got what was comin' to 'em. Folks will be rebuildin' as soon as the problem is cleared up."

"Did all the Wampanoag end up on that ship—even the sachem?"

"The sachem? There are many who call themselves sachem. Far as I can tell very few escaped the muskets. Arrows are little help in a battle of this sort. Any runners will be taken care of by the militia up North."

"You do realize they were on this land long before the white man arrived."

His eyes narrowed. "Ye be one of those sympathizers, eh? Get on with ye then. I'll have no part o' ye." He turned away and picked up a gunnysack full of something, stacking it on top of others.

I ran into Helga on the main road in town, her eyes going wide when she saw me. "What happened to you?"

I saw myself through her eyes, drying red brown mud covering my hair and my clothing, a swampy miasma wafting around me. I was sure I had bruises all over my face. "The dark witch tried to kill me, Helga. If it hadn't been for my energy ball she would have succeeded."

She didn't say anything for a moment, her mouth moving as though words failed her. "If I had known, I..."

"The earth opened up and swallowed me. I couldn't breathe, I couldn't see. It was terrifying."

Helga paled. "She promised me…she said if…if I did as she asked she'd leave you alone."

"She knows you aren't on her side?"

Helga's eyes flicked sideways. "Not exactly. But she knows how I feel about using magic this way."

"What about Samoset?"

"I haven't had a chance to…"

"What have you been doing?" I interrupted.

"Mostly trying to gain her trust. I have to tread carefully. If she suspects my motives, she'll…" Helga turned to look back. "I have to go." She disappeared.

I watched for the dark witch, hoping I wouldn't have another run-in with her. After thinking it over for several long minutes I entered the ether and took myself back to Luxembourg and Kalinda.

"She says she's trying to gain her trust," I whispered, watching Kalinda's expression go from mildly worried to frantic.

"Helga is such a headstrong girl. I should never have sent her by herself." She looked me over critically. "Clean yourself up, Emeline, and then come to my private rooms. We need to talk."

I luxuriated under the stream of hot water, the perfume of my lavender soap and lemony shampoo taking away the swampy smells. I watched the red mud swirling into the drain, trying not to think of blood. By the time I was dressed and my hair combed out more than an hour had gone by. I hurried to Kalinda's rooms, trying to stay out of sight.

Kalinda laughed when I told her how hard it had been to reach her rooms without someone seeing me. "Oh, my dear. I should have explained how differently time moves here. Your month has been over for several days now."

When she gestured to the rose velvet couch I sat down and began to talk. "Lourie has tried to kill me twice. And I have yet to find Samoset. I used the sphere to protect the tribe but I don't know if it worked. Lourie said she's with Samoset now. She told me she's enchanted him."

Kalinda gazed out the window before turning to me. She fixed me with her green gaze, her eyes like fire opals. "I wouldn't trust a word that comes out of her mouth. I have some things to explain to you before we speak of the dark witch. Your assignment was part of a concerted effort that has been going on for several years. This situation has reached a tipping point and must be curtailed. Preventing what happens in future North America is what the coven has been working on."

"I knew that. But what is it specifically?"

Kalinda sighed and sat in an upholstered chair next to me, her bird-like gaze darting around the room. "What happens is a recurrence of what began in Germany during the Second World War, but this time the good guys don't win."

I stared at her. "How far in the future are we talking?"

"Not terribly far. The year 2050 to be exact. But the repercussions will ripple across the globe if we don't put an end to it now." She looked down, her hands twisting in her lap. "The presidential election in 2016 United States was the beginning of the nationalistic mood, fomented by the candidate, I'm afraid. The man ran on the idea that whites were being discriminated against. All the years of hard work put into civil rights and protecting minorities went out the window the following year. People are so shortsighted. The system in place has been very good at pitting people against one another. It is easy when the populace is looking for a place to put their anger."

"When I was back in that timeline I didn't notice anything going on other than nuclear power plants having a few leaks. But then again, when Helga and I accidentally ended up in 2120 it seemed there might have been a meltdown of some sort. And also my sister Jean came into the past from a parallel world—that world seemed more like what you're talking about."

Kalinda let out a long sigh. "I am sorry to say this, but that parallel world was what your world was fast becoming. When you move from one world to another, circumstances can leak through."

"So I'm responsible for this?"

"No, dear, of course not. As I said, this has been going on for several years. Your sister Jean took you there, didn't you say? You cannot be held responsible for every anomaly present in the universe." She smiled. "To continue, this same man is re-elected in 2020, which brings a further collapse of reason. Borders between the United States and Mexico and Canada were closed in 2021. Europe reacted, as did many countries, but there was little they could do. By then most minorities had been ejected from the country."

She leaned forward to touch my knee. "I am so sorry we didn't explain all this before sending you off. We discussed it and came to the conclusion that it was too much information to foist on you. It was only because of your knowledge of early Salem that we decided to send you in the first place."

When she gazed at me I felt like she could see straight into my soul. It was a very peculiar sensation. I was beginning to think there was a lot more to this coven, and this particular witch, than I realized.

"Our people have been moving up and down the timeline for years, attempting to promote tolerance by infiltrating news organizations, social media, television and book publishers—anywhere we could add our messages. The human species is not wired to hate one another, but when entire nationalities are dehumanized it overrides the circuitry."

She stopped for a moment, her sage eyes turning dark. "Nothing we've done so far has stemmed the tide. The baser side of human nature is being exploited, Emeline, used in a purposeful movement that has its inception in power and greed. Yes, we do have tribal instincts, but when we are forced to face a common goal that anger just melts away. Have you noticed what happens when there's a disaster? But with so many disenfranchised it's more difficult. People need someone to blame for their misfortune."

She let out a sigh, her lips pressed together. "The only real way to stamp it out is through consciousness. And you must know how hard that is to implement. This trip you were sent on was our last ditch effort to fix things early on, before the founding of the country. We had such high hopes for a change once the new world came about, but…"

"You make it sound as if you're gods and goddesses fixing the planet."

Kalinda twitched, her eyes widening. "I didn't mean to imply that. A few of us are as old as Job, but we didn't create the world. We are only trying to save the world."

"Oh, is that all?" I laughed at this lofty concept she'd spoken of as if it were nothing. "I hope I didn't make matters worse."

Kalinda smiled and shook her head. "The dark witch and her ilk have been doing their best to create chaos. Lourie is part of the systematic movement to pit one ethnic group against another. The dark witches want power just as the people in government of the future want power. The members of the dark coven have placed themselves in positions of influence in order to widen the divide between people. And it's working."

"And Samoset?"

"As I said before, Lourie is a consummate liar. Lourie has taken a special interest in this timeline for some reason. Perhaps it's because of Helga, perhaps it's something else. But the bottom line is she must be stopped."

"But she was a student here. How did she get accepted?"

"She slipped by us. And with Saffron's support she was able to keep her true identity a secret. But as you must already know, Lourie was not always a dark witch. My theory is she came under Saffron's tutelage and moved away from the light."

"But Saffron is…"

"Yes, Saffron was one of us, or so we thought. It is only recently that we've discovered her true intentions. It began after the fire, although the fire may have come about because of Saffron and her need to destroy us."

"And yet she's still here."

"Do you know the saying, 'keep your friends close and your enemies closer'?"

I smiled. "What can I do to help? I'm willing to travel forward in time if you think that's a better use of my talents."

She looked up, her gaze meeting mine. "We are about to have a meeting with all the covens across the globe. Since you are new here you will not be allowed to attend. After I help you with a few stronger spells to protect yourself, I would suggest you head back. Do not forget that your sphere has yet to reveal its capabilities. But be careful. There are some things that go against the rules of the universe."

Oh great. How would I know if what I decided was cosmically good or bad? "You mean like killing the dark witch?"

Kalinda's light green eyes swirled dangerously. "We are not meant to use that kind of power to achieve our goals. I trust you to know the difference when the time comes." Her eyes met mine. "This dark coven has been working against us for a very long time. Its motives are clear. Destroy everything good."

"But I still don't get why. Is it just about power?"

"That is an age old question. Why do people get caught up in power and greed? There are those who thrive on it, especially in your part of the world. My theory is the youngness of the culture. You just don't see the same attitudes in European countries and others where they've lived through war since time immemorial. To someone like you who questions everything this all must seem unheard of, but to many, power is all there is. Not everyone in a position of influence has been seduced, but the lure is hard to resist, especially with the dark witches whispering in everyone's ear. For those who have succumbed, power is the goal and how you get there is of no consequence."

I thought of my parents' complaints about taxes and the growing divide between rich and poor—capitalism run amok. "What do I do if Samoset's been sold into slavery?"

"We are working to bring the timelines back into order. Once that's accomplished I'm sure you'll find him." Kalinda smiled, her teeth very white against her smooth mocha skin.

"Saffron said he wouldn't remember me."

Anger flashed across her features. "Memories can be resurrected. Love is a powerful force, Emeline. Never forget that. You are far more formidable than you know, my dear. Don't let anyone convince you that being vulnerable is a detriment. Vulnerability is actually an asset—soon you will discover the truth of this. Lourie and Saffron will be dealt with. Before I teach you a couple of spells shall we have a look at your green ball? Perhaps it already holds everything you need."

After carefully examining the sphere Kalinda pronounced me in good shape to head back.

"But what does it do?"

"You've already discovered several things it can do, haven't you? Why should I be the one to spoil your fun? Use it to find Samoset. And when that is done report back. Don't worry about his memories right now. There are assignments in the future in which we will need your expertise. The ability to travel through time is not everyone's forte."

My expertise?

Back in my room I dressed warmly in a long black skirt and sweater and winter shearling boots pulled on over tights. The wool cape I'd stolen from the Parris household completed my outfit. I was ready to face what the fates decided to throw at me.

I was about to leave when Noisette peeked around my door. "*Mon dieu!* You go again so quick? I fear for you, Emeline."

I ushered her in and closed the door. "Don't worry, I have my green energy ball."

Her expression was skeptical. "And the dark witch? How do you keep safe with only this ball you keep telling me about?"

"I'm trying to keep a good attitude. Half my problem has been assuming Lourie could get the best of me. She fights from a place of power, my power is in being vulnerable. I'll be fine."

I hope so." Noisette didn't look convinced when she hugged me goodbye. I listened to her quiet footsteps recede as she descended the stairs, my thoughts more confused than ever. How could being vulnerable help me in any way, especially in dealing with a person like Lourie? But it was Kalinda who said it and I trusted her.

After letting my thoughts settle the answer came. It was simply that deep down I trusted myself and that I was able to love. Lourie had embraced the dark side—any love she might have held in her heart was gone, including any real feeling for Helga or anyone else for that matter. Without love what was the point of anything?

I took one last look around my room before I entered the ether.

Chapter Twenty-six

I tossed the energy ball up and down, trying to determine what else it could do. The surprised look that had appeared on Kalinda's face while she examined it pointed to many yet to be discovered attributes. Would it reveal them or did I have to be in some dire situation before they showed themselves?

Around me the forest stood neutral, keeping its opinion of my activities to itself. Pale morning light filtered through the bare branches of the hardwoods as I tossed the brilliant weightless sphere from one hand to the other. The cedars stood tall, the soothing green of their graceful branches like a balm on my over-anxious soul. The wind moving through them reminded me of dancers swaying to music only they could hear.

On the forest floor cloud shadows slipped by like water, filling in the cracks and crevices as dawn broke. The ball was hot in my hands, and I knew the power inside it was building. *What else can you do?* I whispered, rolling it back and forth from one hand to the other. I heard a clicking sound and felt a shift in my fingers and suddenly it was no longer morning. A waxing moon sent tendrils of cool light into the shadows under the trees. I stared dumbfounded at the pulsing globe in my hands.

I had no idea if I had moved forward or backward in time, only that it was now night instead of day. I placed a few rocks in a circle next to my foot before moving the ball the way I had a moment before. Once I heard a click I looked down. The rocks were gone, scattered as they had been before I collected them. We'd moved backward in time. But I still didn't know how far.

I spent the next hour or so testing, listening carefully for the clicks. I could move it one click or two clicks to the right or the left—right led forward in time, left led backward. Trying to move a pulsing globe that wasn't solid was tricky and took all my concentration. It seemed that each click was roughly a minute, give or take ten seconds or so. I wondered if moving this way through time might be better in the long run—I'd already done too much damage with my meddling. But the precision of it left much to be desired.

"You certainly take yourself seriously," a voice said next to me. I turned to see my doppelganger staring at me out of eyes the same shade and shape as mine.

My tangle of blackthorn had parted to let her in. "You're a mind reader too?"

She smiled and moved one shoulder up. "Do you want to know what happened to Samoset?"

I watched her for a moment, my focus on the thicket in my head. Once the thorns were in place I answered. "I assume he's where I left him."

She shook her head and grinned. "Not hardly, Emeline. A lot has happened since you ran back to the witches."

"I didn't run back...I..."

"You don't need to get defensive. Remember the war?"

"You mean the one that should have happened in 1675?"

She chuckled and made a little moue with her mouth. "A few things got a bit mixed up there for a while. I needed the chaos to keep you off his trail until I decided what I wanted to do."

This did not sound good. I waited for her to continue.

"He and his tribe are in Bermuda. Their owners are not bad people. Unfortunately you can't have a life with him now."

I held back my desire to grab her around the neck. I could use my ball...I could...*no power*, I heard in my mind. Was I supposed to let this bitch ruin my life?

"And don't think of going there, either through the ether or with that *thing* you use. It won't do you any good. He won't remember you."

"I already know that, Lourie. But I'm sure your spells can be undone."

"I wouldn't try that if I were you. His memories of you are not ones you would enjoy him having. Underneath his amnesia he remembers Aimee and her disappearance—unfortunately you look just like the person who took her away from him. I decided after I had my way with him that it would be better for all concerned if he sailed to Bermuda without disturbing memories of the woman he was about to marry. You should really thank me for caring."

"I'm his wife, Lourie."

"His wife? I know what you think you had with him, but it's all gone now, just as he is. Wouldn't you rather focus on your new incarnation?"

"What *did* happen with Aimee?" I asked in as calm a tone as I could muster. She'd told me once but things had changed since that conversation.

"I took her somewhere special to use for my own pleasure. She's quite lovely, don't you think? They would have had such a darling baby together. But then again, her being preggers would have ruined things a bit for me."

When I lunged for her she disappeared, her cackling laugh in my ears long after she was gone. My legs buckled and I crumpled to the ground, tears spilling down my cheeks. If she came back I *would* kill her, unlawful use of power or not. But she didn't come back and as the hours drifted by I realized I had to get myself together. It was a while before I remembered Kalinda's words: *Lourie is a consummate liar.* Was she lying about Samoset and Aimee? I had to find out.

I was in the town square when I thought of asking the mist to take me to the tribe. For some reason there was no one about, the silence unsettling. It was getting close to dark— possibly the settlers were taking care of the wounded and preparing for more fighting? I made sure Samoset was not among the dead before setting off for the forest where I hoped I'd sent them.

When I reached the deeper woods I conjured my ball, letting the mist envelop me. *Take me to where I sent the tribe.* When the mist cleared I wasn't sure whether I'd moved or not—but when I headed to the site of their new longhouses I found only a few buildings still standing. There was no sign of anyone. I visualized the hill above where Samoset had taken me in his canoe and then I took myself into the ether. But when I reached the spot next to the water it was as silent as a tomb, without even the slightest birdsong to relieve the ominous quiet.

I did find signs of a recent fire in the community fire pit close to the edge of the inlet. This clearing was where the tribe lived during the summer months. I heard a rustle of dry leaves just before Aunum appeared, his barks of happiness lifting my spirits. "Where is Samoset?" I asked, bending to rub him around the ears. But he only stared at me out of his soulful amber eyes.

I was dozing at the top of the hill using my cloak as a pillow when I felt a shift or a sound that alerted me to another presence. Aunum barked, waking me fully, my eyes opening on darkness. It was deep night now and a shadow stood there, black against the light from the moon. I moved backward, fear clawing at my throat. But Aunum moved forward, his tail wagging. I heard Samoset's voice, the Algonquin words falling around me like soft feathers. "Samoset?" He didn't move or speak.

I took a step toward him, surprised when he backed away. "It's me, Em—I'm not the dark witch. This was our place, remember?"

He said something in Algonquin that I didn't understand, peering at me with no recognition. I began to cry, trying hard not to let him hear me, but when he moved closer I couldn't hide the tears. He placed one hand on my wet cheek. "Why sad?"

I put my hand over his, holding it there as I tried to stop the well of emotion. "You don't remember me."

He shook his head to say he didn't understand, removing his hand and walking past me. He spread the blanket he'd brought along on the hummock of grass before sitting cross-legged to face east. When I sat next to him Aunum crowded close. At some point I lay back and fell asleep.

The sun woke me, the brightness blinding for a moment when I opened my eyes. Samoset sat as still as a stone, eyes closed and his face turned to the orb rising over the water. It suddenly occurred to me that this was a summer sun, the air misty and warm. I reveled in it, so glad to be here even if this man had no memory of me. I pulled my sweater over my head and tied it around my waist and removed my warm boots. I wriggled my toes in their tights, wanting them off too.

I had my skirt up around my hips and was in process of removing my tights when he turned, his gaze curious but not embarrassed. I continued with what I was doing, getting rid of the offending things before pulling my skirt down again. Once I had completed the changes he nodded, gesturing for me to sit beside him, which I did. When the first rays of sun touched his face I was reminded of an ancient Aztec god. His bare chest glowed like warm honey in the sunlight, the leggings and breechcloth he wore ones I'd seen many times before. But we had never met.

I was leaning close, the piney earthy scent of him drawing me as it always had, when the dark witch appeared out of the ether. Her eyes narrowed, her lips parting to recite the incantation. Aunum barked madly, snapping at her. But before she could finish whatever spell she was conjuring, the ball was in my hands, the mist wafting around her body. She struggled, anger twisting her mouth as she screamed things I couldn't hear. Samoset made a sound, his eyes wide. He glanced at me as he stood and backed away from the mist. A moment later he was hurrying down the hill. He looked up once before he climbed into his canoe, pushing backward out of the reeds before paddling away. I watched him grow smaller and smaller until he rounded a bend and was gone.

I brought my attention back to Lourie who writhed and twisted like a pit viper caught in a trap. I held her gaze as I flicked my hand, sending her tumbling away.

And later when I tried to remember what I'd been thinking or where I might have sent her there was nothing in my mind but my love for Samoset. Whatever I'd done to Lourie had not been done in a fit of rage or anger, but in utter calm. This was how I was supposed to operate the ball, not in some angry frenzy in which I did things too hurriedly. But where had I sent her? And a better question—how soon would she return? I knew my limitations and so far I had not grasped the sphere's full capabilities.

I grabbed my cloak and pulled on my boots, tying the tights around my waist. When I reached the bottom of the hill Aunum began to bark, my attention taken to an older Wampanoag man. He was carrying rushes for the summer *wetus,* his muscular arms full of them. When he saw me he stopped, a frown appearing on his square-jawed features. I immediately recognized Akkom, Samoset's father. I smiled and moved on, knowing that he did not speak English. He'd never been very welcoming. Seeing him gave me an approximate idea of how far back I'd traveled. He was dead now, had been for at least a year.

I had the urge to stay here, to let the natural attraction that had drawn us together in the first place rekindle. I breathed in the summer scents of water plants and wild mushrooms, feeling the air warm against my skin, jumping when Helga abruptly appeared next to me. My reverie evaporated as our eyes met. "How did you find me?"

She scoffed. "I visualized you—how else? Is Samoset here?" she asked, squinting into the forest and then turning toward where Akkom worked.

"He was but I scared him away when I encased Lourie in the mist."

"What? How did that come about?"

"We were together on the hill when she appeared. I wasn't even angry when I did it, Helga. I just sent her away."

Helga smiled. "That's more like it. Now, if you only knew where…"

"…she went," I finished for her. "You always manage to burst my bubble."

She did her one shoulder shrug. "Are we in a time before you arrived here?"

I nodded. "Samoset doesn't know me yet. He barely speaks English. With everything that's happened I wish I could stay and start over."

"And yet soon there'd be two of you. I guess the witch trials haven't begun yet."

She handed me a piece of jerky but the smell of it made

me feel sick. I shook my head, trying not to gag. A moment later she grabbed my arm, and before I could protest we were whirling through the ether. We landed in the woods outside the Salem Town square which was full of shouting townspeople and angry men dressed in uniforms. I folded my arms across my chest against the freezing air before pulling her with me deeper into the woods. "What the heck is going on now?" I glared at her in the dim light.

"How am I supposed to know? Looks like a fight's brewing."

I untied my sweater and pulled it on before adding my cloak. "Why did you bring us here? I wasn't ready to leave that timeline. I don't even know exactly *when* it was!"

She frowned and pulled up her hood. "Do you want to cause another anomaly?"

"No, but…"

"Listen to me, Emeline. We have to deal with Lourie. That's my assignment and I was hoping you'd help."

"Didn't you hear me when I told you what I'd done? Lourie is in the mist. She may be gone for good this time."

Helga made a derisive sound in the back of her throat. "Lourie belongs to a very powerful coven—they've infiltrated every part of government as well as corporations. There are powerful CEO's among their members as well as congressmen. There is no way that ball will keep her contained."

"Kalinda told me to find Samoset. She also said I'm way more powerful than I know. Why do you always doubt me?"

Helga frowned. "Why would she tell you that? Samoset's a lost cause. He won't remember you and he may not even be here anymore. Lourie said…"

"Kalinda told me that Lourie's a liar," I interrupted.

Helga shrugged. "Sometimes she lies and sometimes she doesn't. She has no reason to lie to me."

"I did send her off in the mist, Helga. Maybe that's it for her."

Her expression softened. "I don't doubt you, exactly. I just know her. She'll find a way out of it. I've seen her in way worse circumstances."

"Really? Remember what happened when I trapped you inside the mist? As I recall you couldn't get out until I let you out."

"Lourie has dark magic at her fingertips. Don't underestimate her." She watched me for a moment and let out a sigh as though making a difficult decision. "Saffron's in this timeline, Emeline. She's looking for Lourie and when she finds her the two of them will go back to the future. We have to follow them."

"To the future? That isn't what Kalinda told me to..."

"Forget Kalinda for the moment. You can find Samoset after we discover what's going on in 2050."

"Not sure how the two of us can do much."

"We can spy and see what they're up to and report back to our coven."

"So you take us to Saffron and we follow her to find Lourie?"

"Not quite. I want you to use your connection to Lourie to find her. Then we wait until Saffron shows up."

"And follow their energy signature."

"Exactly."

"How do I do that?"

Helga shook her head in frustration. "Think of her,

idiot. Visualize her and take us there."

"You can't do this?"

"She'll recognize what I'm up to, but she has no idea you can track her too."

"But it wasn't that long ago I sent her into the mist. You think she's already found her way out?"

"I do. Saffron wouldn't be here otherwise."

I stared into the distance remembering my state of mind when I sent Lourie off. I'd felt so good about myself. And now Helga was telling me that it hadn't worked? What did I have to do to get rid of her? I wasn't sure I trusted Helga. What was to stop her from linking up with Lourie and Saffron against me? She thought I was naïve and gullible. "How can I trust you again?" I finally asked.

"If I were against you why wouldn't I go and find her myself? Kalinda trusts me—did she say otherwise?"

"No. But this has all the makings of a trap."

"I have no reason to set a trap for you. I want to catch Lourie and Saffron and I want to send both of them into hell for all eternity."

Her eyes flashed dark as she spoke, tiny sparks of anger shooting from her fingers. A few doubts still remained but I grabbed her shoulder and moved us into the ether. Things would come clear soon enough.

When we landed close to the harbor I saw two men dragging Lourie toward the ship docked there. I turned to Helga. "They're taking her to the boat."

As soon as the men reappeared from below and headed off the ship we hurried down the hill. Helga conjured a candle, lighting it as we ran up the gangplank and toward the hold. We were below when we heard men's voices, the candle skittering away when Helga dropped it. We hid behind a couple of rum barrels.

"I don't think she's down here," Helga hissed in my ear.

But by then flames were licking across the oil soaked floorboards, moving toward the barrels of rum and the gunpowder kegs behind them. "We have to get out of here," I whispered urgently, watching the small blue flames coming closer. "This ship is going to go up like a tinder box." I grabbed her hand and whisked us away, landing in the trees at the top of the hill. It was less than a minute later that explosions racked the earth, dark smoke lifting into the already charcoal sky. I felt the trembling down to my fingertips, backing farther into the woods to escape the worst of it. The ship was now fully on fire, the harbor filled with shouting men with buckets trying to make a difference. But with gunpowder and rum aboard the explosions continued, sending fragments flying and killing people in their wake.

"This is all our fault, Helga. If we hadn't dropped that candle this wouldn't be happening."

"We had to find out if Lourie was below decks. I'm sorry about the candle but it slipped out of my fingers. I saw them dragging her on board. Where have they stashed her? The explosions might have killed her."

"Do you still have feelings for her?"

Helga looked sad for a moment. "We were classmates when we were teenagers—but that was long long ago in a galaxy far far away. You would have liked her back then— she was smart and funny and self-deprecating."

I took that in, not even surprised. "What changed?"

"She got in with the wrong crowd and they took her under their wing. They seduced her with the lure of power. Even back then at the ripe old age of sixteen she had all the makings of a powerful witch."

Another explosion went off and the ship listed to one side. Men shouted and screamed, trying to save their cargo. "She's going to sink," I said unnecessarily. We watched the men trying to right her, their agonized shouting and the chaos going on as men ran aboard and rolled barrels up and off, falling in the water in the process. Gunpowder exploded, lifting two men into the air before they crashed onto the deck and lay still.

"There's Saffron," I whispered, pointing toward the fire-haired woman dressed in brocade robes who had just materialized close to the ship. She looked like a creature from another planet next to the men running around trying to save the cargo and their livelihood.

"She has Lourie!" Helga shouted a second later. But before we could do anything the two of them disappeared.

I followed Helga toward the harbor amidst the screaming and the smoke and the ongoing detonations. The reek of rum was strong, that and the acrid aroma of spent gunpowder. The ship was on her side, men rushing on and off to save what they could.

"Are you sure about this, Helga?"

"Good gods, Emeline. Stop questioning and just do it!"

I visualized Saffron first, her bright hair twisted up and coiled on top of her well-shaped head, the purple brocade robes trailing in the muck. When Lourie appeared in my mind's eye it was as though she'd placed herself there, her midnight blue eyes meeting mine, a smirk on her lips. But by then it was too late—we were already in the ether.

Chapter Twenty-seven

We landed in a war zone, tanks rolling down the middle of the wide street, sirens blaring. People ran for their lives, cars abandoned, the screams of children and gunshots adding to the general pandemonium. It was like being in a holocaust movie except this was real. When I glanced up the sky was crystal blue, the color dazzling, as though thumbing its nose at the human disaster happening below. "Why does god hate us so much?" I heard a woman yell, her tear streaked face covered in dirt.

Helga grabbed my arm and dragged me off the street and into an alleyway.

"Find them, Emeline. Now," she hissed.

I knew where they were. I could see them in my mind's eye furtively making their way down the same street where we'd landed. But a moment later they disappeared from my consciousness as neatly as if they'd never been there. "They blocked me."

"Use that damn ball," Helga whispered.

I held out my hand and summoned the orb, staring into the flickering lights inside it that pulsed and changed. *Where did they go?* A scene began to form inside the green haze—a mid century brick building, a set of winding stairs to a second story. *The orb was now a crystal ball? What else could the thing do?* I peered closer—the building was the only one on the street still intact. In fact it was completely unscathed in a row of burned out hulks with broken windows, splintered wood and gigantic sections of missing bricks.

Helga watched over my shoulder as a door with a smoky glass inset etched with the letters BMC opened, revealing an enormous paneled room filled with witches. And these were not your every day witches. No. The women were dressed in layers of black gossamer that floated about them like feathers, various mythological dragon-like creatures perched on their shoulders. The men wore black, dark hair slicked back like classic vampires, hideous winged and grinning gargoyles on their shoulders. In a strange way the witches were all beautiful—their look of youth flying in the face of what I knew to be true.

"That's coven headquarters," Helga said. "It's where they live and where they do their magic."

I didn't want to ask her how she knew this, afraid of the answer. When I looked again l saw Saffron, her fire red hair so different from the rest of them. Lourie was next to her, fitting in well with the others, a nasty-looking bird-like creature perched on her shoulder. "I'm not going in there," I whispered.

"You have a spell of invisibility, don't you?"

"Well, yes, but I have yet to test it out. You have one too, right?"

Helga nodded. "But Lourie can sense me. She'd know if I was in that room."

"Oh great—so I have to go alone?"

"Someone needs to eavesdrop."

"I hate you right now."

Helga made a face. "Sorry, but if the situation was reversed, I'd go."

"Of course you'd say that."

"You'd best get on with it, Emeline. They may be going over plans that we need to know."

I studied my ball. "Kalinda said my ball could help me with all sorts of things—she urged me to try it out. Maybe I can eavesdrop from here."

Helga frowned. "How does she know that?"

"I showed her the ball the last time I was there."

There was a shout and two men appeared at the end of the alleyway, bearing down on us with guns raised. A shot rang out and ricocheted off a wall, scattering stucco. I grabbed Helga's arm and a second later we were standing outside the formidable Georgian building. Over the door I saw the same three letters. "What does BMC mean?"

She smirked. "Black Magic Coven, but I think the official name is Belgian Medical Conglomerate."

I let out a humorless laugh, backing down the steps, but Helga pushed me forward. "Are you going to do it or not?"

"I thought I could do it from here, Helga. The ball..."

"The ball may show us what's going on, but can you hear what they're saying?"

I stared down at the orb still in my hands. I could see mouths moving but there was no sound. "Well, no, but..."

Helga just stared at me. I sighed and bathed myself in

green mist before saying the words. *Cosmic powers clothe me in light and let no one see me. Keep darkness away until you free me.*

"Can't see you at all," I heard Helga whisper just before I entered the ether.

I landed silently, thank god, in the back of the room, settling myself against the wall. An enormous pentagram was etched into the floor, all the witches seated on chairs within it. Candles lit up the space, the only other light coming from a large skylight in the twelve-foot high coved ceiling.

"The timelines are coming back in line because of the coven's meddling. Kalinda refuses to give up even though she knows she can't win against us."

Saffron's voice boomed, but instead of the other witches looking to her in awe, several had skeptical expressions. She was not feared here as she was in my coven.

"And Lourie being here will alert them further, Saffron," a narrow-hipped strikingly handsome man said, scowling. He glared at Lourie. "She is supposed to be creating chaos back there, not alerting them to what we're up to."

"I want to make more of a difference in *this* timeline," Lourie said, staring him down. "It isn't fair that I'm always doing your dirty work, Rafe. Haven't I been invaluable in the past?"

His smile did not reach his eyes. "I concede your point, but we all have to do our part. The masses have been quelled and the military is about to take over the city. Where do you think you'd be of most use?"

"I do wish I'd been able to manage the death of that one witch in the past. She has some ball that has mystical powers. First one of those I've seen. But if you're talking about here, I would like to go further into the future to make sure our spells hold everything in place."

"I'm sorry Lourie, but the future is off limits at the moment. Only our seasoned witches are allowed to go further afield. Our headquarters are here in 2050—such a good year, don't you think? World markets are on the verge of collapse, hunger is rampant, water is scarce and expensive, causing more fighting—third world countries have already succumbed, others are soon to follow. We have a very short waiting period until witches will be in charge of the world. But in the meantime we must hold steady and be patient. Once witches rule we will be able to reproduce and our numbers will grow. The human race is flawed. Once we're rid of them we can run things the way they should be run."

There was a murmur of agreement. "But first we have to finish the destruction of the planet," Saffron added. "These humans don't give up easily, but they're too stupid to realize that global warming is at the root of their destruction—that and their tribal mentality they can't get past." She let out a low chuckle. "Their survival depends on the fish that are now contaminated with plastic, the agriculture that has turned fields fallow from lack of topsoil and too many pesticides, the meat industry that has imploded because of the rampant use of antibiotics, and the water that is also filled with plastic and many other contaminates. I could go on and on. They have brought all this on themselves by their shortsightedness. They don't seem capable of thinking beyond the present moment. Honestly, all we're doing is speeding things along a bit." A low murmur of laughter moved across the room.

"But what about the other covens working against us?" Lourie asked. "They are meeting as we speak. From what I've gleaned their numbers have grown. Now that Saffron has been caught out, one of us needs to infiltrate Geistigehaus and make sure we know what's what."

"That's true," another gorgeous male witch with high cheekbones agreed. "And I have someone perfect in mind. That is if we can covert her properly." He glanced at Lourie as though the dark witch would know who he referred to, his smile reminding me of a snake about to strike. A vision of him appeared in my mind. He was naked and having wild sex with a flaxen-haired woman in a room not so different from this one. If I could just see her face…

At that point I felt a twitch in my leg and knew if I remained another second my invisibility would be gone. I pictured Helga, the green mist enclosing me before I landed on the steps in front of the building.

She grabbed my hand and pulled me down the steps and between the building and the one next door. Trash had accumulated, rags, metal cans and bags of refuse soggy from recent rain, the odor of dead animal strong. "Some very strange looking individuals went through those doors while you were gone. What happened?"

"They've got someone lined up to infiltrate our coven again. Global warming is feeding right into their plans, Helga. We're destroying ourselves without very much help from them."

Helga let out a strangled cry, staring wide-eyed at the rat that ran by. She muffled the shriek about to emerge from her throat and made a gagging motion, moving toward the street. "Who is the person they've picked to infiltrate?" she whispered, peering out at the tanks rolling by.

"I had to leave before I found out. I had a vision of her with this gorgeous male witch but I couldn't see her face. Can we go now?"

Helga's eyes widened. "A vision?"

"She had hair like yours—straight and the same color. That was all I could see."

"And the male witch?"

"He was beautiful, Helga—they all were."

She stared at me and I felt her probing my mind, her magic like tiny fingers moving through my blackthorn. I clamped down on my mind and shot her a look. "Helga!"

"What?" she smiled innocently. "Before we go I need to steal a paper and a couple of current magazines. I want to see if any of the coven's hard work is paying off."

"I doubt it is, judging from the mess this place is in. Martial law doesn't sound promising."

With a couple of spells Helga was able to distract a shop keeper while we stole a copy of the New York Times, and some older editions of magazines that were lying around. She tucked them under one arm and we left the shop, hurrying down the street and trying to avoid the patrolling cops wearing riot gear.

We stopped in a deserted alleyway between a falling down version of what had been a Macy's and a looted jewelry store, both of us glad to get off the main drag where we could breathe for a moment. Others were doing the same, people huddled together, their wary gaze on the newcomers. When Helga waved her hand they turned away, ignoring us.

The news from the paper was not encouraging. Not only had the United States succumbed to martial law, several European countries had done so as well. The stock market had recently crashed, people committing suicide left and right. When I glanced toward the street, global climate change deniers were out in force, walking with placards around their necks. A moment later the charcoal clouds opened, rain pouring down.

We read on, pressing ourselves against the wall to escape the drenching rain. I read the year old *Economist* over Helga's shoulder, articles titled **Worldwide starvation** and **Water Prices Skyrocketing as Supply Dwindles!** It was the same in Europe. *The Nation* had investigated the beginnings of the current crisis, blaming it on corruption at the highest levels of government. "If only we could go back to 2016," one op-ed read. "If we had paid attention to the signs and decided wisely our world would be salvageable."

"They could be collecting the rain water," I whispered as we shielded ourselves with the magazines.

"Probably has pollutants and radiation in it," Helga answered. She turned to me, her eyes welling with tears. "This is the beginning of the end."

"Don't say that. The coven can make a difference." A second later I was sick to my stomach, bringing up what little I had in it. I shivered in the chill rain that trickled down my neck. Helga stared at me worriedly, watching me wipe my mouth on my sleeve.

"Are you okay?"

I slid down to sit on the ground, trying to control my roiling stomach. "I think reading all this made me ill. I want to go back to the sixteen hundreds, Helga. At least there are still trees and water and animals there. The paper said the animals are nearly all gone. Africa is on fire and the polar ice caps have melted. Oceans are dead and most of the forests have been cut down to use for firewood. The grid has been mostly off line for nearly a year. Some people still have electricity from solar because of Tesla batteries, but the poor are SOL, living like animals in alleyways like those folks." I pointed to the people at the other end of the alley who were huddled around a small fire made of plastic bottles and tires. The smell from it burned my eyes and made me feel sick again. "*The Wall Street Journal* mentioned all the terrible illnesses from the past that are resurrecting their nasty little heads. That rat we saw was probably the last rat standing."

Helga shuddered. "And the fleas on it probably carry the plague."

"Without electricity how can they still print anything?"

"The old way with printing presses and ink. It's tedious, but I doubt they're printing very many papers now. The prices for the ones we stole were outrageous. And those magazines are at least a year old."

"Any articles about injustice?"

Helga shook her head. "I didn't see anything positive anywhere. I don't think the coven has any idea how bad things are."

"But Kalinda said she'd fulfilled her assignment. The coven witches must still be traveling forward in time."

But Helga wasn't listening, her focus on a mangy rat climbing up the wall, claws scrabbling in the loose mortar. When it fell to the ground she screamed, hiding behind me. A second after that a man appeared at the entry to the alley, a gun pointed our way.

"You people need to disperse!" he shouted.

Helga grabbed my arm. I felt the wind, sensed the years sliding by as we moved backward in time.

Instead of landing in the forest as I'd hoped, Helga took us to the coven, our clumsy landing echoing in the dark first floor hallway.

When she saw the disappointed look on my face she scoffed. "Reporting what we discovered takes precedence, Emeline. You'll get back there in due time." She walked down the hallway and stopped in front of Kalinda's apartments. "Are you coming?" she hissed.

I hurried after her.

Kalinda was horrified by what we told her. "I knew it was bad but I didn't realize things had gone this far. We pulled all our witches back for the first meeting and haven't sent new ones yet. I suspect the rate of deterioration has increased in the last months. Time speeds up when things are in decline. How they've managed is quite clever— pitting people against one another and letting them destroy themselves. Whispering in ears about the 'other' is easily done when economies have broken down and people are desperate."

She turned to me. "Those witches you listened to are immortal. But they cannot reproduce. From what you overheard this seems to be one of their goals.

There is a lesson the human race is meant to learn from all this."

"Does the planet have to be destroyed in the process?"

Kalinda smiled sadly. "That is exactly what we are trying to prevent."

"I understand wanting to reproduce, but what else drives them?"

"They are motivated by a Hitler like need to cleanse and purify the race. They want witches to rule."

I tried to imagine a world ruled by Lourie and her kind, shuddering as I pictured the utter desolation this would cause. "What about the meetings? Have the visiting covens come up with a plan?"

"We're still at it. But with this news we will have to speed things along a bit. If you hadn't noticed, all our rooms are occupied, and the hotels close by are full as well. I would take your meals at odd times if you want to get a seat."

I felt sick again, my stomach knotting at the thought of the future. "Can I go back to the sixteen hundreds now? I haven't found Samoset, and…"

"I know, my dear. The atmosphere of the future has depleted you. You must have nature around to feel like yourself again."

I nodded, realizing for the first time how utterly exhausted I felt.

"The witches have been very busy in your absence. I think the timelines are nearly straightened out. You should be able to locate him without much problem."

"What about Samoset's memories?"

"I made sure to tell the witches I sent back to tread lightly. Now that Saffron is gone the timelines have been untangled and memories restored. He will remember Lourie, but he will also remember you. Some timelines may have been erased in the work done to clean it up—for instance the war was never supposed to happen in 1694.

Samoset may not remember events as you do, but I'm sure you can convince him of your identity. Go now and come back once you know that your life with him is secure. I may have another assignment for you, but it depends on several things." Her bird-like gaze regarded me for a moment before she waved me away.

Kalinda was talking to Helga when I left the room. I stood in the hall for a minute to calm my fast-beating heart. Several unfamiliar witches walked by, smiling at me as they headed toward the kitchens. I nodded back, my mind on other matters.

I pictured the forest, the call of birds, burbling streams rushing over rocks, visualizing Samoset and the tribe involved in their daily tasks. *December, 1694*, I whispered. I entered the ether.

Chapter Twenty-eight

A thick miasma of fog lay across the water, the air sultry. Mosquitoes buzzed in my ears and I slapped them away. I heard voices, the sound of Algonquin. The water lapped gently against the canoes pulled up in the cattails. I saw the bowl of mollusk shells sitting on a flat rock, the ones Samoset had brought to me just before I was taken from this time. I'd been here before.

"Em?"

I turned toward the voice, overwhelmed with happiness at the sight of him. "Samoset." I couldn't hug him or kiss him since I was not where I'd planned to go. I could tell by his expression that this was the past before we were intimate—we barely knew each other.

He moved closer, his gaze savvy. "Look different," he said taking my sweater in his fingers. "You leave in other clothes."

I remembered. I'd been dressed for summer the last time I'd been here. It was the beginning of the witch trials, and I'd been whisked back and forth from present to past without any control on my part. So much had changed since then. "I...I may as well tell you the truth. You know I can time travel. I'm here from the future."

He frowned. "Future. You leave to go to future."

"Yes, I did. But I'm another me, Samoset. You and I are married and are trying to have a baby. Many things have happened."

"Wife?"

"Yes. But it's complicated. There's another witch who looks like me who has messed things up for us..."

Samoset shook his head, his fingers working through his long hair. He stared into the distance, his eyes clouding. "Vision of bad medicine in future. Elders angry—blame Samoset and..."

"And me, your wife."

He nodded.

What was I doing here? This would only lead to more confusion in the future, his knowledge of me making our life even more complicated. He'd already had a vision of trouble in the future. And I'd already created a paradox— was I about to do it again? "I should go now, Samoset. I tried to get to the right timeline but this isn't it. There will be a time when you don't trust me because of this other witch who looks like me."

He nodded. "Bad time coming—no game, bad storms, war."

I stared at him. "I don't know what to do. I hope it's all fixed now."

He didn't answer, his dark eyes on my face. I heard a female voice calling him, his mother appearing behind us. She smiled at me before taking Samoset's arm, murmuring something in Algonquin. "Must go. Work now. Come back?"

"I don't know. My other self will be back, I know that. But don't tell her I was here."

Samoset's features clouded further before he followed Weetamoo toward the hides stretched in the sun.

When they were out of sight I conjured my ball and turned it to the right, listening to the clicks as it moved me forward in time. With each click the landscape around me changed, as though I was moving through a movie one scene at a time. The sensation was odd as I stood there in the same spot, leaves falling from trees, turning brown underfoot, snow falling and the air turning icy until I finally began to shiver.

Once the forest floor showed patches of snow, and the branches of the oaks, maples and birches rose like skeletons in the sharp bitter air, I stopped clicking. From my calculations I was nearly a full year in the future. It had been the month of December the last time I'd seen Samoset. But days could make a difference, especially with the possibility of another me walking around somewhere.

Turning, I inspected the clearing where the longhouses had been. They weren't there, adrenaline racing through me until I remembered Kalinda's assurance that the witches were working to get the timelines back in order. I had no way of knowing when exactly Lourie had begun to change things, especially because of my own part in it. Was it my doing that Lourie had come into the past before the tribe began calling me a *Hobomock*, or had that event caused their later suspicions? Several tribe members had seen two of me and two of Samoset that day, not to mention Lourie, who also looked like me.

I sighed, my thoughts tangling in confusion. The only way around it was to head to Salem and find out what was going on in this time. *Be careful*, a voice whispered. I stared down at the ball still in my hands. *Can you talk now?* I asked, but it didn't answer. I kept going.

I had reached the outskirts of town when the ball materialized again, appearing in my hands without being conjured. I'd been thinking of Samoset, wondering about a baby and if I was ready to have one when I was suddenly taken into the ether. What the hell?

A second later I dropped into the Wampanoag village, dizzy and feeling slightly nauseated. Samoset was not ten feet in front of me, using a sharp knife to strip the bark from a birch sapling. "Samoset?" I said warily. He looked as he always did, his hair loose, a stripe of red across one cheek. There had been a recent ceremony.

He placed the knife he was working with on the ground and regarded me solemnly. His brow furrowed as he scanned across my body. "Why you here, Em? Said you go to Grandmother."

Weetamoo stood twenty feet away with her back to me, working to tan a recently stretched deer hide. Numee worked next to her. They'd finally found her. I was about to run to her when two Wampanoag braves walked by, glancing at me as they headed to the forest. "Do they still think I'm the *Hobomock?*" I whispered.

At that moment I saw myself coming across the clearing. The other me was wearing a loose deerskin tunic, a beaded band around my hair to keep it in place. My skin had turned dark in the sun, glowing with health. I noticed that I'd put on quite a lot of weight around my middle. A tingle began at the root of my spine and traveled upward. I felt dizzy, disoriented, a buzzing in my ears. Samoset grabbed my arm to steady me, turning to see the other me walking toward us.

"Go," he said, his eyes wide and worried. And I did.

I sucked in breath as I landed in the woods, bending over to retch in the dirt, my stomach heaving. My last thought of, *take me to where I'm supposed to be*, was imprecise and lame, but in my defense it was kind of like an emergency extraction. And how had I ended up there—obviously in some future time? I was positive the ball had taken me there on its own, which meant it was what…sentient? At least I knew Samoset and I…I let out a gasp.

The realization hit me so hard I nearly fell. I grabbed hold of the nearest branch, recalling the other me who was definitely pregnant and pretty far along from the look of it. I lowered to the ground, afraid I might retch again, but the nausea passed. I hadn't had a period in over two months, but I'd been sure all the time traveling had caused it. Food had repelled me on several recent occasions, my nausea in the alley with Helga another symptom I should have recognized. I'd chalked it up to nerves and that wretched smell of burning plastic mixed with dead animal.

If only this had happened during my first year with Samoset maybe none of this craziness would have come about. The future would be safe and I wouldn't be working with a coven of witches to save the world from total annihilation. Or would I? I was so confused I could barely think. Traveling from one timeline to another in such a short period had scrambled my brain, paradoxes notwithstanding. I pulled myself to standing and put one foot in front of the other, doing what I came to do.

Salem was less chaotic than the last time I'd been here—no ships on fire, no bellowing men, no militia facing off with Indians or with other settlers, no gunfire. The sun was out, spreading thin warmth through the frigid air. But I didn't trust it, my radar on high alert as I pulled my cloak around my shivering body and headed down the cobbled street toward the center of town. Several horses with riders went by, men doffing their hats as they passed. The attitudes had definitely improved since my last time here. In the marketplace tables had been set up and filled with produce and meat and eggs and knitted caps and mittens and other items for sale. I hurried to the nearest one and addressed the young woman standing there. "I just arrived from the south and I was wondering if there had been any unrest of late? My father told me to be careful of the savages in these parts."

The brown haired woman straightened her cap and pulled her dark cape closer. "Savages, you say? Yes, we have them here, but now that they've been settled in the praying towns there has been no more threat from them. There's one of them now," she added, pointing to where the road narrowed and houses crowded close. "He is the leader of the group who recently took up residence in the north of town. Perhaps you would like to ease your mind by speaking with him? He has very good English."

My heart pressed against my rib cage painfully as I tried to draw in a full breath. Samoset was walking up the street dressed in a long black coat—a pilgrim coat by the look of it. His hair was tied back and he had no paint on his face, his leggings and loincloth the same as always. He seemed at ease as he glanced around at the wares for sale, smiling at the townsfolk as he passed, but once he saw me his eyes widened. Instead of hurrying toward me he hurried away, striding up the road so fast that I had to run to catch up.

When I reached him I grabbed his arm. "Samoset, it's me, Em."

He turned, looking me over. "How do I know it is you?" he asked, folding his arms across his chest.

I thought of some memory he might recall, a scene or…"The last time we were really together we made love in the forest by the *wetu* you built for me. It had snowed recently and we found shelter under a cedar tree. And I saw you in the past—do you remember me leaving for my grandmother's house and then reappearing a second later? I know the other witch that looks like me has been around—but I'm not her."

He stared hard into my eyes, leaning forward to sniff me.

"I'm sure I stink—I haven't had a bath for…"

"Smell like Em," he said, watching me.

"Well that's good because I am Em. How did you end up in the praying town? I thought I moved the tribe into the mist."

"I do not remember move you speak of. Praying town is temporary. Longhouses burn and pilgrims give tribe shelter until rebuild. Puritans want tribe to stay, teach children white ways, but pilgrims understand."

"I hope that's true," I muttered to myself. With all the

war and unrest I'd seen these past months I couldn't be sure of anything. And as far as my knowledge of history, all bets were off. That is until I remembered my trip to the future, orchestrated by my ball. "Do you really remember me, Samoset? You don't seem all that happy to see me."

His brow furrowed. "Other witch say things, do things, make me believe things...hard to shake off."

"When was she last here? She messed with time, Samoset. She changed everything, and now I don't know what's real and what isn't. Tell me what's happened in the past two moons."

He stared at me for a long moment before taking hold of my arm and leading me into the forest. It was an hour before we arrived at the hill, our hill. By the time we reached the top I was crying.

When he saw my tears he placed his hand on my cheek. "No reason to be sad, Em. I know it is you. I believe you." He wiped the tears gently from my face and bent to kiss me. When we pulled apart I felt so relieved I was giddy. We sat together and he began to talk, haltingly telling me his version of the past two months.

"The other witch seduced you, didn't she?"

Samoset looked confused. "Seduced not a word I know."

"She talked you into having sex?"

He shook his head. "Samoset know by how she smell, Em. Not the same."

I laughed.

He went on. "Tribe say you *Hobomock*, want Samoset to marry Aimee, Wampanoag woman. Samoset say no, leave if they send you away."

He did?"But I did get sent away, right?"

"*Wetu* for a while until meeting with elders. I come for you but Em gone. Only Aunum."

"I did leave for a while but then I came back. Do you remember what I mentioned—making love under the cedar trees? That's when I came back. Helga was with me."

He nodded, looking down. "After snow Samoset faced with hard decision. Elders angry because of other witch. Elders think summoned by *Hobomock*."

"In other words, me, since I'm the *Hobomock*, right?"

He smiled for the first time. "Elders say *Hobomock* block baby from coming. Say without baby sachem must resign or find new wife."

"But I wasn't around so what difference did it make?"

"Other witch show herself to tribe. Act crazy, say things, upset elders. But I know, Em—I always know not you. I tell elders this but not believe."

"It was me who was blocking having a baby, Samoset. I told you all this, but I don't think you remember."

He stared at me blankly. "Some memories mixed up, some gone. Crazy time."

I nodded and took hold of his hand. "I think I might be pregnant. I went to the future and I saw us. We were living in the deep woods and all the longhouses were there. I…"

"Baby now?" he interrupted, his eyes wide.

"I think so—maybe."

"From snow."

"Yes, from the time in the snow."

He pulled up my sweater and placed his warm hand on my lower belly, cocking his head as though to listen. A minute later he looked up, his dark eyes meeting mine. "Hear heartbeat, Em."

"What?"

He took my hand and placed it on my belly, covering it with his. "Listen—soft like wind in leaves."

And then I heard it—fast, oh so fast, like a feathery rhythm deep inside me.

Our eyes met.

"Baby born in hot time," he murmured, pulling me close.

Chapter Twenty-nine

Samoset and I spent the rest of the day together. It was too cold to spend the night on our hill so he took me to the village where several longhouses were under construction. I clung to him as we walked, afraid he would disappear if I let him go, but he didn't seem to mind, his smiling eyes on my face many times as we walked through the forest following a narrow deer trail. It took hours but we filled it going over the events of the past couple of months. It reminded me of the first time we'd been intimate, the weeks of walking on our way to his tribe. The day I lost my virginity was the day I became his wife—the ceremony later just the icing on the cake. That trip was like a long honeymoon as we came to know each other in all ways, turning me from a girl into a woman in the process. This felt the same, as though we were just beginning our relationship. Except now I carried his child.

"Are you tired?" he asked when I stopped to relieve myself.

"A little. I'm hungry."

"You rest while I hunt. Have rabbit for dinner."

I gagged and then had to turn away to retch under the trees.

"Em sick?" he asked worriedly, kneeling beside me.

"It's the baby, Samoset. It's morning sickness."

"Need food. Not rabbit?"

"Nuts, greens? Not anything that exists right now. It's winter." I smiled, trying to control my nausea.

He nodded and left me standing there, heading under the trees. I waited in the silence, my heart filled with an emotion that left me shaking with joy.

When he came back he was carrying several large mushrooms as well as something that looked like moss. "Cold time food," he said, taking hold of my hand.

There were lots of gaps in his memory, things that had changed since the witches had worked on the timelines. It was confusing trying to figure anything out, and I finally gave up, too happy to even care.

When we finally reached the site of his new village no one was about, tools left in a neat pile for the following days work. The scent of fresh reeds and cattails brought me immediately into the past to when our life had been good. I wanted it back but I'd made a commitment to the coven now…the baby would keep me with the tribe for a while, but eventually I would have to take up my destiny as a witch.

I was exhausted from the walk, dozing while he made a fire and cooked what he'd found. The roasted mushrooms were exactly what my body craved, the strange stringy moss tasty once it was cooked. "Good for baby," he said, watching me eat.

Afterward he took my hand and I followed him into the darkness of a partially constructed longhouse. He placed his blanket down and pulled me to him. "Need Em," he said, his mouth finding mine. His hands ran across my body working at the buttons and zippers. He knew his way around these things now, his fingers sure as he removed my clothes.

"I missed you," I said, reveling in the sensations. "So much."

He smiled when a tendril of moonlight found it's way between an open section of wall, shining in my eyes where I lay beneath him. "Moon in eyes," he murmured.

A moment later his warm lips found my breasts, my belly, sending shivers across my skin. The weight of him pressed against me, his movements becoming more intense as we connected fully. When I cried out he stopped, concern in his dark eyes. "Hurt?"

I shook my head. "Just the opposite." I pulled him closer until there was no air between his skin and mine, our two bodies becoming one as we consummated the joy of finding each other again.

I woke freezing, shivering so hard my teeth were chattering. Snow had fallen during the night and my clothes still lay where they'd been thrown the night before. Samoset's body heat had kept me warm all night but now he was gone. I dressed and pulled the blanket around me, waiting for his return.

He didn't come back and as the hours rolled by I realized I would have to do something to keep myself from freezing to death. I was sure the temperature had dropped to ten degrees or less. I took the blanket with me, wrapping it around my shoulders over my cloak before I headed out. It was then I remembered my ball, conjuring it carefully before thinking of Samoset. It would take me to him.

But the ball had other plans, taking me to Helga instead. She was in the Salem Town square dressed in an ankle length fur coat with a hood and warm boots, mittened hands clasped in front of her.

"Emeline! Where have you been? Kalinda told me to find you, but when I visualized you I ended up here. I've been waiting for almost an hour. What's going on?"

"I've been with Samoset, we spent the night in a longhouse miles from here. He was gone when I woke up and he didn't come back. Is Lourie back?"

"How should I know? I just got here. Kalinda seems to think you're in trouble. Is that true?"

"I didn't think I was, especially after last night, but something's off. Samoset wouldn't leave me alone like that without a good reason."

"I went to the meeting yesterday and from what I heard the coven is gearing up to basically go to war with the dark witches."

"Here or in the future?"

"I don't know. I guess wherever they end up. I'm really worried, Emeline. There's no place safe now that all the timelines have been infiltrated." She grabbed my hand. "I think we should go back to Geistigehaus and get instructions. I don't want to stay here and end up in the middle of a war."

I scoffed. "Been there done that."

"This is different—a war between witches isn't like anything you've ever experienced, believe me."

"And you have?"

Her eyes darkened. "One of these days I'll tell you all about my past."

"I'd love to hear it, especially what happened to your brother."

She grabbed my hand, her gaze in the distance. "Not now," she hissed.

Just before we entered the ether I saw what had spurred her into sudden action. Samoset stood under the trees by the square, Lourie close beside him. She looked exactly like me, even her clothing identical to what I was wearing. And Samoset had his arm around her shoulders, his dark gaze riveted on her. I willed him to look our way, but he didn't pull his gaze from her face before we spun into the ether.

We landed in Helga's room, the warmth like a balm on my shivering body. My mind was still in the past, wishing I hadn't allowed Helga to pull me away—surely I could have convinced Samoset of who I was. "He told me he could smell the difference, Helga. He said Lourie didn't smell like me. He said he always knew."

"Did that little scene just now look like he knew? I'd say she figured out the problem and changed her smell to match yours. You know what this means, right?"

"What?"

"It means we have to kill her."

I visualized my hands around Lourie's neck squeezing the life out of her. "I don't think that's allowed."

"If you don't kill her she'll continue with this. For some

reason she's decided she has to have him. Maybe it's because of you, maybe not. She's always needed a lover to make her feel alive." Helga glanced away and then back again. "I know what's going on! She's using him to make a baby—remember what they said about reproducing?"

"But it's the witches who want to reproduce amongst themselves—he's an Indian. And from what I heard it seemed like it was going to take some time before they could manage it."

Helga shrugged. "Maybe she thinks she can get a head start—I don't know."

As usual Helga had managed to completely freak me out. "I can't stay here. I have to find him and let him know."

"You're not going anywhere until we talk with Kali. She specifically asked me to find you."

I let her lead me down the shifting hallways to Kalinda's rooms, my feet dragging. I wanted to be back in the sweet smelling longhouse with Samoset stretched out beside me. How could this be happening again right after we'd found each other?

"My dear girl," Kalinda said, after hearing my news. "I had my suspicions about the baby. Do not worry about Lourie. I've already sent two witches to retrieve her. Samoset will be all yours soon enough."

"And what about this war Helga told me about? Is it true?"

"Yes, my dear. There is no other solution. But you will not be part of it, even if I have to sequester you on another planet."

"Another…what about Samoset?"

She laughed, a tinkling sound that didn't go with the vision I'd just had of her as a Valkyrie, with wild gray hair that rose like a cloud around her head.

"You and Samoset then, at least until the baby comes."

"But I've seen my future self with the tribe. I'm sure I was only a month away from the birth."

"Well then, there's nothing to worry about, is there? You leave the war up to us. Once the baby comes and you feel ready to return to the coven, we can discuss your role."

"But what if things don't go your way? Those witches are pretty powerful."

Kali's eyes darkened. "And so are we, my dear. You have no idea."

"How soon before I can go back? I'm scared she's bewitching him again."

"You must stay here until she's captured, Emeline. You are too vulnerable right now. The baby you carry is a witch, you know. Lourie could take advantage of that."

"My baby…" my hands went to my belly, "is a witch?"

"Of course. Now rest and eat some good food. I hope the weather will be a bit warmer by the time you go back. The cold is not good for you right now."

How did she know about the weather or the baby, or any of the other things she'd known all along? And then it came to me—the truth of who she was—Kali, the destroyer of evil, and the Hindu goddess of time, enlightenment and death. When our eyes met I saw worlds upon worlds swirling within hers, as though she'd just this moment chosen to show me her true identity. She smiled.

A week went by as I waited for word of Lourie. I ate well, slept well and napped, my exhaustion slowly ebbing away as the days went by. Whenever I thought of Samoset I saw him with his arm around the dark witch. I prayed he would remember what we had together. But what if he didn't?

I was resting on my bed when Helga barged in without knocking. "How are you feeling?" she asked, sitting next to me.

"I'm okay—just lonely for Samoset."

"Do you want to hear about my past?"

I sat up. "I thought you'd never tell me."

She laughed and scooted up beside me, leaning back against a pillow. "Remember the cold witch I mentioned? She was my mother. She taught me everything I know. My brother died when we were on a planet very similar to the future Salem where I freaked out—remember?"

I nodded, waiting for more.

"We were escaping from this very creepy sorcerer who had decided that my mother was his property—he was in love with her, if you could call his obsession love. My mother hated him and wanted my father back, but he was missing at the time." Her eyes glazed over for a second before she went on. "My brother got caught in the cross fire when the two of them decided to fight it out. I was standing right there and I could have saved him but I was paralyzed with fear, afraid my mother was going to be killed." Helga wiped her eyes.

"How did he die exactly?"

"My mother was powerful—way more than I'll ever be.

She used lightning bolts against his sword, and one of them ricocheted off and hit my brother."

"How old were you?"

"Fifteen."

"It wasn't your fault. If it was anyone's fault it was your mother's."

"Mom said the same thing, but I still feel guilty. If I could do it over, I…"

"Emeline?" Kalinda stood in my open doorway. "I wanted to let you know that Lourie is in custody."

I jumped off the bed. "What's going to happen to her?"

"She will be tried and given a suitable punishment." Her gaze went to Helga. "Let's let Emeline get back where she belongs, shall we?" she said, holding out her hand.

Helga rose from the bed, glancing over her shoulder as she followed Kali out the door. "Don't forget me," she called. There were tears in her eyes.

"How could I forget you?" I laughed. "I'll see you soon enough."

I jumped of the bed, tugged on my warm boots and grabbed my cloak.

Epilogue

Finding Samoset was easy, but trying to convince him of who I was proved more difficult. His last encounter with the dark witch had thrown him, and it was exactly as Helga had described—she'd learned my smell, bewitching him easily in his emotionally vulnerable state.

"You say Lourie is witch but smell like Em," he said when I tried to explain. "Not know who you are." He frowned, backing away from me, his eyes going hard. "Make love like Em, kiss like Em, smell like Em."

The bitch had finally managed to seduce him. Fury went through my body as I pictured them together. "You should have known!" I shouted. "How could you let her do this?" I was furious and crying, my hands over my face when he finally grabbed my shoulder.

"If you are Em then there is baby inside," he said softly, placing his hand on my lower belly. A minute later the hard look in his eyes softened and a moment after that tears welled. "Witch make Samoset believe—make…"

I reached up to wipe the tears from his cheeks. "It's

okay, Samoset. It's over now. I'm here and she's in custody." When I stood on tiptoe to kiss him he pulled me roughly into his arms. He buried his face in my neck. "Em not leave again," he murmured.

I didn't answer, knowing that I *would* have to leave again. Hopefully we could get through the birth and the early months without mishap, but after that…

War was coming but I would not be part of it, at least not for the next many months. I hoped beyond hope that the sixteen hundreds would be spared. One of these days I would have to tell Samoset, but for now I only wanted my life back, the knowledge of the baby growing inside me proof that the *Hobomock* was gone for good.

If you want to read more of this series please sign up to be on my mailing list and download a free book! No spam and opt out whenever you like.

https://www.nikkibroadwellauthor.com/